BENEATH

BENEATH

A NOVEL BY

Kristi DeMeester

WORD HORDE
PETALUMA, CA

First Edition

ISBN 978-1-939905-29-1

A Word Horde Book

For the two Js. Always.

Chapter 1:
Atlanta, Georgia 1988

"Snake handling. As in rattlesnakes and Jesus." Cora Mayburn looked up from her stack of notes at her boss, Jimmy Townsend, and picked up her coffee mug. Empty. She hadn't drunk enough caffeine for this conversation. She glanced across the office at the pot left on the burner and sighed. A refill would have to wait.

Jimmy kept his hair long—the tiniest bit of silver glinting among dark brown at the temples—and slicked back from his forehead. He drew a hand through it now and adjusted the gold cuff links on his wrists.

"People love to read about things like this. Makes them feel better about their own shitty lives to know somewhere out there is someone whose life is more fucked than theirs. If they know that there are people who have never seen a television, they can handle one more day of not ramming their car into oncoming traffic." He picked his mug up from where he'd set it on her desk, took a sip, and winced.

"Walters covers the Jesus stuff, Jimmy." She didn't tell him that the thought of even stepping foot in a church made her sick.

"Walters doesn't have the chops for this. He's good for local revivals or if some old lady sees the face of Christ in a potato chip. This is bigger. More interest here."

"I'm no better than Walters."

"That's bullshit, sister, and you know it."

"I imagine there's travel," she said.

"Hensley, North Carolina. Finest little town you'll ever see. Fresh mountain air and quiet and all that shit. Appalachia in all its glory, and only a stone's throw from Atlanta."

"This isn't my wheelhouse, Jimmy. I'm good for politics. Scandal. Reagan Doctrine, or reports on Thatcher, or Swindall and his money laundering. You know that. The church and I don't get along."

"Cora. You've been working for me for, what, ten years now? Fresh out of school and wet behind the ears, and even then I could sense you had chops. I know what kind of reporter you are. You're level-headed. Thoughtful. Honest. This is the kind of story that needs a clear mind. Someone who isn't going to get carried away by emotions and turn the piece into something inflammatory."

She tugged her hair away from her face, let the weight of it fall onto her back, and wished she had something she could tie it with. With the humidity outside, it had already begun to frizz.

He took another pull from his coffee. "It's just a church. Just a religion. Jesus isn't going to bite you."

Cora winced. Her stomach clenched, and she willed herself to focus on Jimmy, on the shape of the words he spoke. She drew breath in and out and forced herself not to think of that terrible, worming mouth on her neck or those hot fingers tugging at her zipper. Forced herself not to think of the Bible verses Mr. Burress would whisper when he was finished or how she would cry at his feet like an obscene Mary Magdalene bathing the feet of Christ with her tears. He had worn the clothes of a holy man, tricked Cora's mother with his soft smiles and Sunday School lessons.

"I don't do the religion stuff," she said again, but her voice was weaker this time, almost a whisper that leaked out from between her lips.

"You did the Garrett Cain story, Cora. People everywhere ate that shit up with a spoon and came crying for more. You *interviewed* the Buckhead Butcher. I mean, Jesus Christ, the guy hog-tied and carved up thirteen women like they were Thanksgiving turkeys. With his *teeth*. This is an opportunity for some exposure with an audience that's salivating for a story like this. If you do this justice—give something that's been salacious for so long a fair shake—there could be Pulitzer talk. I feel it in my bones."

She looked down at her hands. The Garrett Cain story had made her career. Without it, it was likely that she'd still be covering cotton candy news. Cats rescued from sewer drains or ancient grandmothers with the perfect recipe for banana nut bread.

It was Cain's eyes that she couldn't forget. For months after the story had gone to print, she would close her eyes and see them. The iris so dark it blended with the pupil. When she'd spoken with him, he'd stared at her without blinking and there was a sort of gleeful humor in them. It was as if he was speaking to her without words; as if he was willing her to understand that the only thing that kept him from leaping on her, from raking his teeth across her naked breasts was the piece of glass between them, and that wasn't much, now was it?

He claimed that the devil made him do it. She hadn't believed him.

In that tiny, dark closet, when Mr. Burress had asked her to close her eyes and to open her mouth so he could see her teeth, she had come to understand that men could be so, so much worse than the devil. Her eleven-year-old body memorized the hard truths of evil, and he had bent and used her until she learned to shut herself off.

Every Sunday, she watched him with the other little girls, how he ignored them when Bible verses that were perfectly memorized tumbled from their lips, how he smiled when Cora stood, how he praised her even when she messed up.

"Cora, it's a huge story. Something that could mean big things for you. Take it. Expense the trip. Hell, stay in whatever passes for the nicest hotel in bumblefuck, North Carolina and eat lobster every night if you want. This story belongs to you. I want it to go to you."

Cora had not stepped foot in a church since she was thirteen. Not since the last day she had seen Mr. Burress. She stood in his driveway, and he kissed her forehead and told her to be a good girl, that he would miss her, but that God had called him to a new city. That night, she'd scrubbed her forehead until it bled.

Her mother had been cremated just last year, and there was no service. The thought of entering the quiet, still air of a sanctuary made Cora dizzy, and she realized that she was breathing in shallow bursts.

"You don't have to participate. I wouldn't expect you to touch the snakes. Interviews, some research, some time spent observing. That's all. In and out."

It wasn't the snakes that frightened her at all. It was the people and that blind unswerving faith that would prompt them to do whatever it took to quench the fire in their bellies. She imagined that the look that had been in Mr. Burress' eyes, in Garrett Cain's eyes, would also be in the eyes of the townspeople. That thinly veiled hysteria that led men to butcher women or to tell little girls how pretty they were and kiss them in ways they shouldn't.

"I've seen what faith does to people, Jimmy. Seen how it makes them think that God's grace and forgiveness gives them permission to do terrible things. All they have to do is cry and say they're sorry, and Jesus waves his magical beard over their sins, and they can fall asleep with a clean conscience. When you're dealing with radical ideologies, it's too difficult to maintain an unbiased approach. The crazy seeps in. It always finds a way," Cora said.

"That's a load of horse shit."

She shrugged. "Maybe so."

Jimmy leaned toward her and placed a hand on her desk. "I'm not going to force you to take the story, Cora. I'm not that kind of boss, and we're past the point of you listening to anything I say anyway, but I have to tell you that if you pass on this, your career flatlines. Outside of the Democratic Convention—which is duller than a slice of bread—we don't have anything this good lined up for the next year. Unless the governor is caught with his pants around his ankles and his dick inside a hooker, this is the best I've got for a while."

Exhaling through her teeth, she looked at the slow grin spreading across Jimmy's face. He had a point. The very last thing she wanted to do was another exposé on restaurant health scores. Plus, she could get out of the city. Spend a week or two not thinking about the slack, open-mouthed stare when her mother had exhaled for the last time.

"Fine," she said, and Jimmy slapped his hand against her desk. "But I want two weeks to do it, and I don't want you butting in every five minutes to see what I've found."

"Done," he said and then he was gone.

For the rest of the afternoon, she read and re-read the same series of notes and tried not to think of that dark closet or the Bible verses Mr. Burress whispered into her hair when he took her inside.

Chapter 2:
Hensley, North Carolina 1972

Ruth McDowell didn't want her baby to come that night, not under a moon like that, but she knew by the pains tearing across the lower part of her abdomen, the needling right above the most private parts of her, that soon the child would squeeze out and grow into the sin that dominated every breathing creature's heart.

From the floral patterned chair Thomas had bought for her at the Goodwill, she timed her contractions and watched the moon rise over the mountain. It was late October, and the moon sat low in the sky like a grotesque crimson bloom.

For a moment, the sight of the moon frightened Ruth in the way the dark or the threat of the boogey man will frighten children, but she was being silly. She poured herself a glass of water, drank it down in two long, messy gulps.

Ruth walked outside to the porch for some fresh air, her long skirts slapping against bare feet, in the hopes the slight October chill would somehow calm her, smack her back into her senses a little, but the fear building inside of her sharpened at the sight of that terrible moon, and she had to pause for a moment and grasp at the splintered railing of the porch to keep herself from falling to her knees.

A blood moon her mother had called moons like this. Shaking

her finger at Ruth, she'd said, "They call it a Harvest moon, Ruthie, but I know better. Blood on the moon means blood spilt back into the earth. Things with claws and teeth waiting in the shadows to gobble up all your tiny little bits. All that'd be left of you is the bow on your head!" Then Ruth's mother would toss her head back and cackle, the sour smell of her moonshine seeping into the air.

Ruth had closed her ears to her mother's talk and gone back to her Bible verses, determined as always that, while the souls of her mother and father may be damned, her flesh wouldn't mingle with the flesh of the vile and the perverse when God let fly his wrath during the final judgment.

Ruth would stand as a pillar—a beacon even—of light against the darkness. She would follow God's law. She would not drain stolen bottles of moonshine like her mother did until she started giggling and lifting her skirts while the unholy and the holy men in town watched a bit too closely. Ruth would not have rumors spread about her the way they had about her mother. Loose tongues spilling truths and half-truths. *Witch*, they said. *Whore*.

"He marked me. The devil," her mother told her, pointing to her left eye. The small bit of red reflected like new blood against eyes the color of water.

Once, when she was thirteen, Ruth had stood over her mother as the older woman slept, a spoon clutched tight in her fist, and dreamed of slipping the cold metal behind the eye and scooping it out.

But now, as Ruth looked into the great face of the blood moon, she shivered and remembered her mother's words. "Blood moon means the devil's out, walking around, looking to grab hold of little girls' skirts who've wandered home too late. Mind he don't catch you. Nothing the devil likes more than a juicy piece of girl flesh like you."

Another contraction took hold, and she gripped the porch railing harder, the splinters digging into her hands as a high-pitched growl started in the back of her throat and wormed its way out from between clenched teeth.

Ruth's blonde hair was dark with sweat and hung heavy down her back. She normally wore her hair plaited and coiled atop her head, but the pins had hurt her scalp tonight, and she had taken the braid down.

Thomas wouldn't approve of her wearing her hair loose, would call it vain, but he wasn't here any more to frown at her when he was displeased. Ruth couldn't think of a reason the Lord would condemn her for leaving her hair undone.

Her hands shook, and her knees bucked. A splinter dug into the pad of her index finger as she caught herself and she winced. It had been so long since she slept for longer than an hour or two at a time. She knew she should sleep—for the baby's sake—but it had only been two months since the night Thomas had fallen asleep behind the wheel; only two months since she learned he would never come home to her again, and the days passed in quick succession, each one a test of her faith in the Lord. She had survived all of it. She would survive this moment, too.

Granted, she found it difficult to eat, and at nights, when she did finally nod off, she was plagued by strange, grotesque dreams. Images of Thomas, his face mangled and crushed, beckoning to her, his voice garbled by dark bile that seeped from his mouth.

And the snakes, always the snakes that wound around his feet, hissing in what she thought were whispers.

Night after night she prayed, pleaded with God to do His will with her, to please help her overcome these dreams that were surely sent from Satan himself, but her whispered requests fell on deaf ears. Ruth took her Lord's silence as a sign that this was her burden to bear and praised Him for allowing her this opportunity to grow stronger in her faith.

Now, under the light of this moon, Ruth felt the dream creeping upon her, knew somehow if she closed her eyes and re-opened them, Thomas would stand before her, grinning that terrible, mutilated smile, his hands grasping for her belly.

"I cast you out, Satan," she said, wavering on her feet. Another contraction would be along in a moment, and when it came, she would need to be in the house and not standing out here like some dumb cow chewing the cud.

If she'd been thinking clearly, she would have started the walk into town hours ago when she felt the first flutter of pain, but she had thought there was enough time yet. No need to rush. Doc Simpson would have only told her it was too early and not to fret and sent her back anyway.

It would be impossible to make it into town now. Not with the contractions coming this quickly, the knifing pains cutting through her at exact three-minute intervals. Ruth did not want her child born in the dirt like some animal.

For a moment she wished she had a telephone but then dismissed the idea. That machine was good for nothing but idle gossip and fostered laziness among the young people. It was not godly to have such a thing in the house.

Without Thomas to cut it, the grass had grown tall, and under the moon it looked like long switchblades swaying back and forth. Ruth wondered if she walked out into them, if they would cut her, if her blood would drip back into the earth like her mother had told her when she was a child.

The house itself, which Thomas had inherited from his father, sat back from the road, partially hidden by large oaks and ivy that crept skyward and completely covered the eastern side. It was rumored in the town that the house had not been built but had sprung from the ground, a living, growing thing.

Ruth liked the house, liked its isolation and the quiet stirrings of wind that blew through the large windows that faced east; liked the soft light that stole through those same windows at dawn, the scent of grass in the summer and ice in the winter. Thomas had been nervous she would find it too old-fashioned, but when he carried her over the threshold and set her down, his face hopeful, she'd nodded firmly and said, "This will do."

A pain racketed through Ruth's belly, lit her up with a fire that was slowly turning her inside out, and she gasped. Inside of her she felt a strange popping sensation, as if the base of her pelvis had momentarily come out of socket, and then her water was flowing down her legs. She brought her hand to it and then drew back her palm, slick and shiny with the fluid. It smelled of dirt, or brine, or semen, like some essential part of the earth escaping from her between her legs.

Drawing a deep breath, Ruth exhaled through her teeth. Thankfully, she'd remembered to start some water boiling, had sharpened her best butcher knife, and shredded some old towels.

Soon the desire to push would become immense, larger than anything else. It would consume and fill her up to the brim until there was no room. No noise, no sound, just the pushing; the pushing that would tear her, rip her apart to make room for the small, squalling thing that wanted out of the quiet, shadow world of her belly and into this one.

When the moment came, when the pushing finally become more of Ruth than she was herself, she made small, rutting sounds, kept the screams packed down deep inside of her. It was her burden to bear, after all, a woman's place in life to feel the pain of childbirth. Eve and her tree of knowledge had guaranteed that, and Ruth would bear her lot.

And then everything was stretching around this pressure and this pain, and Ruth wondered if this was the way of the world, this pain and not fitting and pushing, and she grunted, pressed her hands against the slickness on her thighs, wondered how the blood moon found a way into the house, wondered how it had managed to bathe her legs in its sanguine light. The blood and the fluid soaked into the towels she'd placed beneath her, and in her delirium she thought she might bleed out. It wasn't possible for her heart to continue to beat under this loss.

But she didn't. After four hours, the small, wet thing squeezed out of Ruth and landed between her legs. The butcher knife, which she'd placed next to her, cut the cord, and Ruth quickly cleaned the child's nose, its mouth, cleared it of the mucous and blood that would surely choke it before turning it upside down and giving it a sound smack across the bottom as Doc Simpson had explained to her just in case.

The child, a girl, gave a startled cry that turned into a thin wail. Ruth brought her daughter to her breast, their blood mingling and marking her skin. As the child awkwardly opened and closed her mouth around the nipple, Ruth dipped one of the towels into the now lukewarm water she'd placed beside her and began to clean her daughter's face.

"Leah," she whispered, and the baby looked up at her pale-faced mother with eyes a dark, verdant green instead of the typical blue.

"Beautiful girl," she said.

At first Ruth thought it was just a trick of the light, that the moon was casting yet another bloody shadow, but as she looked closely at her daughter, she realized what it was that she had seen. Almost lost in the bottom corner of her daughter's right iris was a small fleck of deep red. Marked. As her mother had been.

Ruth looked up at the moon pouring through the large window, her mouth gaping as she shrieked. Cradled in her arms, the baby began to cry.

Chapter 3:
Hensley, North Carolina 1988

"Aren't you scared?"

Leah McDowell kept her hands folded so Mary wouldn't see them tremble. If the girl noticed, Leah would never hear the end of it. Mary had already gone through her induction into the church as a full member earlier that spring and took every opportunity to brag about her adult status.

"No," Leah said and fought to keep the blush from staining her neck and creeping up her cheeks, but it did no good. She could feel the heat just under her skin, and Mary gave her a sharp-toothed smile and tucked a strand of curling auburn hair behind her ear. Her gray dress hugged her body as she leaned forward, her chin thrust out so the angles of her face appeared more severe. Leah had always secretly envied Mary's cheekbones and olive skin and clear brown eyes. So different from her own stick-straight body and even straighter blonde hair and plain face. The only thing to make her unique was the deep fleck of red in her eye, but that didn't make her beautiful. Not like Mary.

"What if you have sin in your heart, Leah? What if the snake can smell it on you, and he wraps around you and *snap*!" Mary clamped her hand over Leah's arm, and Leah squealed.

"Don't do that!" she said, and Mary threw her head back and laughed. It was long and mean, and Leah thought everything inside of her would burn up. She wished Mary would turn back, take the path down the mountain to her own house, but since it was Friday and her mother would be in town doing the shopping for Sunday's supper, Mary had insisted on walking Leah home. She'd claimed she only wanted to help Leah prepare for Sunday's induction. Leah had tried to shrug the girl off, but Mary had ignored her pleas that she had to hurry straight home.

"The devil can smell it on you, and so the snakes can smell it on you, too. Anything bad you've thought or done. Anything at all. That's what my momma always says, but I don't think they really can. They're just fattened up, lazy snakes. That's all."

"You shouldn't say that," Leah said.

"Sixteen means you can get married soon." The girl turned to Leah and puckered her mouth.

Please, just go, Leah thought, but Mary chattered on, and Leah watched her feet shuffle through the dirt and waited for her house—the last house built on the mountain road—to emerge from the trees. Her mother would be waiting, and if she saw that Mary was with her, she'd be displeased.

"That girl is ungodly," her mother had said when Mary came for supper two years ago. Since then, Leah had been careful not to mention Mary's name in front of her mother, and Mary had never asked why she was never invited back for supper.

They were passing the last copse of trees before the mountain landscape thinned out when Mary said, "Tommy Reynolds."

"What?"

"That's who I'm going to marry. Makes my insides funny just looking at him. Carol-Anne said she saw his pecker once because his pants were too small. Said whoever married him was a lucky duck, and she would know. She'd been married for a year already when she told me."

"Don't talk that way! It ain't right," Leah said, but Mary only laughed again.

"If I'm his wife, I'll know all about it anyway. And he already told me he was going to scoop me up and gobble me down soon as he got a chance."

The roof of the house appeared, and as soon as she saw it, Leah began to run. "I have to go. See you Sunday!" She didn't turn back to see if Mary followed, and by the time her feet hit the porch, she knew the girl had turned to go back down the mountain.

She locked the door behind her, pressed her back against the wood, and brought her hand to her chest, but it didn't slow the steady rush of her heart.

Her mother emerged from the kitchen, her face flour-dusted and flushed. "Were you running?"

"Yes," Leah said and hoped her mother wouldn't question her further. She didn't want to lie. Not this close to the ceremony. If the snakes really could sense the sin in her heart, she didn't want the lie resting on her skin like something sweet.

"Come and help me then. Wash your hands first," her mother said, and Leah wiped her palms against her dress and followed her mother into the kitchen.

Her mother had opened the large window over the sink, and a slight wind that smelled of pine and grass swept through the small room. The room was small, painted a dulled white, but it was clean, and Leah loved sitting at the table in the mornings and watching the mountain come to life outside the window.

"There's an onion there that needs chopping," her mother said, and Leah went to the sink and ran her hands beneath the water. Her mother set down the wooden spoon she held and turned to face her. "Your father would have been so proud to see this day."

Leah dipped her head and forced a smile to her lips. She wasn't supposed to be afraid. If she was good, if she was pure, she had nothing to fear. The snakes would pass by her, and God would know she was His faithful servant.

Every Sunday since April, Mary Pharr held the snakes between her hands, and she had not been bitten. It was silly to be so fearful.

"It makes me glad to hear that."

They made and ate dinner in silence. Leah was grateful for the quiet. When her mother pulled down the old Bible from the shelf for the evening reading and prayer, Leah let her mind drift to Sunday's ceremony.

There were two other boys set to be introduced as full members. Jonathan and Beau. Both in her grade at school. Both dumb and plodding and bland as oatmeal. Probably one of them would marry her, and she'd spend the rest of her life caring for their equally plain children. So many other girls at school gossiped about leaving Hensley, about abandoning the Hensley Holiness Church and going to Charlotte or Raleigh or any other place but here, but Leah had never had such desires.

Her mother's voice rose and fell as her prayer continued, and she thought of Pastor Wayne; his dark, curling hair falling over his eyes as he placed his smooth, uncallused hands against her forehead, the back of her neck; his amber eyes burning into her, and his mouth parted as he spoke the verses he'd memorized when he was a boy. On Sunday, he would stand before her, his hand offering her the snake, and she would touch him.

For her devotion to the church, Ruth had found favor with the Wayne family. First Pastor Wayne's father and then Pastor

Wayne himself when the older man passed, and for as long as Leah could remember, she'd known to expect Pastor Wayne for Sunday supper; the smell of the cough drops he carried in his breast pocket flavoring the chicken or the pork chops her mother cooked as the evening meal. It hadn't been until the past year when she noticed him sneaking glances at her, a secret smile on his lips.

Now, whenever he came for supper, her stomach cramped with anxiety, and she fought against the urge to run from the table every time he spoke to her.

"Your mother is a devout woman," he'd said to Leah just that last week as he helped himself to a serving of potatoes.

"Yessir," Leah replied as she stared down into her own pile of potatoes that sat untouched in a congealing heap on her plate. She knew her mother would chastise her later for wasting food, but each bite slid down her throat with the ease of glue, and she feared that another bite would choke her. *It's just a smell. Nothing to be nervous about,* she thought.

"A God-fearing woman," he repeated, his hands bumbling with his fork and knife as he watched her. Leah could feel his eyes on her and couldn't decide if she wanted him to look away or to reach for her under the table, run his hand along the inside of her thighs. The pleasure and the shame of the thought boiled within her, and she gripped her fork and let the feeling of the metal ground her.

"Amen," her mother said, and Leah started, the private place between her thighs gone hot. She kept her head down so her hair might cover the flush on her cheeks.

"Sleep well, Mother," she said and stood. In this moment, she wanted to be alone. To undress herself and let her hands drift over the angles of her body. To dream of things she could never have.

Before her mother could speak, Leah turned and moved down the long hallway toward her bedroom. There were only two bedrooms in the house—her own the smaller of the two—but she liked that it was at the end of the hallway and far from her mother's room. A small bed with a wrought iron frame sat under the window covered with a patchwork quilt her mother had crafted in her favorite greens and cream. A braided rug sat in front of her dresser, and she wished once again she was allowed to have a mirror, but her mother called it vanity and forbad it.

She undressed with care, her fingers lingering against the buttons of her dress, before she let it fall to the floor.

Is this how he would do it? So slowly with patient hands so he wouldn't scare her. He would never want that. No.

Running her hand along the inside of her thigh, Leah marveled at the softness there. A place Pastor Wayne would never touch. Would never see. Was it really so wrong for him to marry? Wasn't it what God intended? For man and woman to come together in holiness? After all, Pastor Wayne's father had married and had children. Leah couldn't understand why his son had chosen to stay alone.

She bit down on her lip. There was no use in dreaming about it. It would never be. She bent to gather her dress, folded it, and placed it in the upper drawer before she tugged a night-gown over her head.

She listened as her mother prepared for bed, and only when the house was silent, did Leah close her eyes. Sleep fell on her heavy and complete.

The dream started immediately. She was lying in her own bed, her mother seated in the old wooden rocker next to the window, the burgundy afghan she'd knitted at the end of the summer draped across her shoulders. "Momma?" Leah whispered, but her mother didn't turn to face her, kept her face trained on the reddish moonlight pouring through the window.

"Momma?" Leah repeated, but her mother only drew the afghan more tightly around her shoulders.

She felt as if some icy hand was pushing against her chest, holding her against the mattress. Why wouldn't her mother look at her? What was she staring at?

Leah followed her mother's gaze toward the moon. She'd seen moons like this before, and while Mary Pharr told scary stories under their light that did nothing more than make the other girls giggle nervously, something about the moon was terrible. The color was off, had painted the room in strange tones of crimson.

She tried to sit up, to get out of the bed and go to her mother, make her turn away from the window, but she couldn't. That hand pushed against her, and she began to thrash.

"Don't," she said, but still, she couldn't move.

She heard their rattling before she saw them. Their scaled skin and diamond-shaped heads emerging from the darkness, crawling down the ceiling, pouring from under the door before slithering their way onto her bed, their bodies the width of her arms.

Leah closed her eyes, told herself to wake up, but when she opened her eyes, the snakes were still there, their eyes winking reddish in the moonlight, the tongues darting out and lapping at her feet, then her thighs, as they made their way toward her.

"Please, oh please," she began, but the snakes came even closer. They wound around her legs, her arms, draped themselves across her belly. The low hissing filled the room, and Leah thought she might go mad from the sound of it. It gnawed at her, chewed at the last edges of her sanity, and she began to shriek, but the hissing only grew louder. It sounded like laughter now.

She waited for the snakes to make their way to her mouth, to force themselves inside of her, their muscles flexing against her throat, but they didn't.

In the corner of the room, her mother sat inert, but there was movement in her lap. Something shifted under the afghan, and when Leah saw what it was, she screamed again.

A larger snake, his back marked with alternating diamonds of black and green, unwound itself and crept out of her mother's lap. The snake was enormous, at least the length of a grown man, and Leah watched the great muscles contract and release as it pulled itself toward the bed and up and over the footboard.

"No, no, no," Leah repeated, but the snake only kept coming, its mouth stretching back and back, the fangs exposed and sharp.

When the snake went under her skirt, Leah didn't understand, but when she felt it push against the stretch of fabric covering the most private parts of her, the cloth ripping in a long, slow succession, she remembered the dirty stories Mary told at school. The stories of what boys did with their things when they got excited, how they got all swollen and hot before they shoved them into that aching place.

Leah had blushed when she heard and turned away before she could hear anything else. She knew it was wrong to listen to such sinful things, but something inside of her caught fire when she thought of the things that men and women did together in the dark. Surely Pastor Wayne lay heavy under the sweat of such thoughts as well, and the idea of him thinking of her like that in the dark had made her wish he'd never taken the church when his father had died.

Now this snake was pushing against her, stretching her apart, and it hurt, it hurt, and the world was crashing down around her, and surely she would be ripped in half, but the snake didn't stop, and her tears tasted of salt and honey.

Her screams woke her, and she sat up, tried to make sense of the smeared dark in front of her. She brought her hands to her legs expecting to find the snake, but there was nothing but her nightgown and her tangled quilt.

From the hallway came a small shuffling. The sound of something trying to not make much noise, of something tip-toeing while holding its breath. She blinked once. Twice.

"Momma?" Leah whispered. The thing in the hallway gave no response.

I'm dreaming again, she thought and pinched herself.

No. She was very much awake.

The doorknob shifted before turning. Asleep. She was asleep again. She had to be. She closed her eyes and opened them, but the door still moved.

I will die, Leah thought. *I will die here in the dark, and the door will shut again, and I will always be here in this room, in this house with that awful thing.*

The door opened, just a crack of darkness from the hallway spilling into the bedroom, and Leah pulled her knees to her chest and shut her eyes. She thought of the Angel of Death, how it visited the houses of those that were not marked in blood and took the first-born children. She thought of this story now as the door opened just a bit more. She closed her eyes.

If I am very still, it won't see me. If I am very quiet, it won't hear me, won't come and take me away, she thought, but her teeth had begun to chatter, and she bit her tongue, the blood warm and sharp in her mouth. She opened her eyes.

The door stood gaping, the thing behind it still pushing

hard. A scream twisted in Leah's throat, her breath failing.

And now the thing was stepping through the door, and the Angel of Death, and the snakes, and the blood, and *I will die here, I will die here*. Leah found her voice and screamed as she had in her dream.

"Leah!" her mother said and flipped on the light. A dull, yellowed glow flooded the room and cast dark shadows beneath her mother's eyes.

Leah could not form words, blubbered as her mother came to her, took her by the shoulders, and shook her.

"Stop it, Leah. It was just a dream," she said.

"The Angel of Death, and the blood…" she trailed off into confusion, and Ruth frowned at her daughter.

"You had a dream. That was all."

"There were snakes. One of them…" Leah trailed off, and her mother pushed her hair away from her face, smoothed it back as she had when Leah was a child.

"Hush now. It was nothing. Get a drink of water and go back to sleep. There's nothing here."

Her mother stood, her mouth set in a firm line. She did not look back and closed the door behind her.

"Just a dream," Leah repeated, but even now, the feeling of cold, damp scales lingered on her skin, and she swiped her hand over her thighs. It did nothing to dissipate the sensation.

The house had gone quiet again; the only sound came from the window. An autumn wind rustled in the big tree in the yard, and Leah almost laughed. *How normal,* she thought. *I should be afraid of the dark, of the wind. It would be normal to be afraid of those things. Instead I'm afraid of snakes and the Angel of Death.*

She thought of the book of Grimm's fairy tales she'd taken from the school library. The tales were dark, blood-soaked things, and she'd been surprised the library kept a copy. She'd hidden the book under her mattress so her mother would not find it and she drew it out now and read of Sleeping Beauty who had stayed quiet, buried under the darkness of sleep and dreams. She had stayed quiet, but it hadn't saved her from the King who'd weaseled his way between her thighs.

Leah lay awake for a long time listening to the wind. When she fell asleep at last, she did not dream.

Chapter 4

It was early when Ruth and Leah started down the mountain. The sun had not yet touched the grass, and dew clung to the blades, washing them in silver. Her mother was quiet as they walked, the only sound their shoes crunching against the rocks scattered along the road that led down the mountain and into town.

The air was cold and held the hint of the first frost. When Leah breathed it in, it tasted clean instead of the tang of deep rot that it usually held. The road was dark, surrounded on either side by monstrous red spruce trees, and somewhere deep amongst those shadows came the low hoot of a great horned owl. *Up past his bedtime,* Leah thought and shivered as an icy wind bit at her ankles. Her mother had insisted that she wear tights under her dress, and now, she was glad she'd listened.

At intervals, the rising sun peeked out from between tree branches. Muscadine vine and black-eyed Susans choked in the undergrowth alongside the road, and Leah had the sudden desire to stop, to wander off the path and away from the church. She wanted to crawl in amongst the wild fruit and flowers and sleep forever, entwine herself with the berries and roots and forget the feel of the snakes against her skin, but her mother marched onward, and Leah hurried to catch up.

When the spire of the church finally appeared, Ruth stopped and turned to her daughter. "God will know the truth in your heart today, Leah." Her eyes glinted, hard and cold, and she wrapped her fingers around Leah's arms. "Should the serpent bite you, it is His will and your faith that will determine your fate. If His Holy Ghost does not move through you, your lot will be cast with the wicked. The black sins of your heart may go unnoticed, but they will not go unpunished." Ruth paused, her eyes softening, and then continued, "Do you understand?"

"Yes, Momma," Leah replied.

Ruth nodded and released Leah. "Good," she said.

Her mother was afraid. For her. The thought made Leah flush.

They began to walk again, and as they came down the mountain, the forest gave way to the town itself, and then the church that rose out of the trees and the dirt in solemn dominance.

It stood at the heart of the town, its white paint standing stark against the gray buildings that served as the post office, the grocery store, the solitary gas station that served cold sandwiches and hot coffee Sister Maguire more than often scalded and had to be sipped in quick gulps that did not account for taste or enjoyment.

Sister Maguire lived alone with her two daughters in a small room attached to the back of the station. Her girls, Anna and Deborah, had invited Leah for dinner once. Leah had not wanted to go. It was well known at school that Anna and Deborah were crawling with head lice, but her mother had forced her, and sure enough, Leah had come home with the telltale nits in her hair. For weeks after, the other girls stuck their fingers down their throats and made gagging sounds whenever Leah entered the classroom.

Ruth walked ahead of Leah and didn't notice the furtive

glances darted toward her and her daughter as they made their way to the church, but Leah saw them. She always did. Ruth's lips were pulled tightly against her teeth into a permanent frown; her chapped cheeks sunken, the skin there sucked tight against the bone. Leah wished that just once her mother would smile when they walked down the mountain to the church. When her mother smiled, it was always when they were alone.

Standing just outside of Sister Maguire's station were Mary Pharr and Tommy Reynolds. Their heads were bent together, Tommy's tow-colored hair clashing with Mary's auburn, and Leah's stomach clenched. If her mother caught her standing alone and unsupervised with a boy like that, she'd whip her till she couldn't stand.

"I'd just die if she was my momma," Mary said as they passed, and the words, with their barbed intentions, hooked into Leah. She felt tempted to rush upon them both and push them to the ground. Maybe grind Tommy's face into the dirt and yank the curl right out of Mary's hair.

"Leah, come along," Ruth said.

"Yes, Momma."

The church rose in front of them, the plain white clapboard dusty like the rest of the town. Pastor Michael Wayne stood at the door greeting his congregation as they entered the church.

"Sister McDowell," he said and pulled a yellowed handkerchief from his pocket, mopped his forehead, before stuffing it back into the breast pocket of his coat.

"Pastor Wayne," Ruth said and extended her hand, which he limply shook before turning to Leah.

"And little Sister Leah," he smiled, his lips pulling back into an awkward smile, a dark lock of hair falling over brown eyes with dark, tangled lashes. He had a natural boyishness that made him something akin to handsome. Leah had the sudden image of his mouth against her neck, his teeth in her hair, and she had to look away.

"A joyous day for you, no doubt," he continued, and with her eyes trained on the ground, she nodded. Pastor Wayne would want her to be cheerful, would want her to be bright-eyed and jumping in her enthusiasm to take up the snakes, to show the entire congregation the strength of her faith, but all she could do was keep her eyes down and smile weakly.

He grasped her wrist and squeezed, and Leah thought again of the snakes in her dream and froze.

As Ruth led her daughter into the church, he spoke again. "Such a joy to see two God-fearing women."

Ruth gave a tight-lipped smile in appreciation of the compliment without noticing the pastor's eyes burning against the body of her daughter.

But Leah saw. And she smiled.

Chapter 5

"And these signs shall follow them that believe: In my name shall they cast out devils; they shall speak with new tongues. They shall take up serpents; and if they drink any deadly thing, it shall not hurt them; they shall lay hands on the sick, and they shall recover," Pastor Wayne screamed from the pulpit as spittle flew from his mouth, flecking those in the front row with white bits of foam. He spoke as a man possessed, a far cry from the quiet, unassuming man who greeted Leah and her mother at the door.

The snakes stayed quiet in their boxes as he rained his fury upon the congregation, but during prayer, they began to move; their coiled bodies making strange kissing sounds as they unwound themselves in preparation of the ritualistic passing; the hypnotizing song of their rattles sending the crowd into a frenzy of moaned prayers.

"Praise Him," they shouted as the rattles beat louder.

"Take my sins, Jesus," came the voice of a lone woman, lost somewhere in the crowd, which had become one entity. The wet beating of a singular heart.

Pastor Wayne lifted his hands, calling his children to be silent before he thrust his hands deep into the boxes, hauling one snake toward the light over his head in triumph as the choir behind him broke into song and the members beat tambourines against their thighs.

One by one, he pulled their bodies from the dark box and set them down among the congregation. Drunk on their belief, they took the deadly snakes in their hands as they sang along with the choir, pulling the coiling bodies close to their faces as they shouted their belief into the symbolic face of the devil.

Overcome with the power of the spirit, the women and men danced while the snakes curled over their arms, their shoulders, their necks.

"Are you washed in the blood of the Lamb?" they screamed against the power of the devil as the tongues of the Holy Spirit broke over them and forced them to the floor of the old church.

Ruth swayed on her feet, her lips moving soundlessly over the words that had inhabited her. Soon, the Holy Spirit would overtake her, and the garbled language would pour from her lips in long guttural issues that rose and fell in a kind of dark music.

At the front of the church, Pastor Wayne stood, his arms outstretched, his eyes fluttering as he called his children to him, and they came, surrounded him with raised arms and small cries of supplication.

Leah stood frozen beside her mother, her eyes trained on the snakes. Their tongues darted in and out, and she remembered her dream, the feather-light feeling of those tongues flicking over her skin, taking her in bit by bit.

Something inside of her broke loose.

Then it was time, and her mother was pushing her into the crowd, and Leah was swallowed up, the congregation's hands against her back, her arms as they pulled her towards the altar. Her dress clung to her uncomfortably, her chest and lower back wet, and she allowed herself to be carried on their hands toward the front of the church.

She wished she could strip the dress off, cool the slick skin on her back against the wood floor, but the hands and voices urged her forward.

She stood under Pastor Wayne now, and a small bead of sweat worked its way from his hairline, down his nose, before dropping against her arm. She wanted to bring her tongue to her arm, to take him into herself, but she stayed still. He was shouting, and the muscles in his neck corded against the strain. She thrust her tongue against her teeth and refused to think of what it would be like for him to push his body against her own.

Pastor Wayne pressed his free hand against her forehead and wrapped his fingers into her hair. She marveled at the coolness and closed her eyes, leaned into his hand, which smelled of his cough drops, but of something else, too, some deeper earthy smell that made her think of trees or the clean, early snow that sometimes fell in November at the top of the mountain.

Someone behind her had begun to beat a tambourine in slow, steady succession, and all around her the voices lifted. Pastor Wayne's fingers bore into her, his voice racketing through her skull.

His hand was on her neck now, kneading the muscle there, and she leaned into him. The fear that had grown in her belly, such a strange, grotesque thing, had vanished, and it was only the feeling of his hand, his smell surrounding her. A lock of hair had fallen across his eyes, and she had the desire to push it away, but she kept her hands still.

"Child," he whispered, his voice barely audible, but she heard him. The others did not, but his voice was not for them, only for her, and then the snake was on her, wrapping around her arm, her shoulder before bringing its head to rest against her collarbone.

Its skin was hot, and the shock of it brought back the fear, and she remembered her dream, remembered the snakes pushing against her, threatening to open her from the inside, and she stiffened.

Later, Mary Pharr would swear she saw Leah laugh when the snake bit her.

Chapter 6:
Atlanta, Georgia 1988

When Cora opened the door to her apartment, the air that rushed out to greet her was thick and warm. The power had gone out again. Fucking cheap wiring.

She wrinkled her nose against the smelll—mildew and spoiled meat—and using the dim light from the hallway, she fumbled her way toward the kitchen where she'd stowed a spare flashlight for moments such as these. Her landlord was always apologetic, but more and more frequently the shitty wiring jobs meant nights spent in weak candlelight eating cold Chinese takeout so it didn't spoil. She could have gone out, but there was no one to meet for dinner, and she hated the pity stares the servers gave her when she told them she would be dining alone.

Getting out of town was starting to look better and better. She shone the flashlight into her tiny living room, the yellow light making her off-white couch look nicotine-stained. Against the far wall, a series of bookshelves dominated the space, and other than the couch was the only furniture in the room. She'd never bothered with a T.V. The news was old by the time she watched it, and the sitcoms were cheesy or boring.

Her bedroom was equally spare. No prints or artwork colored her walls. Nothing to indicate she actually lived here. She'd never intended to stay long, but it had been three years, and she still had not tried to make this place her own.

In an hour, she'd packed a suitcase—slacks and blouses that would not wrinkle, a few pairs of sturdy flats—and emptied the remnants of her refrigerator into a trash bag. A few times, the lights flickered, and she thought they would come back on, but her luck had apparently gone to shit, so she threw the rest of her things together in the dark.

How many times had her mother asked her to come home in the years before she died? There was too much space in the old house, too much quiet. She could use the companionship. She missed Cora.

It would have been easier than moving to the city as soon as she left college. Easier than eating cereal for dinner and learning how to take a five-minute shower to save on her water bill, but she couldn't live in the house she'd grown up in. If she'd been back inside of that bedroom, the bedroom of her girlhood that held her stained past, the echoes of her nightmares, she would have gone crazy.

Of course, the house belonged to Cora now. She'd hired a cleaning service to empty it out, to box up her mother's belongings. She'd rented a storage unit and found a realtor to put the house on the market. The house had sold in two weeks. All without Cora having to step foot on the property. There had been no one to tell her she shouldn't.

As she stood in the doorway looking back into her dark apartment, she thought of the people living in the rooms she'd once inhabited. Perhaps another little girl slept in the same room where Cora once slept. She hoped the little girl rested easy and undisturbed.

Jimmy had offered to pay for a flight, but she'd told him

she wanted to drive. It would give her time to think about her approach to this story. The truth was she was hoping to delay her arrival for as long as possible. The lie had come easily, and he'd believed her and handed over the company card for gas and meals.

She needed the hum of wheels on the highway. She needed to vanish into the sound so she could pretend that she was not afraid.

Chapter 7:
Hensley, North Carolina 1988

P astor Wayne sat in the McDowell living room. Ruth had asked him to come, asked that he say a prayer for her daughter, and he'd agreed.

It shouldn't have happened. He'd not the fed the snakes in eight days. Weak and lethargic, they should have done nothing more than curl themselves around the arms of his congregation, their tongues tasting the air. It was what his father had taught him, and he'd never wavered from those old lessons. Never.

For years people left the services comforted with what lay in their hearts. Their skins went unmarked, and their souls were clean. Perhaps deep down they understood what was happening. Perhaps they never thought of it. But every week, Michael made certain the snakes were placated. And now, they'd opened their mouths. He thought of Leah's smooth, pale skin, her neck exposed and her head tipped toward him. How her mouth had opened so slightly when the snake bit her.

He clenched his hands against his lap and waited for Doc Simpson to emerge. Ruth paced before him, and he wanted to snap at her, to grab her by the shoulder and force her to sit down, but he kept himself still.

"It is God's will if she survives." Doc Simpson lumbered

back into the living room. His hands shook as he wiped his face with a large handkerchief he pulled from his pocket.

Michael almost laughed. *God's will. Shouldn't have bitten her in the first place,* he thought but kept his face smooth. His mask in place as it had been since his father had taught him how to lead this church. Before he'd stopped believing. It had been a long time now.

"She's feverish but resting," Doc Simpson said, and Ruth swiped at her eyes.

"Thank you, Doctor. Bless you."

The old man nodded and made his way out, his cane wobbling as he picked his way around the larger rocks on the old road down the mountain.

Ruth watched the old man through the living room window. "I knew this would happen," she said.

"The snakes will bite, Ruth. It is only God's will that holds her to this earth." The doctor's words fell from Michael's mouth. A learned routine.

Ruth set her lips in a grim line. "That may be, but there is unspoken sin in that child's heart. Why else would she…"

She didn't need to finish. Pastor Wayne knew the stories about the girl's eye. The most common being that Ruth herself had lain with the Devil, and the speck of red was the mark of Satan.

It was absurd to think of this woman, with her steadfast belief and conviction, as someone who would allow herself to be taken in by dark forces. He'd known Ruth McDowell all his life, had sat at her table for years. Ruth may be naïve to the ways of the world and a bit harsh in her beliefs, but she wasn't wicked.

Of course he'd heard stories of such things, had even seen a demon cast out of a young boy during a tent revival, but the devil was usually quick to make himself known. If the girl did have a demon within her, it had remained quiet for the past sixteen years.

Even now he found it unsettling that despite everything, he still believed in the Old Testament version of Satan. That evil could grow and walk among people. It was the only thing that frightened him.

"Do you believe in spirits, Pastor?" Ruth's eyes were fixed on something just beyond his shoulder. He turned and saw only the large window that provided a view of the yard, the grass long and swaying in the breeze.

"The Holy Spirit is a remarkable power, Ruth. You know that as well as I do."

She brought her eyes to meet his. The hollowness there made the hairs on his arm bristle. "I don't mean the Holy Spirit."

"I'm afraid I don't understand," he said, but he understood perfectly well.

"Ghosts, specters, phantoms. Spooks, as my mother called them. Do you believe it's possible for such things to exist in our world?"

"The devil can take many forms. He is a roaring lion. He walketh about seeking whom he may devour. I'm sure it's possible that what we of the flesh deem a spirit may be nothing more than a demon manifested. A servant of the devil meant to make us fearful, to bend us towards belief in the dark realms where he dwells. You know the scriptures as well as I do. Perhaps better." The smile he offered was meant to reassure her, to calm her fears, but her eyes were wild.

"And you believe that?" she asked and crossed to the window where he stood. Her footsteps were loud against the wood floor, and the sound pierced him. His head ached, and he wished for a glass of water.

"I do," he said. Watching her made him nervous. Her movements were erratic and jerky, like watching a bird caught in a cage.

Outside, the sun had begun to set, and shadows crept across the grass. He'd been here too long. If he left now, he may make it back to the church before the sun vanished completely.

Before him, Ruth brought her hand to her chest. A flicker of gold caught the light, and her hands twitched over a delicate chain necklace. Two faded gold rings hung there, and she passed her fingers over them.

"Do you always wear both?" he asked, and she jumped.

"Both?"

"Yes, both rings." He gestured to the chain. He had not seen her wear it before, and Ruth didn't strike him as a woman given to the vanity of jewelry, but since he'd brought Leah home, carried her through the house and to her small bedroom at the back of the house, Ruth's hands had found the rings again and again, her fingers stroking the gold circles.

"Oh," she paused, brought her hands down. "No. I've not worn them since the night Leah was born. But it felt right to wear them today. Thomas would have been so proud to see her enter the church."

"I see," he said.

"I believe," she said and turned back towards the window. "There is sin in the world. Some of it as black as night, and when you die, it's not erased. Sometimes, it's so vast, so great, that it lives on without the body. Grows, feeds on its own without the aid of the flesh," she said.

"Ruth, this is blasphemous," Michael said, but his mind drifted to the girl resting at the end of the hall, to the smell of her hair as he laid her on the mattress, the arching curve of her chest against his own.

"My mother always said there were things in this world that were blacker than hell. Things the devil himself didn't want and had sent back. Things that walked only at night when there was no moon." She sighed. "Just the ramblings of a crazy drunk woman." She laughed then, a clear, high sound that set his teeth on edge.

"Stop, Ruth. You're over-tired. Leah is sick. You should eat something, get some rest. This is delirium talking. Nothing more. Pray tonight, Sister Ruth. God will help you." He spoke to her, but he didn't believe. It could have been a dry bite. But perhaps it hadn't. More than likely the girl would die in the night.

"Listen to me, preacher," she said and wheeled back toward him, brought her face so close to his that he could feel her warm, damp breath. "The Lord has helped me through these sixteen years, and I have given full faith to him. The serpent has not seen doubt or sin in my heart, but there are things that move in the shadows, and they have come to my door. They have called my name. They have called my daughter's name."

He looked away from her, took a step back. "God would not have you believe in such things, Sister Ruth. His wrath is great, and such words and thoughts do not go unpunished. You've always been a faithful member of the church. Rely on that faith now, and let it soothe you. It's the fatigue speaking." The words fell from his lips easily, with authority even, but he had begun to sweat, could feel it slicking across his lower back. He didn't like her like this, all wild-eyed and twitching. She looked like a woman broken.

"Thomas came to me. He told me she was marked. That the serpent would see it and take her for his own. That she had always belonged to the darker world, that evil begets evil, and that for all my efforts, she would still be taken. Before he died, he told me that the town was poisoned. I didn't believe it, of course, but today, I knew, I knew when she reached for you..."

Her words made him uneasy. Reminded him of what his father had told him before he died. The book that his father had buried. The one that Michael had still not gone looking for.

"I think you need to lie down, Sister," he said, and he reached for her arm, but she jerked away.

"I'm not a child," she hissed. "I know what I've seen, what I've heard. And the serpent has left its mark on my girl; his teeth have marked her flesh for his."

"What's happening?" Leah stood at the hallway entrance, the bandage over her wrist the color of rust. Her hair had come undone and fell in tendrils around her face. The pallor of her skin made her eyes look an even deeper green.

He should have looked away, but he didn't. Sometimes, at night while he lay in his small bed, he thought of her. Thought of her neck slipping out of the blue dress she always wore, of the slow smile that she only sometimes allowed to break over her face. He would bury his face against his pillow and grind his teeth until the pain became too much to bear. He could not be rid of the visions and despite the heat that built in his abdomen, the sight of her also made him sick to his stomach.

"Back to bed, Leah," Ruth said, and Leah turned without question and moved back down the hallway. Moments later, he heard the door latch.

Ruth turned to him. "It's a sign. She shouldn't have woken."

"Sister Ruth, it will be dark soon."

"Of course," she said, and he noted the weariness in her voice.

"I'll pray for you and for Leah. God will watch over His faithful believers, Ruth. If anything, I believe that."

She only nodded and opened the door for him; let him out into the late afternoon where the shadows grew.

He walked down the mountain, his eyes sharp. The sun had begun its descent, and he imagined he felt something moving in the forest around him. Something with teeth and claws that watched and waited for the blackness before it leapt upon him. He thought of Ruth's words, of her ghosts that came scratching in the night, and he began to hurry.

He was not a superstitious man. His father had made sure of that, and while his faith in the snakes had been lost long ago, he still believed there were strange things in the world.

Once in the safety of the church, he could laugh at this, perhaps even rebuke Ruth in his mind for her belief in such things as spooks and spirits, but for now, the sun was setting, and he hurried.

Chapter 8

Ruth was glad to see Pastor Wayne go. She could see the judgment in his eyes. He thought her blasphemous. Maybe she was. Only, she couldn't shake the sound of Thomas' voice. She was certain it was him. Despite the years since she'd last heard him call her name, she knew the sound like she knew the beating of her own heart.

She needed to clear her head, wanted to take a long walk through the woods around the house as she had when she and Thomas were first married, but the thought of stumbling around outside in the growing dark frightened her. She locked the door, and went to the kitchen, taking the faded afghan with her.

Some tea would help. She retrieved the old pot, set it on the stove, lit the pilot light, and sat down to wait.

For a long time, she'd told herself that they were only dreams. Nightmares and nothing more.

As the date of Leah's acceptance as a full member of the church approached, the dreams came more and more frequently. Thomas stood before her, his mouth smeared with blood, and his hands grasping her skirts. His voice ragged and his breath filled with the smell of rot.

When she woke, she could still smell the sickly scent of de-

cay. It would take her rising and going to the porch to breathe
in the sweet mountain air, and even then, she could not forget
the burning sensation of his fingers against her cheek.

Standing, she checked the teapot to be sure that the water
was not yet boiling and walked down the hallway to check on
Leah.

Leah had curled up in the corner of the bed, her knees pulled
against her chest, the blanket pushed off of her. Ruth tucked
the blanket around her and smoothed a lock of hair from her
face. She held her hand under Leah's nose, and the rush of air
over her skin relieved her.

"My baby," she said aloud, and Leah shifted in her sleep, the
smoothness of her forehead suddenly creasing as she frowned.

"Watch over her, Lord. Keep her safe. Let her do Your will
and stay far from the path of the wicked. Be a guide unto her
feet lest she stumble or find herself in the devil's snare." She
brought her lips to Leah's cheek and withdrew quietly.

The kitchen was cold. Soon, winter would be upon them,
and she had not yet hired anyone to bring her firewood. So
many things she'd let slip because she was tired, the dreams
seeping into her waking life and distracting her.

She took down the faded blue mug she always used and
poured the boiling water into it and took a moment to warm
her hands. Maybe Pastor Wayne was right. Maybe the dreams
were nothing more than a product of her anxiety. Standing,
she took the mug and walked to the living room, pulled the
old family Bible down from the shelf and flipped it open.

In the dim light, she read the words and let them soothe
her. Of course she was tired. Pastor Wayne was right. These
weeks leading up to Leah's birthday had made her fearful.
Any mother would worry about her daughter. Her visions of
Thomas were nothing more than bad dreams. She needed rest.

Time for Leah to heal. Nothing more.

The absolute quiet in the house made Ruth sleepy, and she closed her eyes and drifted.

The scratching came in time with the full dark, and Ruth, who had been dozing, started. She closed her Bible, set her mug on the small table next to the armchair, and listened. At first there was only the sound of the wind, but then it came again, a small flurry that sounded like a rat caught behind the wall.

Just a dream, she thought and stood, held her breath, and listened. The sounds started again, a steady *scritch, scritch, scritch* that made her think of someone slowly dragging their fingernails against plaster. Back and forth. Back and forth.

"Stop it," she whispered and brought her hands against her ears. "I cast you out in the name of the Lord. In His blood have I been washed, and it covers and protects this house. In His name I rebuke you."

She didn't know why she would pray. Probably it was just an animal, but her skin went cold, and she knew whatever was outside was something else altogether.

From inside the wall, the slight sounds grew stronger, sounded like teeth working against the wood. Something was trying to gnaw its way out, was trying to find its way into the room with her.

"I know what you are, demon. In His name I rebuke you!" She brought her fist against the wall.

When Thomas' voice came through, she began to cry. "You're not real," she said.

"Not real," the voice repeated. Her husband's voice as close as breath, and she wrapped her arms around herself.

"Oh please, Lord."

"Please, Lord," the voice whispered back in an obscene mocking meant to shame her.

"No, no, no, no." Ruth clasped the Bible to her chest. Her mouth tasted fetid, and she ran her tongue across her teeth. "Thomas is dead. He is not part of you, demon. I cast you out. I cast you out."

"Men are easily led. Isn't that true, Ruth? Your father was easily led, and then your mother after him. Your father, with his Bible and his insatiable taste for all those little boys? How long did he fight it, Ruth, before he gave in? How long was he able to ignore those filthy thoughts before he found the first one and paid him to keep quiet? Do you think those boys grew to like it, Ruth? Do you think they felt important that a man like your father took his time with them?"

"Stop it!" she shrieked, and the voice ceased. All was quiet once more. Outside a coyote yipped, was close enough to the house that Ruth could hear it panting.

Sobbing, Ruth picked herself up and walked back to the kitchen. The light was cheery, and she went to the sink, ran the water, and splashed her face. Her skin burned, and the water cooled her.

She would put on another pot of tea. There would be no sleep tonight.

Tomorrow, she would go back into town and have another talk with Pastor Wayne, but for now, she would stay vigilant. She sat down at the old table Thomas' mother had given them on their wedding day, laid the Bible open next to her, and began to read. If she heard any other sounds that night, she would pray.

In her bedroom Leah slept on, but had her mother gone back in to check once more, she would have seen that her daughter's eyes were open, the small fleck of red glowing in the darkness.

Chapter 9

Leah had no dreams for three nights, or rather, she didn't remember her dreams. She remembered Pastor Wayne's smooth fingers wrapped around her neck, but that was all.

Her mother had told her what happened. How the snake had bit her, but she had no recollection of the pain. No memory of Pastor Wayne carrying her up the mountain. For two days, her mother made her stay in bed to be certain she was getting better, and yesterday Doc Simpson had come up the mountain to check on her.

"A miracle," he'd said and patted her on the shoulder. "A pure heart."

Still, her mother had made her stay in bed, and she'd spent the day watching the sunlight streak across the room, her fingers drifting over the bandage that covered the two small puncture wounds. She flexed her calves and arched her back and thought of Pastor Wayne.

When her mother called her for breakfast, she rose without the usual early morning slowness. Her muscles felt lithe, as if she could run the entire distance down the mountain without tiring. She bent at the waist and tensed her abdomen, and the thought of her body moving in such a way made her blush. Pulling her dress over her head, she made her way down the hallway.

She brought her fingers against her neck and ran them along the flesh there. It was as if Pastor Wayne's fingerprints had burned into her skin. She could still feel them resting there. When he had looked at her, just before *it* had happened and ruined everything, his eyes showed his unspoken heat, and he had seen hers. They shared a secret now.

If I was a just a year older, it wouldn't be so bad. Laura Bryant was married when she was seventeen, and no one blinked an eye. But of course, Laura had married Nathan because she was in the family way. All of the girls at school knew. The town would not stand an unwed mother, and so Laura had married Nathan Watkins in a small, quiet ceremony last year.

"Leah," her mother's voice snapped her out of her girlish daydream. "School this morning. Hurry up now." Ruth turned towards the sink, busied herself with the dishes there, but Leah had already seen the dark circles under her mother's eyes.

"You didn't sleep last night," Leah said.

Her mother's shoulders tensed. "I slept just fine. Now eat your breakfast. And mind that you say grace before you begin. And be sure you clean your wrist before you go. And put a new bandage on it," Ruth said and snapped a dish towel over her shoulder. She kept her back turned.

"And drink your juice," Ruth continued. "It's good for you."

Leah lifted the glass, took a large gulp and grimaced as the pulp slid down her throat. For the third time, her mother washed the same glass. "I'm sorry, Momma," she began, but her mother put her hand up, stopped her.

"Now isn't the time, Leah. School won't wait."

"But…"

Ruth whirled to face her daughter but still did not meet her eyes. She fixed them on some spot just beyond Leah's head. "What did I say, Leah?"

"Yes, Momma." She finished her breakfast quickly. The oatmeal was cold and lumped in her throat. Several times she thought she would gag.

When she finished, she took her bowl and rose, but her mother stopped her once more. "Leave it," she said.

Without a word, Leah did as she was told. She'd known her mother would be angry.

Of course, she had the thoughts about Pastor Wayne, but it wasn't as if she'd actually attempted to carry the acts out, knew that it would be impossible, and surely God understood that? Surely Momma had worried about her only girl and was happy to see that she was better?

Tonight Leah would pray and read her Bible for an extra hour. She would banish the thoughts from her mind. Maybe then her mother would see the goodness in her and everything would go back to normal. Back to the way it was before the dreams, before the dark circles had appeared under her mother's eyes, and she wouldn't meet Leah's gaze.

In the bathroom, she unwrapped her bandages. Other than the two small puncture wounds, the skin was unmarked, and there was only a slight purplish bruising around the holes. She might have bumped her arm against something sharp. Once more, she took note of how she felt. It was strange that she should feel this healthy. This alive. As if somehow the venom that should have shriveled her had actually energized her.

The mirror did not reveal the face of a girl fallen ill. Her cheeks were rosy and looked as if she had pinched them only moments before. Her eyes sparkled as if they held some delicious secret that begged telling. For the first time, Leah felt pretty.

She smiled at the elfin girl in the mirror, and the girl smiled back. For a moment, Leah imagined she saw the girl wink—the same wicked wink Mary Pharr had given her. She started and brought her hand against the mirror. It was solid and did not yield under her fingers.

It would not do to dally about here all morning, so she washed her face quickly. As an afterthought, she pulled a brush through her hair. She wished she had a ribbon—a blue one with lace edges—to put in her hair, but her mother did not allow such vanities. Instead, she braided the long strands and tied them off with a simple black band.

They prayed as they always did before she set off for school; her mother begged angels to stand sentry around her daughter and asked God to help keep Leah's thoughts pure and her actions committed to His service. After both woman and girl said amen, Leah kissed her mother goodbye and set off on the old mountain road alone.

The air was cold and damp and tasted of woodsmoke. The leaves had only just begun to turn, and here and there bright streaks of crimson stood out among the green.

Leah tested her muscles by running part of the way. She was surprised to find she felt faster than normal, almost as if her feet were not touching the ground but skimming across the top of it, some unseen force pushing her forward.

Giggling, she pushed herself to go faster, and she panted, her mouth open as if she could draw the whole world into herself.

As she neared the bottom of the mountain, other children joined her on the road, and she slowed to a walk. They wouldn't understand, would call her a weirdo or a freak, and even though this new strength made her feel as if she was floating, she did not want their hateful words directed towards her.

Mary Pharr waited at the bottom of the mountain where the old road became Jessup Road. Her lips were stained bright red. Leah could see them from where she stood.

"Well, smack my bottom, Leah McDowell. I could've sworn that you'd be laid up in bed for the next two months after the way that snake took after you."

"It wasn't that bad," Leah said, and kicked at a leaf in the road and watched it go skittering off into the grass.

"Wasn't that bad? Tommy said that snake would've killed a man twice your size. Guess your heart is nice and pure," Mary said and pursed her lips. "Notice anything different?"

"It's pretty. Where'd you find it?"

"Silly! It isn't lipstick if that's what you're thinking. That would be sinful." She grabbed Leah's hand and brought it to her mouth and quickly took one of Leah's fingers between her lips.

"What was that for?" Leah said.

"Go on and taste it."

"What? Why?"

Mary rolled her eyes. "Oh for goodness sakes, you big baby. Just taste it."

Leah did as she was told and quickly swiped her tongue across the dark pink smear left on her finger. "Raspberry," Leah said.

"Exactly. You know those wild ones that grow right at the start of the mountain? I just crushed a bunch of 'em up. You want me to do you?"

"It's okay," Leah said and quickened her pace. In her mind she kept replaying the image of Mary leaning over to Tommy and whispering in his ear. The sour feeling that had filled her stomach several days before came rushing back.

The vigor that had filled her that morning was fading, and

a heavy fatigue had begun to spread throughout her bones. She wanted to lie down in the dirt, to dig until there was a hole big enough to tuck herself into and sleep and sleep and sleep. Away from the light and the harsh tones of birdsong and Mary's incessant, needling voice in her ear.

"Suit yourself," Mary said and shrugged.

They walked on in silence. Underneath her bandage, Leah's wound throbbed. She could feel each distinctive puncture wound, and they felt as if they were growing wider, ripping and tearing as they opened.

Are they letting something out, or keeping something in? The thought bothered her, and she cradled her wrist with her other arm and tried to ignore it.

"So anyway," Mary babbled on beside her. "Did you see what Pastor Wayne was wearing Sunday? My momma said that no self-respecting preacher would wear a tie that color of red, but she figured God would forgive him because he's so studied in his scriptures. Does he take it off normally?"

"What?"

"At dinner. Does he take his tie off? My momma always says that men should never undress in front of ladies that aren't their family, but I figure that with as much as he's been at your house for dinner, you must be used to seeing him in all states of undressed," Mary said, a sly grin playing at her lips.

Mary tucked a strand of perfectly curled blonde hair behind her ear, and Leah had a sudden, intense desire to grasp her by the throat and rip every strand out of her head one by one.

She could be on her in three seconds, could push her down into the dirt. Mary wouldn't know what was happening until Leah was on top of her. Maybe she would put her teeth against Mary's throat, taste the sweetness of those crushed raspberries with her tongue before wrapping her fingers through Mary's hair. Leah wondered if Mary's blood would be pink instead of red, the same color as her lips, like an overgrown doll bleeding out onto the dirt and gravel.

From under her eyelashes, Leah watched Mary flip a lock of hair over her shoulder. A sudden pain shot through her jaw and at the same time, a low snarl fought its way out of her chest.

The sound startled Leah out of her reverie, and she brought her hand to the cool trickle of fluid seeping down her jaw line. She swiped her hand across her face, wiped the drool against her thigh, suddenly ashamed of the things she'd been thinking. Her heart hammered, and she swallowed. Something was wrong. Something bad was happening.

Leah ground her fists against her eyes. When had she started thinking like a crazy person? Before long, she'd be pulling the wings off of flies and drowning rats in bleach like Daniel Brighton had started doing last year. His parents told the town they'd sent him to live with an uncle, let him get some rest, but everyone knew that they'd really shipped him off to the Stonewall Jackson School for Boys. Daniel was probably being fed his breakfast by a nurse right now with his hands bound behind his back.

Forcing herself to breathe deeply, Leah rubbed her temples and tried to think of something else, anything else other than the vein throbbing just under the pale skin of Mary's exposed neck.

Her heart slowed, and her skin felt cooler. Perhaps her body was still healing, or the run down the mountain had been too much.

"I wouldn't know much about that, Mary," she said. "I trust that you know more about undressing before other people than I do."

Mary stared at Leah and her mouth opened and closed like some dumb fish. Leah smiled and left Mary standing in the middle of the street alone.

Her wrist still hurt, but she felt a little better.

Chapter 10

P astor Wayne knew she was coming. A journalist who would write a story about his church. It had happened before. When his father was still alive, another journalist came and sat among them, his head bowed and his fingers moving over a small notebook, black ink scrawled on the page.

Later, Michael had hunted down the article and read the lies about their faith. He imagined how the readers gasped as they read of children being married off to their brothers. How they ate dirt and believed the devil walked among them, clothed in flesh. Stupid. He'd stopped before he reached the end. If his father ever read the article, Michael never knew, and his father never spoke of it. It would have been easy enough to uncover the real truths of what his father did, but the journalist hadn't stayed long enough, had taken what he needed for a razzle-dazzle story, and printed it in some rag of a magazine that next to no one read.

He had not told anyone about the letter he'd received from Jimmy Townsend, editor in chief of the *Atlanta Voice*, figured it would be better if no one knew the reason for the woman's sudden presence amongst them. He'd only agreed because Townsend had promised "monetary compensation" for his time, and the weekly tithes had been thin lately. Saving people from eternal hellfire and damnation had profited his family his entire life, but the older folks dropped smaller and smaller amounts in the plates each week, and he needed something more if he wanted to keep himself afloat.

If some journalist wanted to shout to everyone in Atlanta that his religion was a scam, it was no skin off his back. Not here, in Hensley, some six hours north. His congregation would never read that article, and the people who did would shake their heads and wonder how anyone could be so gullible and then go on about their miserable lives. That's how faith worked. To believe in something unbelievable to keep yourself from the threshold of despair.

No one would question the journalist's presence. A stranger in town was fairly common. People often passed through. They stopped over at Sister Maguire's place for gas and a coffee. Sometimes hunters ventured through on their way up or down from the mountain, but people didn't stay long. Certainly not overnight if they could help it. It might be nice to look out over the picturesque landscape for a little while, but Pastor Wayne heard them whisper to each other as they left. He'd heard their snatches of conversation, heard them say that something about the town gave them the creeps, and they sped off as quickly as they had come.

Of course, the journalist would want to interview him and the members of his congregation, but he knew that when it came to outsiders, the town may open their doors to passersby, but they didn't take kindly to people poking their noses where they didn't belong. He had no worries when it came to that.

He'd done what he could. He'd spent the morning scrubbing the sanctuary of the church from top to bottom, had made sure that the snakes had been fed—an extra mouse for each of them— and they moved sleepily, like cats dozing in sunshine. Everything looked idyllic. Picturesque. A postcard of a quiet, sleepy town.

Now, he waited. He knew the journalist would come to the church first, and he stood on the steps and watched.

The town was quiet today. The children were all at school, and Sister Maguire had closed up the store for lunch. The silence was eerie, and he took a small Bible from his coat pocket, began to read, his mouth forming the words.

It had been ten days since the snake had bitten Leah Mc-Dowell, but he'd seen her just that morning, walking down the mountain with Mary Pharr at her side. She hadn't looked up to see him watching her, and his face and neck flushed at the memory of her light body pressed against his. An image had flashed through his mind of her standing in the center of a field under silvered moonlight, her skin bare and glowing, her hair down and flowing past her waist, her arm dripping blood against the dirt. It had made his mouth water.

When the journalist's car—a silver Camry coated with a fine layer of dust—finally pulled up, he'd made his way halfway through the book of Revelation. The woman and her child, and the great dragon waiting to devour her son. He thought of Ruth and Leah, a woman and her child; he thought of Ruth and her belief in the dragon that was devouring her daughter. He thought of Leah, the fleck of red in her eye, the slip of creamy throat coming out of her dress. He shook himself, and watched as the woman climbed out of her car.

She had long dark hair that curled about her waist and browned skin. Her eyes were a deep brown, and he found himself watching them as she took in the church and the forest beyond. Her clothing was plain: a cream blouse over tan slacks. No jewelry adorned her throat or hands, and he noted her bare fingers.

"Michael Wayne?" she said and extended her hand.

He stiffened. "It's Pastor Wayne. I assume you are from the *Voice?*"

She withdrew her hand, took a step backwards. "Yes. Cora Mayburn. My apologies if I've offended you, Pastor Wayne."

"No matter, Ms. Mayburn." He appreciated the flush working its way up her neck.

"Yes, well," she stalled. She looked up at the church and clasped then unclasped her hands. "I was hoping," she continued, "that I could ask you a few questions before I observe tomorrow's service."

"Follow me," he said and turned, but she did not move. He stopped and turned back. "Ms. Mayburn?"

She blinked as if confused and then smiled. "Of course. Lead the way."

The church was dark and smelled of Murphy's Wood Soap. Beneath, there was the same musty scent Michael knew from boyhood, and he breathed deeply. In a few days, this woman would be gone, her article written and then forgotten. If he wanted food on his table, it was a necessary evil to have her here.

"It seems that you have plenty of room," she said, and he laughed.

"God has blessed us with a roof over our heads, and a floor under our feet. It's humble, but it serves its purpose."

He led her through the sanctuary to the small door in the back left corner that led to the Sunday School classrooms and his own quarters. "My office and rooms are back here. We can talk in the office. I can offer you tea, if you'd like some."

"Thank you," she said and followed him down the narrow hallway, her footsteps thudding against the worn carpet.

"Please," he said and opened the door for her and gestured to a chair placed across from a battered desk.

He watched her take in what little there was of the room. The only other furniture apart from the chair and desk was a bookshelf that ran along the back wall, its shelves sparse and sagging in the middles. He'd placed a small hot plate on one of the shelves and a worn teapot on top. He switched the plate on and hoped she would be quick with her questions. He still had to finish tomorrow's sermon.

Pulling a notebook and pen from her bag, she said, "I hope you don't mind if I take notes. I know that recorders are all the rage now, but I'm stuck in my ways, I suppose."

He nodded.

"How long have you been the pastor here?"

"Ten years."

"And before that?"

"I was a member."

"I see. What of the previous pastor? Did he leave the church?"

"No. I took over for my father when he passed on."

"Was the church also categorized as a Holiness Church under his direction?"

"Of course it was." He almost spat the words. Her questions were more than pointless. Simple and stupid. He expected her to recoil from the fierceness in his voice, but her face remained smooth and her voice even.

"Have you lived here in Hensley all your life?"

"Yes, but all of this strikes me as irrelevant to your point, Ms. Mayburn." She was wasting his time, and he readied himself to stand and bid her good afternoon.

"How many times have you been bitten?"

"Excuse me?"

She leaned forward in her seat. "I think, Pastor Wayne, you heard my question perfectly, but I'll say it again. How many times have you been bitten?"

"Ten times."

She paused. Opened her mouth and then closed it before

she spoke again. "And what do you think that says about your relationship with God? Your belief system?"

Heat flooded up his neck and cheeks, and he stood then, his hands trembling at his sides. "I think, Ms. Mayburn, that if you've come to poke fun at our faith here instead of gathering facts as would be expected from a reasonable journalist, that you ought to get in your car and go back where you came from."

"I'm sorry, Pastor Wayne. I'm not poking fun. In fact, I pride myself on being a fair and equal-minded journalist. My point in being here is to present your faith in the realism that it deserves. The realism demonstrated by how closely a pastor's belief system aligns with the faith he preaches, but I cannot do that if you refuse to cooperate with me."

"I will answer what questions about our work here that I can. I can promise no more than that," he said and took his seat once more.

She nodded her head. "I understand."

Behind him the teapot began to whistle. She fell silent as he poured her a cup and offered her a small box of sugar packets, which she refused.

"We follow the Lord's word. It is no great mystery what we believe here." He pulled his Bible from his coat pocket, set it on the desk, and tapped it with his forefinger. "Through His divine guidance, we are saved, and through His instruction, He saves us from the flames of hell. It His will that keeps us from that torment. It is His will that saves us from the serpent's bite. The handling is a testament of our faith and belief in God's will over our lives." He wondered if she could detect the rehearsed cadence in his speech. So many years ago, his father delivered similar phrases. Probably in the same seat he occupied now.

Her eyes darted around the room, and she shifted in her seat. "And if the followers are bitten? If they die?"

"If they have no fear, no sin, in their hearts, God will protect them." How long ago had he stopped believing in those words?

She paused, weighed the possible answers to her next question before finally asking it. "What about your own bites, preacher? Are those instances of fear?"

"Humans are flawed, Ms. Mayburn. Eve's sin marked us from the beginning as flawed creatures, but each time, God has saved me from death, and I praise Him for that." What he really meant was that he'd been too hasty in their handling or had overfed them or had made some other equally dumb mistake that led to their teeth in his arm and hands. It helped that Doc Simpson kept a stash of antivenin in the instances of such mistakes.

"Can I see them?"

"What's that?"

"Can I see them? The snakes?"

He paused and thought of the ten coiled copperheads and rattlers in the dark boxes in the little room at the back of the sanctuary. It was probable that at least one of them was dead. Three, maybe four months was about as long as the snakes lasted. If he was lucky.

He sighed. What did it matter if he showed her? "This way," he said and stood.

Cora was stuffing her notebook back into her bag. when a horrible keening broke the silence of the afternoon. He stumbled forward, and Cora turned to face the door.

He knew that voice.

Pushing past Cora, he ran through the sanctuary before throwing open the double doors at the entrance of the church. He gritted his teeth as he took in the scene. Another salacious tidbit for Cora's story. In the middle of the street was a group of children who circled around a girl in a blue dress.

Leah. It was Leah.

She was screaming, her mouth open and bright red against white teeth, her right arm dripping blood into the dirt. It took him a moment to realize she wasn't simply bleeding. She was squeezing the blood from her arm, looked almost as if she was nursing the earth with the bright drips. Again and again she squeezed, and she dug her fingers into the flesh and pressed a bit more blood out of her and let it fall to the dirt.

If Cora Mayburn had come for her story, she'd found it.

"Leah," he shouted as he ran down the steps and into the street. The children, with their pale, frightened faces, parted to let him through, and he gripped the girl by the arms, pulled her to him. She felt light. Hollow. Like something he could take in his hands and crush.

"I'm taking her in the church. Mary Pharr, go up the mountain. Get Sister Ruth and bring her here. As for the rest of you, get yourselves home," he said.

The children didn't move. "I said, go!" he said, and they all scattered.

He turned to Cora. Her face had gone still, and she stood motionless on the steps. "Help me get her in the church," he said and threw his shoulder under Leah's. Cora joined him, lifted Leah from the other side, and the girl hung between them. She smelled of iron and wet earth and honeysuckle.

Her screaming faded to a whimper, and it sounded as if she was muttering "Get them out, get them out," but he wasn't sure.

"What is she saying?" Cora said.

"Nothing. She needs to lie down. I have a cot in my room at the back of the church. Can you help me carry her that far?"

"Yes."

He shifted the girl's weight so his legs could do more of the work than his arms. Between them, Leah babbled, her eyes rolling up to show the whites. He tried not to see the small swelling of her breasts straining against the fabric or the wet tongue hidden behind her bloodied lips. He looked away but not before he noticed Cora staring at him, her eyes reflecting a shade darker in the dimly lit sanctuary. Flushing, he turned his gaze to the door at the back of the large room.

By the time they had Leah in the room and laid on the cot, the girl had fallen quiet, her eyes fixed on someplace that neither he nor Cora could see.

"I need to bind her arm. There are towels in that drawer there," he said and pointed to a large cherry dresser in the corner of the small room.

The rusted smell of blood was thick, and Michael swallowed hard against the lump forming at the back of his throat. What could have possibly happened to make Leah scream like that? And why had the children just been standing there? If Leah had an accident, had cut herself on something, wouldn't one of them have gone looking for help instead of standing around her with their mouths open?

Guilt could do this to a person. Make them crazed as they grappled with whatever internal demons they'd conjured for themselves. Perhaps Leah believed she should have died. Perhaps the girl had some terrible sin in her heart. He looked down at the fleck of red in her eye. For a moment, it seemed as if she smiled at him, and then she was looking past him, her mouth moving silently.

"What happened here, preacher?" Cora's voice was soft but firm.

"I reckon she must have fallen, cut herself on a rock," he

said, but the idea was implausible. It was her right arm that was bloody, and there were red stains under the fingernails of her left hand. Half-moons crusted with dried blood. No. Leah had done this to herself.

"Her mother will be here directly. It may be best for you to take off before she arrives. Ruth won't like having a stranger see her daughter like this."

"Shouldn't she see a doctor?"

"We have a doctor. He'll be along soon. I'm sure of it."

Cora frowned. She looked down at Leah and then back up at him. He could tell she didn't want to leave, but these were not her people. She had no right. Anger flared through him, and he flexed his hands.

"We'll continue this some other time," Michael said. He pointed to the door. "I trust you can find your own way out."

"Of course," she said, but her eyes were still wary. He wanted to spit at her, to tell her to get out of his room, out of his church. She didn't understand. Whatever she thought she saw, whatever she thought she understood were nothing in the face of everything he had given—everything he had *sacrificed*—for his church. His entire life swallowed and decaying inside the belly of a snake.

He turned his back and counted to five. He did not turn when he heard the door click behind her but kept his eyes trained on Leah's mouth.

Even now, he thought of pressing himself against her, of tasting the blood on her lips.

He imagined she would taste of wild raspberries.

Chapter 11

Cora had had only vague sketches of what to expect as she'd pulled onto the gravel road that led to Hensley. She anticipated small houses with front porches where mothers sat shelling peas or fathers sat cleaning guns. A clapboard meeting house at the town's center that would shine bright in the early fall morning. Children in drab clothing: the girls in long dresses or skirts and the boys in button-downs with Peter Pan collars.

Pastor Wayne didn't fit cleanly into the image she had constructed of a backwoods, fundamentalist preacher. In her mind, she'd imagined a corpulent, bulbous-eyed hellfire and damnation minister who was old enough to fart dust. With his razor-edged jawline, chestnut hair, and amber-colored eyes, Pastor Wayne was none of those things.

His calm manner had eased her nerves at first, but as she stared up at the church's steeple, the old fear crept through her hard and fast. It would be easier to run, to get back in her car and haul ass back to Atlanta where there were no churches she had to go into. No ministers to interview.

When she crossed into the sanctuary, her stomach had turned over, but she found that if she focused on his back, she could manage to keep walking. Her legs still shook, but she was able to keep going without collapsing.

It had been better in his office where she could distract herself with the books on the shelf behind him, the letters blurred and unfocused as she tried to make out the titles. Even still, her questions had been scattered and stupid, like a first-year journalist fresh out of school.

Then there was the girl. The way Pastor Wayne's eyes passed over her body. His lust a raw, exposed thing. Every part of her had gone hot watching him look at this girl, and she wanted to cradle the limp body against her, whisper that she could take the girl away from all of this and keep her safe. All of the things she wished someone had done for her.

But she had left the girl there, in that tiny room, laid out on a bed like the defiled princesses in so many fairy tales.

Tomorrow, she would come back. Tomorrow, Cora would talk to the girl and see if she could figure all of this out. If it had been a simple injury, Pastor Wayne wouldn't have asked her to leave. No, he was hiding something.

Now, with the road humming pleasantly underneath her wheels, she realized that she had every muscle in her body clenched. Between her shoulder blades, a muscle spasmed, and she brought her fist to the spot and pressed against the tightness moving down the center of her spine.

That night, in the cheap motel bed, she would dream of snakes and little girls with blood under their fingernails. She woke up screaming.

Chapter 12

"Preacher. Look at me." Leah lay before Michael, her hair spread across the small cot.

"Your arm needs attention, Leah. Can you remember what happened?" Michael knew he should wait for Doc Simpson, but the dark smears of blood needed pressure, and so he pressed a towel to the place where she'd ripped herself open.

"Please. Just listen to me," she said. Her voice fell to a whisper, and he bent, his ear next to her mouth, and her breath fell hot and damp over his neck.

"You understand something about darkness, don't you, preacher? How once that door opens, it can seep out. Infect everything it touches? How quickly it spreads, and you standing with all of your knowledge in the pulpit, screaming to your sheep how it must be torn out by the roots.

"No escape. Nowhere to find shelter or to seek solace once it opens its teeth and goes searching for the weak."

"You're hurt, Leah. You should rest. Your mother will be here soon, and Doc Simpson will get you sorted," he said, and she brought her hand to his thigh, wrapped her fingers around him and squeezed.

"Don't you like me, preacher? Don't you like the way my

skin smells of sea salt? How my neck slips out of my dress, all of that creamy flesh unmarked and clean? How long have you imagined what it would be like to be the first? To taste?"

In the long suspension of seconds between the beating of his heart, he'd thought of tearing open her dress, burying his face against the hard angles of her sex, breathing in her scent, but his hands shook, and he couldn't bring himself to act. Her eyes were all wrong. The red fleck had grown immeasurably larger and threatened to drown out the green with the leaking of blood-tinged scarlet.

When she began to scream, he thought the room would come crashing down over the both of them. Her hands found her wound once more, and she clawed at the flesh there.

"Get them out! Oh, please! The snakes are inside. They got inside!"

He pressed her body to him, clasped her wrist as the blood spurted over his shirt and shoes, and held her paper-thin body flat against the cot as she flailed. A few moments of her life leaking over him, and she went silent, her eyes fluttering into the back of her skull. He was thankful for her silence, but her body was still melded to him, and he shuddered.

Once she was still, he sat beside her and ran his hands through her hair, brought his fingertips to his tongue as if doing so would allow him to taste her. Shame flooded through him, but he could not stop himself. Before he could think his fingers traced the top button of her dress. It would be nothing to open it up, to see her flesh laid bare, but Doc Simpson or Ruth would arrive at any moment. He folded his hands together and waited.

When Ruth arrived, Leah had fallen asleep. By then Michael had cleaned Leah's wound, rubbed antiseptic into the lacerated edges of her flesh, and re-bound her arm with torn strips of a towel. The entire time, he watched her chest rise and fall.

"What happened?" Ruth said. With her she brought the smell of wood smoke, and Michael wished he could go outside, be away from the smell of this girl's blood, the burning touch of her skin.

"Not sure. She was standing in the street screaming." He didn't want to tell Ruth about Leah's wounds: how she'd dug into the punctures left by the snakes; how she'd dragged her fingernails through her own skin. He didn't want to tell Ruth about how she screamed about the snakes, that they were inside of her and must be torn out. If he told her all of this, it would only feed Ruth's delusions further. The last thing he needed was Ruth McDowell screaming about ghosts and demons during the Sunday service.

"Mary Pharr said she went crazy. That there was no reason for her to start screaming like that, but she did, and then there was blood. She didn't know how it got there, but she said there was blood." Ruth drew in a ragged breath before continuing. "Unwrap her arm."

"Sister Ruth, I don't think that's the best idea."

"Unwrap it, preacher."

He did as he was told. Slowly and with care, he unrolled the bits of towel and placed them on the bed next to the sleeping girl.

When Ruth saw her daughter's arm, she turned pale. "There is something inside of my daughter. My baby."

"Sister Ruth, please."

"The voice. It came again. It knew things, preacher. Things it shouldn't have known. And now it's inside of my daughter. It saw her, and it knew she was weak, knew it could come into her. She's always had the mark upon her. Always."

Pastor Wayne took Ruth's hand in his own. It was rough, the

fingers bony and the skin callused, and he wondered if his own felt too smooth, too soft: the hands of a man who had never known hard labor. "Leah had an accident, that's all. She's feverish and delirious. Sending her to school so soon was probably more than her body could take. Your daughter is sick, Ruth. Nothing more."

"An accident," she repeated, but her voice was dull and flat, and she dropped his hand.

"Yes, that's all. I think for tonight you and Ruth should stay here in the church. I can sleep in the office. It wouldn't be good to move her now. She needs the rest. Both of you do."

"Thank you, preacher."

He left her then and made his way to his office. He shut the door behind him and then locked it. He couldn't explain why he felt the need to do so, but he felt safer with the door separating him from Ruth and her stories.

He marked time by watching the walls. Once, he tried to open his Bible, but he knew the arrangements of all the words, and it offered him no comfort or insight.

As the hours passed, the shadows elongated, stretched strange fingers toward unknown places his eyes could not see. He wished now he'd not told Ruth and Leah they could stay. Granted, it may have been dangerous to move the girl, but wouldn't she have been more comfortable in her own bed? He could still smell her blood.

Again, he took up his Bible and flipped to Revelations. Read of the whore of Babylon, envisioned Leah robed in deep-jeweled purples, astride the scarlet dragon, her tongue tracing against its horns. He closed his eyes, breathed, but the image would not leave him.

He thought he might pray, thought he might take up the old words he learned as a boy, but he couldn't bring himself to do it. It had been so long since he truly prayed.

He sat in the chair and looked across at the place Cora Mayburn had sat that morning. Outside his closed door, something whispered. He wouldn't let himself try to make out the words.

That night, he would not sleep. Would instead listen to the whispering between the walls, the voice of a girl telling him of places not seen, things not felt. And he would cry out with no one to hear him.

Chapter 13

Cora dressed slowly the next morning. Her limbs felt heavy, as if the arms and legs she pushed through her navy blouse and black jeans were not her own. Twice, she had thought she would be sick and hovered over the toilet with her hair braided through her fingers and her eyes squeezed shut.

Today, she planned to go back to the church. With luck, she would be able to talk with the girl and her mother. If Pastor Wayne would speak with her, she wanted to talk to that pedophiliac fucker, too. There was something odd going on with the girl, some element to this story that went beyond uncovering the truths behind the mystery of snake handling.

Even if no one would talk to her—surely word had spread of her presence—she could at least play the quiet observer. After yesterday's events, she imagined that the little gas station and store at the base of the mountain would be a goldmine for gossip, and sometimes a silent presence was forgotten. Most of her stories were the results of doing nothing more than fading into the background. A bland smudge against an even blander setting.

Her face was pale, a ghostly reflection of what it should be, and she brought her hand to the mirror to be sure it was really her, that she had not vanished during the night. For a small moment, the glass felt spongy beneath her fingers, and she jerked her hand away, her breath catching in her throat.

But the glass, of course, was only glass, and her face was her own, however sleep deprived, and she could hear Jimmy's voice telling her to stop being such an insufferable coward and pull her shit together before her story was swept out from underneath her.

"Idiot," she muttered and pinched her cheeks, raked a brush through her hair, and gathered her notebook and keys. Breakfast was two aspirin. Coffee she could get later. The drive would do her good, would clear her head.

Before she left, she went to the phone on the table next to the bed and called the front desk. "Good morning. I'm calling to see if there have been any messages left for me? Room 138."

"Just a moment."

She tapped her fingernails against the table as she waited. If she went to the church first, that would give her time later in the afternoon to make her way through anyone else who might be willing to talk with her.

"Miss? Only one message. From Jimmy Townsend. Reads 'Hope the hotel doesn't give you bed bugs. Or V.D. And try not to let those fuckers convert you.'" The receptionist cleared her throat, and Cora couldn't help but smile. Of course Jimmy wouldn't have listened to her request for no contact, but at least he wasn't pumping her for information.

"Sorry about that. His sense of humor can be rather…intense," Cora said.

The receptionist's voice remained clipped. "Have a good day, Miss."

She thought of calling Jimmy back, but he would be in the Furlitz meeting and weasling his way into a story about a local plastic surgeon turned organic farmer. Real heavy-hitting shit.

She checked her reflection one last time before hurrying out the door.

Once she was inside her car, she punched on the radio, turned the volume up so that bass pounded her ears. Judas Priest's "Devil's Child" pumped through the speakers, and she laughed at the DJ's obscure choice, notched up the dial just a bit more, and sang along.

Despite the sunless, grayed morning, the drive was lovely. Trees dripped a vermilion carpet of leaves on the blacktop, and sugar maples blazed out in the final throes of glory before winter's temporary death. Cora cracked her window, breathed in air laced with ice and the late autumn smells of smoke and earth.

In twenty minutes she was pulling into the gravel lot outside of the tiny store at the bottom of the mountain. Two cars, an old Ford and an even older Dodge, were parked in the lot, but otherwise, it was deserted. Cora hesitated. She had been sure that the entire town would be out today. After all, wagging tongues would need to find other wagging tongues to divulge rumor and idle chatter, but the town was quiet. Dead.

Stepping from her car, she adjusted her blouse and tucked a loose curl behind her ear. Options were limited. She could go into the store and try her hand with the people who had ventured out, or she could drive over to the church and see if Pastor Wayne was more amenable to her presence. Or she could climb into the car and drive back to the hotel, maybe find a liquor store on the way there, pour herself four fingers of bourbon and wait for the alcohol to settle over her like a coat.

But then the door popped open, and a tall boy with a rakish grin bounded onto the porch, descended the stairs, and took a sharp left onto a worn path that led up the mountain.

"Of course," Cora mumbled. She had forgotten that the town itself, while housing the store, the school, and the church, had very few actual residences at the foot of the mountain. One house with a massive front porch stood to the right of the church, but other than that, Pastor Wayne's congregation and Sister Maguire's customers would live on the mountain and walk to town. No reason for a car. She locked her doors and walked quickly to the store.

The porch stairs creaked beneath her weight, but no one noticed when she entered the store. She slipped behind an aisle of flour and sugar, the bins open and waiting, only no one was buying today. The store, while obviously old, was scrubbed clean, and smelled of burned coffee and yeast. The counter-top held a cash register and a variety of baked goods, golden crusts leaking sugared bits of golden apple or bloodied stains of cherry.

All around her, conversations fluttered, voices cresting and falling to whispers, and she settled herself, closed her eyes and tried to focus on a single voice, to follow that bright thread out of the dark.

A woman's voice, high and quavering, rose out of the din, and sliced through the air with the harshness of condemnation. A voice of accusation. A voice of quiet violence.

"Never could trust Ruth. Living up there all alone on the mountain with her girl. Acting all high and mighty. She always was queer, but after her husband died, wasn't nobody who didn't think she was all right in the head.

"Her daddy, you know, was a fruit. I heard tell from Mable—she's got cousins in Beaufort—that her daddy found himself in a heap of trouble with some boys in town, but money does all the talking that sin doesn't want to admit."

"But her girl," another voice chimed in, but was immediately drowned out by a crowd of others shouts and protestations.

"She ain't grown. Can't blame her," a tinny male voice said, but the arguments resumed without paying him mind.

"Mary Pharr saw the whole thing, poor lamb. Said that Leah was panting like a dog in heat and dribbling spit all over herself. And then she just started digging in her arm. Ripped her bandages off and used her teeth to tear those holes wide open. And what's worse," the speaker dropped her voice now, whispered the rest.

"What's worse is that Mary said she saw something *moving* under there. Something black and liquid."

The crowd fell silent and exhaled a collective breath. Death and despair had crept among them, and their words were miniscule and pointless in the face of such creatures. These were the people of the snakes; the people who waited for the cold flicker of a forked tongue, for the smooth whisper of snakeskin against flesh, but this girl and her mother led them to fear, and they sucked it down, imbibed on it like desperate men.

"Abomination," another male's voice echoed in the silence.

"Brother Manley, she's merely a child. And Mary Pharr has always been given to stretching the truth. I once saw that girl wink—actually wink—in church."

Cora waited, concealed in her aisle. If she made her presence known now, the people who crowded the store would see her as nothing more than a gossip or a sneak, and their words would be forever lost. She wanted to talk with the woman who mentioned what Mary Pharr had seen, and perhaps even more urgent was the need to talk with Mary herself. Even if the girl was a liar, Cora could work her until the truth came tumbling out of her. Ask enough questions and any liar was bound to trip up. The confessions always came quickly after. Almost some sort of penance or desperation for Cora to know they weren't all bad.

"I've watched that woman pray, Sister Robinson. Ain't nobody who prays like that. Her head shaking back and forth and muttering to herself. Can't even make out what it is she's saying. Sounds like another language to me," the man—Brother Manley—spoke again.

"Speaking in tongues is all. It's the foundation of what we believe," the woman replied.

"Mable said that Ruth's momma was a whore, too. The men paid her, she said. The whole town thought she was a witch. That she'd worked blood magic on all of the ladies' husbands, and that at night, they couldn't control themselves and would go hunting for her like animals. That whole family is marked by the devil himself," the first woman spoke again.

"Jesus Christ," Cora whispered. For such an isolated town, the congregation knew a thing or two about the goings-on of the outside world. Dumb bunnies they were not.

"I'm telling you. That woman—and her girl—ain't right. You mark my words, there's something rotten inside the both of them, and it won't take long for it all to come leaking out," Brother Manley said. The door opening and the stomping of boots signaled a new gossiper under the guise of a customer, and Cora took advantage and slipped out.

The air had gone colder, and it bit against her bare skin. The town dangled on the edge of mass hysteria. Cora could sense it, an abyss opening, darkness reaching to grab at the ankles of minds already given to fanaticism.

There was a story here, but Cora couldn't be sure of her angle. Certainly Jimmy had sent her here to cover the religious aspect only, but this had the makings of something much larger—a Salem witch-hunt repeated. At the center, a young girl accused of possession and a lustful preacher. Jimmy would love it. The readers would love it. And even better, Cora wanted to write it, wanted to peel back the layers of these townspeople and rebuild them word by word until the bare truth lay exposed. More than anything, she wanted Pastor Wayne flayed to the bone, and his shame presented for the world to see.

In the parking lot, she hesitated. Her feet pointed toward the church, but she turned away from the large building and toward the worn path that led up the mountain. She wasn't sure where to find Leah or Ruth, wasn't sure which of the houses belonged to them. She was bound to find someone along the dirt road, and she figured they could point her in the right direction. Of course, that's if they didn't look at her as an outsider and tell her to pound sand, but she figured she would try her luck and see if anything landed right side up.

Had she looked into the woods though, searched through the dark trees, she would have seen a blurred form, a girl in a bloodied blue dress, hurrying up the mountain.

Chapter 14

Ruth spent the night curled around her daughter's slight, sleeping form, her hand pressed against the girl's chest, measuring her breaths. She dreamed of Leah as a baby, how her laugh echoed through the spaces left by Thomas' absence. Leah as a little girl spinning as fast as she could before collapsing into giggles. Leah learning to sew, her tongue poking out of her mouth, as she threaded her needle. Leah pressing her lips against Ruth's cheek, whispering her love into Ruth's ear.

When Ruth woke, her eyes were wet, and Leah was gone. The threadbare quilt had gone cold, and Ruth sat up, threw on her dress and her shoes.

When had Leah left? Ruth had always been a light sleeper. Frequently, owls or the scream of a cougar would wake her, but somehow, Leah had slipped out unnoticed.

Hurrying down the hallway, she rapped on Pastor Wayne's door.

"Pastor Wayne?"

"Sister Ruth?" he replied, and the door opened quickly. His eyes were reddened, the thin skin beneath darkened like a bruise. His clothes were rumpled. He had not slept.

"She's gone."

"What do you mean, she's gone?"

"She's *gone*," Ruth repeated. Her chest tightened with the weight of what she told him. Her girl, her broken, little girl, was wandering somewhere on the mountain right now, and there were things in the woods, her mother had said. Things in the woods that wanted their teeth and tongues inside of little girls.

"Where could she have gone?" He turned from her, grabbed at a dark coat hanging from the back of his chair.

"I don't know. The mountain," Ruth started but then stopped.

"She can't have gotten far. Surely someone has seen her."

Ruth laughed then. The tethers that held her to the world snapped, and something inside of her broke open.

Once, when Leah had been five, Ruth had found her daughter bent over a dead crow, her fingers buried inside the dark feathers, seeking out meat and bone. Her face smeared with crimson. Ruth had pulled the girl away, dragged her home, kicking and screaming the entire way that she was *so hungry, Momma, let me eat, Momma.* That night, Leah had slept like one in the grave, and in the morning she had forgotten the taste of death on her tongue and was cheery as she ate the oatmeal Ruth set before her. But Ruth had not forgotten, and she pictured her daughter now, her mouth tearing at flesh and feathers, her cheeks bloodied.

Something bad has happened.

"Ruth. Look at me now. We'll find her. She'll be fine," Pastor Wayne said.

She didn't respond, only followed him into the morning mist. It was easy for him to say the words. He had not seen what she had seen, had not known what she had known.

"He is a god of vengeance. Of wrath," Ruth said, but Pastor

Wayne did not hear. He scurried before her like a rat. Like something that crawled naked and mewling from the earth and scrabbled along seeking soft flesh.

"I see you," Ruth whispered, but still he hurried along. She knew him clearly now, the raw desire so naked in the glint of his eyes when he turned to face her and give an attempted glance of reassurance.

"Dirty, dirty," she said, and he did not hear and turned away. Unaware. Naïve. So much like her father. He had tried to hide, too. But something had seen him. Something that moved in the dark. The thing her mother had spent so many nights trying to find finally creeping out of its hole, and Ruth knew that somehow it moved among them now.

It had carved her father's sins on his flesh, hadn't it? Laid his shame bare so that all may know. Her mother, too. Their bodies peeled open like ripe fruits. She'd found their bodies wound together, their eyes plucked out, and their tongues missing. It terrified her, but she had not gone looking for the thing that had done this to her parents.

She'd put her mother and father to ground, and no one had dared to cast a word of accusation her way. Even when Ruth fled her hometown, no one came after, and if people talked in the dark of their beds of her, it didn't matter. Not in the face of something so much greater.

Her god was a god of vengeance, after all, and she was nothing more than His humble servant. It was the only thing that kept the terrible thing her mother had found in the dark at bay.

"She can't have gone far. We'll find her. Someone will have seen her if she went up the mountain," he said.

Yes. Those ungodly people. Burning with their lust and their lechery and their wantonness. They would have seen Leah.

Many of the men made it a special point to see her, to train their eyes on her breasts, the crest of her sex where her dress sometimes clung when she walked. And what would those men have done to Leah if they caught her in the woods alone and afraid? They dreamed of it at night. Ruth was sure. Dreamed of their teeth against her bare neck, their fingers wound through golden hair as they grunted and heaved and pumped their seed into her pretty daughter. Pastor Wayne would have dreamed the same things. Ruth screwed up her face and spat. Pigs.

"Would she have wanted to go home, Sister?"

She wouldn't respond to him. He was one of *them*. No better than the men of the town.

"Ruth, you must answer me. I can't help you if you don't," but Ruth only stared back at him. She wouldn't speak with this false prophet. Let her blood run into the dirt, let her very flesh melt from her bones. She would not do it.

"We'll go up the mountain. She may have woken and wanted her own bed. We may find her at home, asleep in her own blankets. She's just a frightened child who wanted to go home, Sister."

"It is no child. Not anymore, " she said, and she could have wept. Leah was surely gone. Something else lurked behind her daughter's eyes. A demon cloaked in her skin. She knew it. Her mother had told her it would happen. All of those years ago. She said there was something asleep beneath the town. That she'd heard it moving, heard it coming awake. One day, it would lay claim to her, to Ruth, to any daughter Ruth bore.

She would follow him up the mountain, but if there was a girl curled among the quilts of Leah's bed, Ruth would rend her in half, would tear with teeth and fingers until the beast was no more and blackened blood rained over all. God would see her through.

She'd run away the last time. She would not do so now.

Pastor Wayne moved ahead of her with haste, and his voice fell like lead among the mist. She brought her fingers to her lips to stifle her laughter. The fool was calling Leah's name. It would have many names now, none of them belonging to her daughter.

She had heard the names as a girl. Her mother's whisperings in the night carried their names into her room where they wormed under her skin and boiled inside of her. Those names wanted saying, wanted to be spoken aloud, and she had held them back with her teeth, her sweat and her prayers seeping into her sheets. *Sitri, Paimon, Asmodeus.* Even now, her mother's foul whispers sounded in her ears, and she clamped her fists over them, willed herself to not hear.

"Leah?" Pastor Wayne called again. Ahead of them, something stirred, a female form moving quickly through the forest.

"Shit!" the woman said and turned back to them, her hand pressed to her heart. She was dressed in a dark blouse and pants, and Ruth frowned. This woman was an outsider.

"Ms. Mayburn," Pastor Wayne called to the young woman, and Ruth glanced at him sharply. Why would he know such a woman? A woman who spoke vile words and dressed to show the angles and curves of her body? A woman steeped in sin.

"You scared the ever-loving Christ out of me," she said and then blushed a deep crimson. "I'm so sorry. But you did frighten me. It's incredibly quiet up here," she said, and Pastor Wayne nodded. The woman turned her eyes to Ruth.

"Ruth? I'm so sorry that I don't know your last name. I was actually looking for you. If you don't mind, I'd like to ask you some questions."

Pastor Wayne stepped between them and raised his hands. "I don't think right now is the best time, Ms. Mayburn."

"Of course not right here in the woods. I could accompany you home, and we could speak there?"

"I'm taking Sister McDowell home now for some much-needed rest. She should not be disturbed," he said. A brief look of annoyance flitted across the woman's face, but then she smiled.

"Of course not. Perhaps some other time."

The sky seemed to push down against Ruth, a bloated ugly thing, and she darted her tongue across her lips and tasted death in the air. Leah—*it*—was nearby. The girl's scent cloyed and turned fetid under the smells of earth and moss. Ruth whipped about expecting to see her daughter standing just beyond the trees, but nothing in the forest moved.

"It's here, preacher. Watching us. Waiting to see what we'll do. She's left her mark everywhere like some dog in heat."

"Sister, let's get you home. I'm sure Leah is there." He took her arm, but she moved away from him and bared her teeth.

When the earth swelled with the sounds of screaming, of the ripping and tearing of flesh, Ruth sobbed aloud, a solitary moan that spoke of all that the woman had known shattering. She turned her eyes to the sky.

"Let it come then. Let it come."

Chapter 15

The sky was still dark when the thing inside the girl woke. She couldn't see them, but outside she knew that clouds choked the heavens, the stars blinking out one by one until there was only darkness, only shadow. Beneath her, the Great Worm moved, his ancient stirrings resounding deep within her, and she called to him now, sang to him in a tongue long forgotten.

The townspeople would call her devil. They would gather with their snakes and speak gibberish, their faith tied to some unending, blind delirium. In the end, they would draw blood from her, scatter her bones on the mountain, and she would seep into the dirt, poison the ground and the water until they too foamed and spat and returned to the earth. But the great eye would be opened, and they all would rise again, as they always did, among blood and venom and darkness.

The girl—Leah—had been born of all of these things, the blood-red mark a totem that shone as a beacon. Years ago, another woman had come looking and found her. Had found the Great Worm. She had always acted as his emissary, his eyes and ears in a world that had long forgotten him, but the Great Worm had not woken when that woman called. Now, it was time.

The girl had guessed at her presence, could feel something else, this *other,* moving in the blood, unfurling delicate tendrils of thought that darkened all they touched, but she didn't understand what had come awake within her. Certainly, she didn't know how to control it, and it stretched inside the girl's skin, luxuriated in the smooth movements of this youthful form.

Beside the girl, a woman slumbered. Her mouth had gone slack, and she mumbled in her sleep, her brow furrowing. The girl's mother. So fervent and devout. So easily torn open and cast aside. She would pull the woman's tongue out when the time came.

Down the hallway, she knew the preacher sat, his eyes roving over page after page of scripture. His lust for the new form she inhabited rolled off of him in waves, and she ran her hands down the girl's body and dipped her fingertips in the deep hollows left by the girl's hip bones.

Eventually, the preacher would come to her broken as every man must. This holy man who drew his faith around him like some protective mantle. How easily led. How easily distracted.

It was always the same. For millennia, it had been the same.

She rose, careful not to disturb the sleeping woman, and dressed. The old blue dress went over her head, and the brown shoes laced tight on her feet. The bandages covering her arm were unnecessary, and she tore at them, crumpled the gauze and let it drift to the floor. The flesh on her arm was unmarked except for a faint streak of purple. The reminder of a bruise. Nothing more.

Slipping from the room, she closed the door behind her, and moved down the long hallway toward the sanctuary. The preacher's room was at her back, and she could sense the serpents, coiled and sleeping in their boxes.

She went carefully. Behind her, a faint murmur rose. The preacher wondering aloud, his words falling into the silence. Something like a prayer, but not quite. She could have laughed at the preacher's desperation, but she moved forward, passed through the gloom of the sanctuary that smelled of wood soap and dust.

The door made no sound when she left the church, and the early morning mist swallowed her. Around her, the town still slept, and she hurried. If the townspeople had been awake to see her, they would have imagined they'd seen a spirit, the disembodied form of a girl on the verge of womanhood drifting up the mountain, but the townspeople slept on, drew their blankets about them as their dreams grew darker.

Mothers screamed as they clutched their dead children to their breasts. Young lovers cried bitter tears as they watched the other betray them, their fingers tangled in another's hair, their lips pressed hot and tight against someone else. She stepped lightly and smiled as she felt the town shudder around her.

The girl would wake soon. She could feel her even now, a slow, hesitant reaching. She hadn't the strength to keep the girl from overtaking her. Not yet, but soon. The townspeople would see to that. They would recognize the girl for what she was and cast their accusations like hard stones at her feet.

Around her, the mountain road fell silent. The early morning birds' songs dropped away and the small rustlings of furred animals ceased as she approached. A crow flew above her, all oil-winged and dark-eyed and razor-beaked. It flapped its wings once more and then fell to the ground like a stone. She walked on, and all around her the animals lay themselves down, their breath coming no more.

"And the teeth of beasts I will send upon them, with the venom of crawling things of the dust." She spoke these people's holy words aloud and smiled at their foolishness. To believe so emphatically in ancient words that they couldn't possibly understand. Words that had existed before their prophet walked the earth, before he had descended into the earth to uncover their truth and corrupt it with his own meaning.

The preacher and the mother had woken. She could feel them moving behind her. And another. A woman. All on the mountain now. All seeking something they would not find.

"They will come to know," she said, and everything that lay beneath began to scream.

Chapter 16

"A cougar," Pastor Wayne said, but he didn't believe it. The screaming pitched lower, turned into the deep, guttural death groans of an animal.

"No, preacher," Ruth said.

His vision blurred. Verdant trees suddenly blackened and leaves curled into decay and death in the air. The bright black -eyed Susans and goldenrod and delicate flowers of Queen Anne's lace rotted and fell to the ground. Shadows gathered against the dim sun. Morning falling backward into night. He blinked, but the vision did not leave him.

Cora glanced back at him. If she saw the forest as he did, she gave no indication, but her fingers curled in on themselves, her arms rigid at her sides. *Fight or flight*, he thought.

"We should keep moving," he said.

"She'll find us all the same," Ruth said but moved forward into the gathering dark. They walked on, silence absorbing their footsteps.

"They're dead. All of them. Holy shit." Cora's voice startled him, and he stumbled.

Before them, the dead stretched outward. Animals, small and large, staring up at the sky, dark eyes large and unblinking.

"What could do something like this?" Cora said, but no

sooner had she spoken than a voice emerged from the darkness before them.

"Momma?"

"I'm coming, Leah. Momma's coming," Ruth said and stepped over the bodies of the dead. She walked slowly toward the sound of her daughter's voice, her shoulder drooping as if carrying some heavy weight, but she moved all the same.

"Don't..." Michael started, but the words died in his throat as Ruth disappeared. Leah was just a girl. A sick girl. It was his own weakness, the stress of a sleepless night that had darkened the world and prickled his skin and set his stomach churning.

His own mind demanded that he think this way. Evil stalked the world in the hearts of men. There was no beast set loose among them, no demon seated in the heart of this girl to bring chaos and confusion and violence. There were unexplained things, but they were not here. Not walking among them on the mountain.

His eyes closed against the abominations that lay on the forest floor, against the blackened sky. Behind his lids, he saw Leah again, laid on the cot before him, her hair framing her face, and her eyes wild.

Blind to the world, he licked his lips, pictured the trees flamed out in green as birds flitted from branch to branch as the town rustled awake. He pictured the church, the quiet pews with folded hymnals filled with what his father had called "the old-time traditionals." Slowly, the tightness building in his chest relaxed and the frenzied heartbeat beating a rhythm against his ribs eased. There was an explanation for this. Something simple. There were no devils here.

"Preacher?" Cora Mayburn squeezed his elbow, and he opened his eyes. Her closeness startled him—the heat and pressure coming from her hand a strange feeling—and she quickly moved away, her eyes searching his face.

His eyes were no longer shut, and the nightmare world had not vanished. His stomach heaved, and he swayed on his feet, clutched at the dark sweater Cora wore. Underneath the smells of rot and death, he could smell her perfume. Tea roses. Or lilacs? Something light and floral. It reminded him of his mother.

"Whoa there. Take it easy, preacher. Should we stop?"

"I'm fine," he said, but her fingers wrapped firmly around his forearm, and she guided him forward. He wanted to turn and run. Get himself far away from the girl Ruth had gone to find, but he let Cora lead him.

"Poison. Has to be. Or acid rain. Some kind of invasive species. That's what killed everything off. It's not like this down the mountain. No dead plants or animals there. Something got to this spot and infected it," she said.

"Must be."

They trudged on, the mountain road curving sharply to the right. Ruth had disappeared around the bend only minutes before, but to him, it felt like years had passed since she'd gone. He let Cora lead him, and he matched his steps to hers.

"She needs a doctor."

"Leah has seen a doctor."

Cora shook her head. "I mean *they* need to see a doctor. Both of them. Trauma can throw anyone into shock, and Ruth has seen more than her share of it these past few days. A doctor could help to figure out whatever this thing is. Or at least could prescribe something to help them sleep."

"God will see them through and give them solace." He spoke the words, but he knew how hollow they sounded. How disingenuous. He stood in the midst of death. There was no comfort in his forced platitudes.

"I'm sorry for what I'm about to say, but that's bullshit, brother, and you know it. Turn a blind eye all you like, but that," she thrust her chin in the direction Ruth had gone, "is a sick woman. Plenty of people would break under less. You saw the way she was mumbling to herself. The way she took off. You're a man of the people, preacher. You want to protect your sheep? Keep them from harm? Get her a doctor. A *real* doctor. Not some wrinkled prune with a medicine bag."

He laughed at that, and she glanced up at him and smiled. He wished she wouldn't.

"You may be right, but for now, Ms. Mayburn, we should find Ruth and Leah."

Voices drifted out of the gloom. Ruth murmuring and Leah responding. Despite everything, Michael's blood quickened at the thought of Leah. Her body stretched in the dirt, her hair tangled and falling to her waist. Her eyes fever-bright. Cheeks flushed. Arms opening to him and drawing him down into the earth. Burying him in decay and silence. How sweet to sleep, to lay down his heavy burden. Yes. Lie down and never rise again.

He looked before him and saw mother and daughter crouched in the dust. Their hair tangled and matted, their skin hanging from their bones as if they had aged years in the span of minutes. Two sister crones come to meet in the woods. They spoke in hushed tones, fingers tracing strange shapes in the air.

"What are they doing?" Cora said. For the first time, he heard fear in her voice, and an obscene laugh bubbled into the back of his throat. He swallowed it down. Bit back against the urge to turn to the woman next to him, and press his teeth against her throat. Something terrible and sharp moved through him.

He thought of the temptation of Christ in the desert. How the devil came to him and offered power and promised kingdoms that would kneel in fear and awe.

"Get out," he whispered, and something curled around his heart, squeezed for one beat. Two. Three. Phantom fingers traced down his spine, over his lips, and he gasped as his heart sputtered under their invisible grip.

As quickly as the feeling came, it was gone, and he gulped air, filled his lungs and gagged against the stink of it.

"She's fine, preacher. Just a little disoriented is all," Ruth called over her shoulder. Their hands were still. There were no symbols drawn in the mist by the spiderlike twitching of their fingers.

Cora looked at him, and just for a minute, he could see panic rising in her eyes—a wild stare that flitted from object to object but did not truly *see*—but she turned away. Of course she would not want to him to see her fear. She would want him to believe in her rejection of belief, to trust that her scientific logic was all that guided her, but Michael knew that in the face of the unexplainable, even the most unwavering doubter could be converted. It was only a matter of what the person accepted as truth. Both good and evil had their beauty.

Together, they walked on toward all of the things they did not understand.

Chapter 17

"A deep itch. Like a bite I can't scratch. But it's there. And I can feel it now. All of the time. Under my skin," Leah said. Her throat was raw, and she dreamed of water. Swallowing and swallowing until her insides felt like they could contain no more and her stomach gone all sloshy and cold.

Around them, dead crows lay heaped in small piles of black feathers. Had she done this? Called them down from the heavens and laughed as they flung themselves at her feet?

"Hush now. You're disoriented," her mother said and gathered her close, and Leah wished—for as long as possible—that she could go back to being a child, forget that *thing* burning in her blood and the nightmares of snakes crawling inside of her. Forget the heat between her legs when Pastor Wayne glanced her way and the shame that twined deep in her belly when she dreamed of him.

"Why did you come here, Leah?" her mother said.

"I don't know. I don't know why I'm here. I fell asleep. I was so tired. And it was so dark, and I was cold. I smelled water. I woke up, and I was here. On the mountain. And I couldn't remember." Tears burned in her eyes, and she let them fall. Her mother stroked her hair, and she looked at Pastor Wayne.

He stood before her now, his face drawn and cautious. There was a woman beside him with long folds of dark hair and dark eyes. She was pretty in all of the ways that Leah wasn't. Curved in the right places and dark lashes and long legs. When the woman smiled at her, it was with lips pinked and glossed.

There was something inside of her. It was sleeping now, but she knew it would wake again, and she wasn't sure she could hold it back. She wasn't sure if she wanted to. Underneath everything, she knew that it felt *good.*

"We should take her home. Let her rest," her mother said.

"I think she really should see a doctor," the woman said.

"You don't get to think about my daughter." Ruth whirled, her hands clenched at her sides, but the woman didn't flinch.

"Both of you have been through quite a bit. But if you don't think your daughter's health is worthy of your attention and care, I'll certainly mind my own business," the woman said.

In her few years, Leah couldn't recall anyone speaking to her mother that way. If anything, people in town would turn tail and run to avoid Ruth's cold stare, but this woman met her mother's eyes and didn't look away. Leah kept her eyes cast downward, but she smiled. If the woman wasn't so beautiful and standing so near Pastor Wayne, Leah thought that she might like her.

Finally, Ruth sighed. "Perhaps in the morning. For now, this girl needs her own bed. Preacher? Could you help me lift her?"

Without hesitation, Pastor Wayne moved toward her mother, but there was no smile of reassurance or extended hand to help her up. Instead, he grasped her under her arms as he would a child and hoisted her up roughly. If he saw her wince or heard her small cry, he gave no indication. This was not the man Leah had come to know during her girlhood. The kind man with a gentle smile and soft word for all he met. There was something hard about him, something dark in his face that aged him. Once she was on her feet, he turned and began walking back down the mountain.

"Preacher? Will you walk with us?" her mother called after him.

"I think I'll go home as well, Sister Ruth. We're all in need of rest. And reflection." He did not turn back when he spoke, and Leah felt a twinge of despair in her stomach. She had not forgotten the heat between them, the snakes that spilled over his fist and arm as they sought out her soft flesh. She made a small noise in the back of her throat. Perhaps to call him back to her, but he kept walking.

The woman kept her eyes trained on Leah, and she did not watch the preacher's back disappear around the corner.

There was a clattering, clicking noise that echoed through the trees. All around the three women, the dead animals opened their eyes. Feather and claw scurrying away or taking flight as the crows called to each other with voices that seemed lost. The air suddenly choked with wings and the ground creeping with small animals seeking their holes.

"Resurrection," her mother said, and the woman brought her hands to her mouth.

"How," the woman said, her eyes still looking upward.

But Leah knew. The thing inside of her understood. And it was beautiful.

"Leah. It's time to go," her mother said and took her hand. Together, they walked home and left the woman standing in the forest marveling at the sky. None of them thought to look down into the earth.

Beneath them, something ancient opened its eyes.

Chapter 18

*I*t's not real. It's not fucking real. Things don't just come back to life. They were dead. You saw them. Quiet and still and rotting on the ground. All of them, too. Not just one or two natural deaths or a part of that circle of life kumbayah bullshit either.

Cora watched as the birds disappeared into the grey morning, and the animals found their holes and hid.

Leah and Ruth were long gone. They'd left Cora standing with her mouth open like some dumb asshole. Only after long minutes of watching the skies clear did she come to her senses and realize she was alone.

Part of Cora wanted to follow them up the mountain, find some way to speak to Ruth or, even better, to Leah, but Ruth would never allow it, and if she pressed too hard, wouldn't allow her near Leah at all. Another part of her wanted to go back to the church and talk with Pastor Wayne about what they had seen, but she doubted he would see her either. Either way, the entire situation was fucked.

Instead, she began the slow walk back down the mountain. Moving carefully over exposed roots and loose rock, she watched the landscape come back to life. Bright yellow and airy white flowers dotted lush greenery. It made her shiver.

She doubted there would be a telephone anywhere in the town. *The town technology forgot.* When she got back to her hotel, she'd put in a call to Jimmy. Ask him if he had ever heard of anything like this, and if he hadn't, he could hopefully do some research for her. Maybe find any other places with inexplicable flora and fauna death followed by instantaneous and complete reversal. Perhaps a strange toxin or chemical released from a plant nearby or some kind of poisoned water run-off that could even lead to hallucinations in exposed individuals. There had to be a reason. Something that made sense and wasn't wrapped up with the supernatural.

She turned the ideas over and over in her head, but none of them explained why or how everything came back to life.

Before she drove back to the hotel, though, she planned on finding a bar. Hell, one of those drive-through liquor stores would suffice if they even existed in this part of God-fearing Appalachia. Jameson was what she needed. A bar would be best. Couldn't trust herself with a bottle. After the morning she'd had, killing several drinks and blacking out were the most likely scenarios. The safest ones, at least. The front desk manager had given her the eye when she checked in, and he was at least two hundred pounds overweight and still had most of his own teeth. The most handsome man in a fifty-mile radius. Outside of a fundamentalist, snake-handling preacher who wouldn't know what to do with a woman even if she threw herself at him, he was the most likely option. With enough Irish whiskey in her veins, even the front desk clerk might have an opportunity if loneliness decided to strike.

Cora didn't see the snake at first. It curled in the center of the mountain path, brown and black diamonds streaking across its back. Only when the rattle began, did she freeze.

Poisonous, she thought, marking the triangular head. The snake turned to her, its rattle a furious staccato in the background, and unhinged its jaws.

Don't move, don't move, she thought, but the snake uncoiled and crept toward her.

She thought back to her days in the Girl Scouts, scanned through anything she could remember about snakes. Give it space. If there were leaves or bushes nearby, move out of the way so it could escape. She backed away, hoping the snake would flee for the groundcover, but it followed her.

Her neck went hot. Who would possibly find her out here if this stupid thing decided it was worth the trouble to bite her? Leah and Ruth had no reason to come back down the mountain, and Pastor Wayne wasn't coming back up here after what they had seen. That was for certain. Unless some wayward, backwoods redneck decided to go for a mountain stroll, she was fucked six ways to Sunday.

The snake paused before her, and its rattle grew louder, as if the sound had crept into her brain to press against the soft tissue there. Sound becoming pain. Still, its jaws opened wider, the teeth no longer only the two fangs up front, but endless rows of tiny barbed hooks stretching back and back.

"Please," she said. It would open her up with those teeth, burrow deep inside and attach itself somewhere deep and tender. Her tongue was heavy in her mouth, and she tried to swallow, choked instead.

She closed her eyes, listened for the dry rustle as the snake made its way toward her. Like something trying to not make a sound.

No. If she was going down, she was taking a piece of that thing with her. Whatever the hell it was. She hadn't spent this long fighting tooth and nail for every scrap thrown her way for some apocalyptic harbinger of hell and damnation to swallow her up.

When she opened her eyes, the mountain path was empty once more. The snake, if it had ever been there at all, had moved on. She began to run.

A bottle of whiskey then. Definitely a bottle.

Twenty-seven minutes later, she was inside her car, her blouse sticking to her back despite the air that had grown progressively colder since the morning. It took her more than a few miles to find a gas station, but when she saw the phone booth, she almost cried from relief. Her hands shook as she dropped the quarters in the slot and dialed Jimmy's direct line. She hoped he was in the office and not in a meeting and held her breath as the phone began to ring.

"Speak of the devil," he said. At the sound of his voice, the familiar, comfortable timbre, she began to weep.

"What's going on, Cora?" She heard the creak of his office chair and the sound of his door closing.

"I'm sorry, Jimmy. I just…" She drew in a breath. If she couldn't get herself under control, what did that say about her ability to even finish this story? That was to say, if she even knew at this point what the story was. The girl. Leah. She was the important thing. The thing that made her want to stay and figure out what the hell was going on.

"Listen, kid. If you're having a tough time, just come on home. It's no big deal. Really. There's plenty of other shit happening here in town that people would just love to poke their noses into."

"I'm fine. Really, I am. Just haven't had much sleep lately, and these people. It's enough to get anybody spooked."

"They're just people, Cora. Remember that. Just people caught up in something bigger than themselves. That fervency can be frightening. But it can also be a beautiful thing."

She shook her head and wondered how much further she'd have to go before she would be near the hotel. On her way to Hensley this morning, she could have sworn she saw a package store.

"It's more than that, Jimmy. There's something else going on. There's a girl. Her mother thinks she's possessed. The town thinks it, it too. Real mass hysteria stuff." She left out her suspicions about Pastor Wayne and her need to expose him. She needed to figure everything else out first.

"Okay. So take that angle. Hysteria in Appalachia. Sexy it up with the snakes and the symbolic connections to the devil. Boom."

Of course he wouldn't think about the well-being of anyone involved. The possibility that a young girl may need some psychiatric help. And her mother. Couldn't forget about her.

"If nothing else, Jimmy, you're dedicated to the story," she said, wiping the tears from her cheeks.

"No one ever said I had a heart." She tried to laugh at that, but what came out was a choked imitation. She took a deep breath.

"You're right on that. There's more to it than that, though."

"Please tell me the preacher is running some backwoods brothel where the women read you Bible verses until you come. No. Don't tell me. I may die of happiness."

"Jimmy, I'm serious. There's something majorly strange about this town. Some weather anomaly or acid rain or biological oddity. I saw it. It's more than people getting carried away by the mythical battle between good and evil and using that as a crutch to explain away what they don't understand."

"I'm listening."

"I watched all of these plants—the ones up on the mountain—die. Just curl up and rot away. Like there was poison in the ground, and they couldn't get enough of it. I'm talking within minutes, Jimmy. Everything was dead. The trees, the grass, the flowers, the *animals*. Shriveled up like it was the middle of fucking winter. But what's more, it all came *back*," she said. Even as she spoke, she realized how crazy it sounded. Illogical. Impossible.

On the other end, Jimmy had fallen silent. She'd expected something more from him. Maybe a "holy shit" or a "no fucking way," but all she could hear was the sound of Jimmy breathing and perhaps the sound of ice clinking against glass. It made her thirsty, and she licked her lips.

"I know it sounds crazy. Like some meth addict's wet dream, but when have I ever given you bad information? I *saw* it, Jimmy. There's no way around it."

"I believe you, Cora. I do. But I've never heard of anything like this. Things don't just die and come back to life. Unless they're Jesus fucking Christ, and if the second coming is happening, I'm up shit creek without a paddle. I have lain with a man and the Good Lord will condemn me to burn in the fiery pits of hell along with all of my other male-loving compatriots. Actually, it might be kind of fun. Club Med with fire dancing."

"Just look into it, please Jimmy. Put Brunner or Matheson on it. Tell them it's a special project, and I need to know of any cases of sudden flora or fauna death and immediate resuscitation. If there's anything out there that remotely resembles what's happened here, I want to know about it."

"Of course. We'll be in touch if we find anything at all. The biology nerds would love it if there's a natural component to what's happening out there." He paused. "Take care of yourself, hey Cora? I can't have my top reporter losing her marbles in the middle of bumfuck nowhere."

"Thanks, Jimmy. I appreciate it. I really do," she said. They said their goodbyes, and she listened for the click as he hung up the phone. If she knew the way he operated, Jimmy would have the information she needed by sunrise the next day. Brunner and Matheson would be working late tonight. Poor idiots. Of course, they had known what they were in for when they signed on with Jimmy. She had, too. No social life. No family. Something her mother had never ceased to remind her of whenever Cora went to visit.

She climbed back into her car, her muscles sore and her mind fogged, and she thought of her mother. Thought of how she'd been so proud when Cora had gotten hired. She wondered if the loss of her mother would ever stop hurting.

Neon lights flashed up ahead, and she turned on her blinker, glanced at the clock on her dash. 1:24. There were worse sins than getting piss-ass drunk before five o'clock on a Thursday afternoon in the middle of absolutely nowhere. After all, she had just seen the impossible, and that deserved a little liquid memory fog.

"Good Lord, forgive me," she said and pulled into the empty lot.

Chapter 19

Ruth brought her daughter home, scrubbed her clean—the white washcloth and bathwater turning a dingy brown—and tucked her into bed. Several times, she thought of pushing Leah under the water, holding her there until her thrashing went still, but she found she could not do it.

They had not spoken on the walk home. Placing one foot in front of the other, Ruth had listened to the wind, to the birds with broken songs that came from throats dead and rotting only moments before and wondered if the ground would simply drop out from underneath them. If the dirt would take them back into itself and swallow down all of the horrors they had seen.

She had thought she would pray when they returned home, but after she had stripped her daughter down, cleaned her body and wounds, slipped the white nightgown over Leah's head, she found the words would not come. Locked inside of her, they twisted into something obscene, and she held them back.

Through all of it, Leah was complacent. Quiet. Her eyes followed Ruth's movements, and when she went to leave the room, the girl clung to her, and Ruth sat with her until she fell asleep.

Even with Leah comfortably asleep, Ruth could not rest easy. Leah was safe, breathing easily in the next room, but Ruth's skin itched, and she washed the porcelain mug that she had left in the sink the day before and dried it with her apron.

She did not see the snakes at first, but she heard them. The sound of something dragging itself along on its belly echoed around her. She turned and watched as they made their way past the stove into the far right corner of the room before curling up like house cats.

"I see you," she said. The snakes flicked their tongues at her and settled down for what appeared to be a long rest.

"It was Eve who spoke to the serpent. But how was she to know it would understand her? That it would have her do unspeakable things? There was no one else to talk to," she spoke, and the snakes winked dark eyes at her.

"Can you taste our sins? Could you taste mine? Would there be punishment for all that I've seen? All the secrets I've locked away?" She extended her arm, but the snakes coiled into themselves, their bodies intertwined in an endless circle. She thought of walking to the knife block, pressing the butcher knife to her wrist, and letting her blood drop onto their backs, but she didn't think it would matter. They would not have her.

Once, she would have imagined this was a sign of her faith; that God smiled upon her and kept the snakes from her flesh. That she was pure. A holy sigil of the almighty power of His grace and His mercy, but now there was only the stink of unworthiness and the idea that something had turned a great eye upon her and seen only emptiness.

"My mother spoke of you. Wanted to bring you into this world. She tried and tried to open the door. Blood and sex leaking out of her like honey from the comb. You heard her, didn't you? And you came," she said.

In the other room, something vast and dark slept in the skin of her little girl. It had gone silent for now, but for how much longer? When Leah woke, would the beast come with her? Or would it stay hidden and quiet? Biding its time in the places where the world didn't look too far or too deep.

The snakes remained curled in their corners, so she put the mug away, walked to her own bedroom, and sat on her bed. The wedding ring quilt she'd made before Thomas proposed was tucked tight under the mattress. She did not bother to cover herself but lay on top of it, her shoes still on her feet, and closed her eyes.

If the snakes were going to come, let them come. She slept.

When she woke, the house had gone dark, and the moon shone bright and silver through her window. There was a light in the kitchen, and someone hummed something slow and tuneless. She felt as if she recognized the song, and she pushed herself onto her elbows and listened.

Woozy and sleep-laden, she swung her feet onto the floor, and whatever hummed stopped for a moment. Ruth had the distinct impression it was listening, waiting for the tell-tale signs of her coming awake.

It came down the hallway. Feet moving lightly over the wooden boards, and the hushed swish of a skirt.

"Leah," Ruth said, and the footsteps paused just outside of her door.

"I didn't want to wake you," Leah said, and Ruth turned to her daughter, took in the slight form, the blonde hair come loose, a spot of dried blood on her cheek.

Just her little girl. Her Leah. The girl she had nursed and loved and fought for all of these years. For so long, she had ignored the gossip and whispers of the town because Leah was the fixed point around which her world revolved. She was all that mattered. Even now, as the snakes wound up and around Leah's legs, their tongues tracing her thighs, she wanted nothing more than to open her arms to her and breathe in everything she knew about her girl.

"I don't know why I was ever afraid. I always thought it would be painful. The promise of teeth and poison. But there are other things that crawl along on their bellies. Things that live in the dark with their eyes and ears closed. Sleeping. So terrible when they wake. So beautiful," Leah said.

Slowly, Leah stepped across the room, her hands outstretched.

"Pray with me, Momma," Leah said and sat next to her, twined her fingers through Ruth's.

Ruth turned her face away. When the snakes touched their flesh to hers, she began to weep.

Chapter 20

Leah woke to silence in the house. Moonlight filtered through the window, and she lifted her hand and let fingers drift through the shimmering light. She remembered the mountain, remembered the taste of blood on her lips, the smell of death thick in the air, and she smiled.

She squirmed under the quilt and lifted her nightgown so she could press her hands against her stomach.

"Where are you?" she whispered, and she felt something twist inside of her. "What do you want?" she said, but she already knew. Already understood what had come to live under her skin.

Not the devil. No. Something much, much older. More beautiful than even that fallen angel.

She curled into herself, covered all of the soft, delicate places of her body, and listened to the long, slow sounds coming from the kitchen. The wound on her arm throbbed, but the feeling was not painful.

For so long she'd been quiet. Careful. A good girl to make her mother proud. Her shame burning within her as she tiptoed around the things she wanted.

And now...

"All this and more," she said and giggled. The sleeping princess and the monster come to her door. Everything. She could have everything.

The snakes crept closer to her door, and she peeled back the quilt. Why had she ever been afraid? What they carried inside of them was lovelier than anything she'd ever known.

"Oh, please," she said. A request. An invitation.

When their cool skin slid over hers, she closed her eyes and listened to all of the things they could give her. All of the things *he* could give her. The Great Worm.

"The whole world," she said and thought of Pastor Wayne moving above her, his hair against her face, his lips pressed to her throat.

Why fight so hard for something that had never brought her any joy? Why fight for a belief her mother had passed on to her? A belief to which she'd never laid any claim.

The snakes wound their way over her legs, her belly.

She sighed.

"Yes."

Chapter 21

When Pastor Wayne stumbled out onto the main road, the town had gone quiet. The usual bustle of people coming and going from Sister Maguire's store, their arms laden with sugar or milk or coffee, was absent. Children should be running about, shouting and laughing as their mothers looked on, distracted by their own conversations—swapping recipes or instructions on how to remove grass stains from white cotton—with the more godless gossiping quietly behind their hands. The church doors should be open, a few believers trickling in and out to kneel in the quiet of the sanctuary and whisper their prayers into the sky.

He'd closed the doors to the church before he left, and he did not think he would open them. Not today. As he walked down the steps, he wondered if he would ever open them again. Even the slight sounds of those whispered prayers would itch just under his skin, and he was afraid that if he heard them, he would scream, his fingers twitching with the desire to tear out the throats of those seeking God.

What would it be like to simply gather the few items he called his own, lock the doors, and walk away? Find a city with people who didn't know his name and who didn't think of snakes and the desperate holiness that clung to his fingers when they saw him? He could find a job, get an apartment, and forget about this town, this life. Live quietly and die quietly, and when he went into the darkness, not worry about what came after.

His faith was weak. Had always been weak. He couldn't remember a time when he truly believed the things pouring from his father's mouth every Sunday.

He brought his hands to his face as if he could keep the eye of God from seeing his quavering, puny cowardice. Because that's what it was. This need to run, to hide, was proof he knew nothing other than turning tail.

The girl waited for him at the base of the stairs, her knees tucked carefully beneath her as she played with a long, blonde curl. He pretended not to see her, but she stood and stepped toward him. She still fidgeted with her hair, and he wished he could smack her hands and shout at her to be still.

"Mary Pharr," he said, and the girl winced and cast her eyes downward to study the dirt.

"Preacher. I wanted to. I thought I would. I wanted," she stuttered and stopped. His muscles burned and his head ached, and he wished the girl gone, but she stood before him, and he sighed.

"I'm quite tired today, Mary," he said. She nodded and lifted her head. Tears stained her cheeks. It was his duty to hear the voices of his congregation: their concerns, and guilts, and sins, and doubts. No matter how much easier it would be to run.

"Come inside then," he said and unlocked the front door. He intended to take the girl to his office, pour a glass of water, and take an aspirin, but she sank into the first pew she came to.

Sobbing, Mary buried her face between her hands. The sound echoed through the church, and he had the idea that the walls themselves were mocking him.

He hovered beside her. Could he get to his office and return before she noticed? He would come right back, and in twenty minutes, the iron band around his head would have eased, and he could listen without wanting to grab her shoulders and shake her until her neck snapped.

He shifted his weight forward, but the girl grasped his arm and pulled with a strength that surprised him.

"Preacher. I'm dreaming about her. Every night. She comes with the snakes and opens me up with her teeth," Mary said and shuddered. Her fingernails sliced into his arm, and he wondered if his blood beaded beneath her fingers.

"There's only the dark, and it sounds like the ground is breaking open and everything is opening up, and she's laughing and whispering and telling me to be still. Be a good girl. To open my mouth."

Michael's head pounded, and he brought his hands against his temples and squeezed, but the pain beat back from within. It made him lightheaded, and he forced himself to breathe and to focus on the air filling him up.

He did not need to ask her who it was that came to her in the night, who it was that stalked through her dreams. Mary brought her fingers to her mouth, and his blood stained her lips, her cheeks.

"I wake up with her eating my tongue. I can still feel her. Lying in bed, I can still feel her weight against my chest, and I can't breathe. Please, preacher. I don't know what to do. She won't leave me," she said and leaned against him.

"It's just a dream, Mary. It means nothing," he said and went to stand, but once more, she took his arm and held him in place. Cocking her head, she watched him, and he thought he saw something in her eyes change. The color going black or the pupil dilating suddenly.

"You would have me pray. Wouldn't you, preacher? Pray and ask that God cleanse me of these wicked thoughts. You would tell me it's my fault. That I brought this upon myself, and now I'll pay for everything that came before.

"Say it out loud. Tell me all of the thoughts you've locked up in your head," she said and pulled his hand against her sex and held it there. Mary's hand was unnaturally hot, and he tried to pull away but found himself locked against her heated skin.

"Mary. Stop this. You're confused."

"Surely you've heard about me, Pastor Wayne. From the boys. From the girls, too. That I'm bad. Wicked. Sinful. About what I've done when people ain't looking. Did I tell you that I *like* it when she takes my tongue inside of her? That she presses against me, and that it feels good when the snakes push my legs open? Don't you want to feel good too, preacher?" she said and pumped herself against his hand.

Michael tore himself away from her and fell into the aisle. His legs worked uselessly underneath him. Laughing, Mary sat in the pew watching him as he scrambled away. She stayed seated and watched him go.

"We'll be waiting, preacher. You've called us many things over the years. Witch. Demon. Devil. Spirit. Haunt. But we are awake now, and you'll know what we are," she said.

He turned for the back of the sanctuary and made his way to the door that led to the main hallway that would take him to his office. *Get away, get away, get away.*

Hiding from Mary like some scuttling bug was the only thing driving him, and he broke into a trot halfway to the door and reached his arm forward, afraid that he wouldn't find the knob, but then the metal was against his hand, and he pushed himself through.

The door closed behind Michael, but he could still feel

Mary's eyes on his back, and he wiped at the line of sweat that had worked its way down his cheek.

"Please," he said. The deep quiet of the church answered him. These manifestations of evil, of the devil, of whatever it was that had taken root, these were things he had only read about, heard whispered among his congregation when the nights were dark and long and the big cats screamed on the mountain.

That night, he picked up his Bible and read the same verse over and over but the words washed over him without meaning, the small cot and blanket going hot beneath him, and his body burning with what was surely a fever.

Chapter 22

The girl who used to be Mary Pharr sat in her pew. Her eyes burned in the dark, and she listened to the preacher man not sleep. Sometime after midnight, she rose and walked to the door, placed her hand against the wood, and traced a cross into the grain.

"Oh, preacher," she said and turned away. He did not feel her when she went, but there would come a time when he would feel and know all of them. All of the still, sleeping things still hidden under the earth.

She stopped just outside the church and knelt, pressed her body into the dirt and brought her tongue to the grit, and opened her mouth to what lived there.

It came into her. And it was good.

Chapter 23

"Whiskey?"

The pimple-faced ball of grease at the front counter pointed vaguely toward the back right corner of the store without looking up from his paperback and grunted.

"Thanks a heap," Cora said and wound her way through the maze of half-empty boxes of vodka toward what she hoped would be her salvation.

"Please, for the love of all that is good in this world, have something that doesn't come in plastic. I don't care what it is as long as it's not fucking bottom-shelf bullshit," she said and sidestepped a puddle of standing water. Above her, the ceiling dripped from a large section of tile that had browned and rotted away. A hole large enough to stick her head through leaked in large dribbles, and the water was a deep brown. The color of rust. Or blood.

"Nice," she said, but beggars can't be choosers, and soon enough she was standing in front of a row of—thank God—glass bottles with labels she actually recognized. She grabbed the Jameson and turned but thought better of it and doubled back to the shelf.

Might as well get two. Seemed like she would need it if things kept going the way they had been so far. And by that, she meant absolutely off the rails, deep in the shit nuts.

Fuck it. Make it three.

"Having a party?" the cashier said as he dog-eared his book and peered at the bottles she'd piled on the counter.

"Something like that," she said and handed him one of the hundred-dollar bills she'd stashed in her purse. Better to travel with cash is what Jimmy had always told her, and she'd trusted him on this.

"The good stuff, too. All the parties I go to it's only ever Hunch Punch made out of Everclear or some shit somebody cooked up. To be honest it tastes like dog dick. Nothing like this stuff."

Cora nodded and wished he would just bag up her stuff and hand her a receipt so she could be out the door, but he only stood there, turning the bottle over and over in his hand and looking at her. He licked his lips.

"Sometimes, when ain't nobody in the store—and that's pretty much all the time—I like to think about what I'd do if a girl came in here. By herself. I could trap her, you know? Lock all the doors while she's hunting for whatever she came in to buy. Wouldn't even notice me doing it. Come up behind her real quiet like. She wouldn't even feel it. At first. But later she'd feel it. A lot. A whole awful lot." He smiled then. A mouthful of green teeth, and her stomach lurched. Behind the counter, he'd unzipped his pants and was working the hand not holding the bottle against himself, and he revealed himself to Cora, flashed a mass of pale flesh that made her want to retch.

Cora glanced at the door, and he watched her do it as he pumped his hand faster and faster. She couldn't be sure, but it didn't look as if the door was locked. Surely she would have heard him moving, but she had been navigating boxes, focused on finding the whiskey.

"That's what I think about. Oh, yes. When nobody's look-ing," he said and tipped his head back. His Adam's apple bobbed as he swallowed, and Cora thought of grabbing one of the bottles, breaking it against the counter, and drawing the ragged edge across his throat. If she gutted him like the animal he was, how long before anyone found him? Her hand crept across the counter, and she wrapped her fingers around the neck of one of the bottles.

His breathing had gone ragged, and his eyelids fluttered, his mouth gone slack and working soundlessly. Shaking, Cora drew her arm back and raised the bottle over her head. If she gave herself time to think, to wonder if she was strong enough to do what needed doing, to wonder if there were security cameras, to consider that the door really was locked, she may never leave this place. She paused and pressed her fingers against cool glass.

She brought her hand down and across in a wide arc.

The bottle glanced off his temple, and he toppled, landed on his back with a loud whump. She counted to ten. To twenty. When she got to fifty and was certain he was out cold, she peered over the counter. He lay on his back, his hand still wrapped around his puny dick. Cora resisted the urge to spit on him.

"What the fuck is wrong with this place?" Her shoulder ached from the impact of hitting him, and she rotated her arm.

She had no desire to stick around long enough for him to wake up, so she hurried for the door. It didn't matter that she was leaving without what she came for. She was *leaving* and that was all that mattered. The door swung wide when she pushed against the handle. He had not locked it.

"You little cretin. I hope your dick rots off," Cora said and turned back for the whiskey she had left on the counter. If there even was a security camera—which she highly doubted—it would have captured everything he had done, too. No way would he call the cops for three missing bottles of Jameson when his mug was on camera beating it in front of a stranger.

Once she was in the car, she unscrewed the cap and took a long, hard pull. Maybe there was something in the water. Something that had gotten into the supply, tainted it, and turned everyone in a fifty-mile radius crazy. Made them see things. Hear things. Act in ways they wouldn't normally, or act on the secret things they kept locked away.

Maybe this was why she had seen things, too. One more deep pull and the whiskey settled hot and slick in her stomach, her nerves easing into something like numbness.

Another theory for Brunner and Matheson to test. Spores or fungi or bacteria could worm their way into anything. Maybe she was the wrong woman for the job, and what was actually needed in this strange town that believed in the terrible intertwining of serpents and God was not a journalist but a scientist.

When the sun rose tomorrow, Cora would return and ask her questions. Listen and watch and try not to think about the dark world of the occult and the unspoken parts that led only to nightmare. For now, there was only the promise of ice and the remaining whiskey and sleep.

She drove on into the dark.

Chapter 24

Asoft wind blew through the forest, but nothing moved. No leaves drifted from the tops of trees. No grass bent to kiss the ground. The animals slept, and all of the things that belonged to the night stayed hidden, watched with bright eyes from the holes that kept them safe from what moved out in the open.

Leah walked along the path, her feet soundless against the hard-packed earth. Ruth shambled beside her, her hands outstretched, feeling the air as if it could guide her, hunting for any sign, any signal that would show her the correct way.

As she walked, tree branches snatched at her hair, snagged her dress as if they were telling her to stop. To turn back and away from what her daughter was taking her to do. Brushing them aside, Ruth kept her hands in front of her, feeling along the path and listening to her daughter move ahead of her.

She'd thought there would be pain when Leah pressed her thumbs into her eyes, but there had been only the light and then the dark, and the soft pop of her optic nerve separating, and the smell of blood in the air.

It was better this way. For Leah to pluck out her eyes and feed them to the snakes. It would be best if she couldn't see them when they came. And Leah had promised they would come. The Great Worm and his children.

She could feel and taste them now. They tasted of fear. Of death.

Ruth's mother had not been able to open the door to the terrible things that lived beyond, but her granddaughter had. Leah. Her girl.

Earlier, Leah sat with Ruth and prayed, spoke in hushed words of everything that moved underneath and of the wonder and beauty they could bring. The love and the sin and the clean and the dirty all coming together to create something greater. Something they had never been able to understand.

"There is no such thing as sin. As redemption or punishment," Leah had said, and Ruth swallowed down this new truth. She had not cried, and the world felt like a safer place now that she couldn't see it.

"Here," Leah said and knelt, and her fingers scrabbled against loose rocks and dirt and roots. "Help me, Momma."

"I can't, Leah. I can't do it."

"Momma," Leah said, and Ruth wanted to hug her daughter, to pull her tight against her chest until the thing that stood before her was her girl again, but it was done. When a beast opens its mouth, there is no shutting it.

And Leah had promised her it would be beautiful when he woke.

Together, the woman and girl dug. Down and down and down until their fingernails ripped away and their blood joined with the dust of the earth, and what slept there drank of them.

Slowly, the ground opened around them, and there were things down there in the dark. Things that moved and spoke with words that slid over Ruth like oil. Soft and wonderful and warm.

Cocooned inside the earth, Ruth listened to their voices,

but this would not be a rebirth. There would be no hardening chrysalis to keep her from harm as the winter months came. No glorious flowering in the spring. No. This was not a renewal, but she would serve her purpose.

Once, when she and Thomas had first been married, he had found a snake pit. Dozens of bodies heaped one on top of the other. A single, writhing mass of scaled creatures moved together as one. She'd shrank back when he brought her to see it, but he'd pressed forward.

"When I was a little boy, I read a story about this. People would dig a hole, fill it with snakes, and throw someone down there. As punishment or for revenge. Terrible, terrible thing. I didn't think much on it then. Just a boy reading adventure books, but seeing it now. Like this. It's a terrible thing," he'd said, and she'd taken his hand and squeezed until her knuckles turned white.

"This town is poisoned, Ruth. That preacher is no holy man. He stands up there, and he says the words, but he doesn't mean them. I've been thinking lately. That we should leave," he'd said, and together they'd watched the snakes.

Two days later, he was dead.

She hadn't left. There wasn't anywhere else to go.

He hadn't understood how beautiful it could be. How lovely when everything finally came apart. She understood now.

Ruth thought of Thomas' hands in her hair and the sound of his voice in the middle of the night. The way he would reach for her in his sleep.

It had not been Thomas that had come to her in her dreams. The terrible, bloodied visions. All that time that it took for her little girl to grow up, she had thought that it was him. Coming to warn her. To protect his family.

It had not been Thomas, and the thought made her want to

weep and laugh at the same time. There were other things at work, and the birth of a girl with a blood-red mark had helped to usher it in.

Perhaps this was her mother's final act. Even as the creature had taken her, the old woman had planted a seed that had opened a doorway that could not be shut again.

She thought all of these things as the snakes came into the pit she dug with her daughter and wrapped themselves around her.

She remembered them all. Her mother. Her father. Thomas. Leah. All of the little things that made up a life of sin and joy and sorrow.

Deeper and deeper into the earth she drifted until her mouth was full of the snakes; her teeth clamped down and the scream inside of her died away as they ate of her body.

Ruth would not be born again, but she would feed them as a mother feeds her children.

When the screaming began, Ruth wept, and they swallowed her tears, too.

Chapter 25

*B*urning. *Something is burning.*

Pastor Wayne opened his eyes. For a moment, he thought that he was in his childhood bed, his mother and father sleeping just down the hall.

Only, this was not his old bedroom, and Michael had buried his mother and father some ten years past. He shook his head and raked his hands through his hair. He had not expected to sleep, but when he sat on his cot, it had come on, immediate and deep, and taken with it the horrors of the previous day.

Rolling onto his side, he pushed himself up and swung his feet to the floor. As he moved, something knocked at his door, and he jumped.

Mary. Mary Pharr. He had forgotten about the girl he left sitting in the sanctuary.

A chill crept up his spine. Had she not left? Had she been there this entire time, just outside of his door waiting for him to wake up? Holding his breath, he stood and listened.

Again, something knocked.

"Mary?" he called, and whatever was on the other side of the door did not answer, but it laughed. The high, tinkling laugh of a girl, and the sound of it made him want to curl into a ball and go back into the memory of being a child. Back into a place where his mother and father would protect him from the monsters in the night.

"Go home, Mary. It's late," he said, and he hoped that his voice did not sound as weak as he felt. He fidgeted and waited for her to respond, but whatever was outside the door had gone quiet.

It was the smell that made him open the door. An acrid odor that made him nauseated. He covered his mouth and nose with his shirt and moved to the door and paused before throwing it open.

There was no one there. No Mary Pharr crouched down, her fingers and lips stained red as he had imagined. Only that smell moving heavy and dark through the room.

Glancing up and down the hallway, he stepped out and turned right. The odor thickened, became palpable, and he realized what it was.

It was the smell of flesh burning. Of something live and wriggling tossed into flames. The smell of a hundred winter nights with his father as they skinned and dressed the rabbits they caught. His father's voice guiding him, showing him how to skewer the meat, how to hold it over the bright, dancing flames.

"We eat what we kill, boy. It's like spitting in the face of the Creator to take something from his earth and not use it," his father had said, and the smell had washed over him. It had not made him hungry.

Michael could hear the flames now, a quiet crackling that led him back into the sanctuary. He moved down the hallway and passed the two doors that led to the Sunday School classrooms for the children. Pausing at the entryway of the sanctuary, he glanced into the vast room, and the smell overtook him.

In the center, directly in front of the pulpit, a rectangular crate fashioned from rough wood stood, and a fire raged inside of it. Orange flames licked at the corners, and the wood there smoked and blackened, but the crate itself had not yet begun to burn. The flame only consumed whatever was inside the crate.

Pastor Wayne knew what lived there. The dark bodies that he brought forth each week. The congregation's faith and sin bound together under the moving, scaled backs of those creatures that rattled in their box. Teeth and venom and fear. He passed them around his congregation every Sunday, and his people praised him for it, lifted their voices and hoped they would be chosen, prayed that this week, God would press his holy finger against their bodies, mark them as worthy of selection.

"Test us," they said and hoped for the sharp sting of poison entering their bloodstreams.

And now, the creatures burned.

Another memory of his father came to him then. The old man leaning over the body of a copperhead, the point of his shovel buried against its neck. The round black eye staring up at him as if in accusation.

"You have to burn them, Michael. If you don't, three more will spring up in its place. You have to burn a snake to keep the other ones away. A wild snake is different from the ones we keep. You understand?"

"Yessir," he'd said and helped his father build a fire. Michael hadn't wanted to touch the snake, and he'd used the shovel to pick up its lifeless body and throw it over the flames.

"The head, too," his father had said and watched as Michael slid the head onto the shovel and tossed it into the fire as well.

Michael sat in the front pew, his eyes still on the flames. It was the same pew he'd sat in as a boy—his mother in her best hat next to him—and he watched the snakes burn. When the time came, he would smother the fire and bury the bodies behind the church so the big cats wouldn't come sniffing around.

Michael sat in the same pew that held the memories of his father's preaching, but his father did not stand in the pulpit anymore. Now, in this moment, there was only the sound of the snakes burning, the popping as flame turned the skins to smoke.

When the doors to the church slammed open behind him, he did not turn. The thing crept in on four feet. He could hear the slow shuffle of each one. It came to sit behind him and breathed foul air into his ear. Still, he did not turn, and together, they watched as the snakes became smoke and drifted upward.

"What are you?"

It reached out, touched his shoulder, but it was not a hand. No fingers grasped at his flesh and bone. Just a slight pressure that receded as the creature leaned away, the pew creaking beneath its weight.

"Turn and see, Michael," it said, and the rank smell of its breath overpowered the burning. The deep, sulfurous smell of swamp water. Of something that came from deep beneath the ground.

"What are you?" he repeated, but the creature did not respond, and he listened as it left the bench, moved back down the center aisle, the doors closing softly behind it.

Only when it was gone did he realize he had bitten through the inside of his cheek, and blood filled his mouth. He brought his tongue to the spot, wincing as he traced the raw edges his teeth had left.

Rising, he went to the box and looked down at the snakes that now smoldered. Had they known that death was close?

Had they felt it in their skins when the flame ignited; in those first moments before the fire took them, did they know that it brought destruction?

Would he know, would he understand when his moment finally came?

Chapter 26

Cora slept without dreaming, and when she woke, all she remembered was a vague, amorphous gray. A mist that cradled her as she slept, and she dressed methodically.

Based on the things she'd seen—or thought she had seen—the day before, a cold dread should be building in her belly, but she felt at ease. Calm. Rested.

The restorative miracles of whiskey, she thought and laughed. Despite mewling hunger in the pit of her belly, she felt better than she had felt in quite a while. None of it made sense. She should feel like road kill.

The hotel phone rang, loud and insistent, and she jumped. She let it ring twice more before she lifted the receiver to her ear.

"Yes?"

"Cora, it's Jimmy."

She slouched forward and rubbed her fingers over her forehead. "I hope you have good news for me," she said.

"Brunner and Matheson are on it as we speak."

"Hey, if they're at it, could you have them take a look into the possibility of hallucinogens? You know, natural occurrences. Something in the water, or a bacteria that could be airborne. Cause hallucinations only in the area. Or a local plant everyone decided would be great in salads."

"Like ergot in the Salem witches? I'll have them check. But, Cora, if it was a plant, you would have had to have eaten it, too. Only makes sense if you saw the same things that everyone else saw."

She thought back to her first meeting with Pastor Wayne and the tea he had served. It had been loose-leaf. No sachet with a brand name stamped on the small paper label. Who knows what he had given her. Perhaps one of the church ladies dried her own mix and passed it around the congregation.

"The preacher gave me some tea. During our first meeting. It could have had something in it," she said, and Jimmy sighed on the other end of the phone.

"Cora, didn't your mother ever tell you not to take candy from strangers?"

"I hear you. I hear you. But it's possible, right? Seems logical that if the entire town was exposed to the same toxin, whether it's in the air, the water, or ingested in food or drink, it could lead to mass hallucinations or at least bizarre behavior. Or that it would affect some more than others. Or that some have been exposed and some haven't."

Her brain cycled through the possibilities, and the fear she had felt the day before became a tiny, insignificant thing. Here was her explanation.

"Jimson Weed. My mother called it the Devil's Snare. Lots of people who lived off the land or were just dirt poor would gather it, boil it, and eat it. Spend the next few days fucked out of their minds. Wander around with their dicks flopping in the wind screaming about how there were holes in the sky. Places where the dark could come through," Jimmy said, and Cora glanced out the window. Hadn't she closed the curtains the night before? She couldn't remember now. Through the glass, outlines of pines reached jagged lines into the gray sky.

"They use it in voodoo ceremonies supposedly. Haitian zombies. You never know, Cora. There's weird shit out there in the world." He paused and the sound went muffled as if he'd put his hand over the receiver.

"I have to go. You're headed back there today, aren't you?"

"Definitely. Figured I'd poke my nose around a little bit. Talk to some more people. Test some of these theories."

"Good. I'll be in touch if we find anything interesting. In the meantime, be careful. Like I said. Weird shit out there. Never know what people might be capable of," he said and hung up.

Fifteen minutes later, Cora turned off of the highway and onto the dirt road that led to Hensley. The car bounced through rut after rut, threw her violently to the left, then the right, and she wished for better shocks as her head knocked against the window.

She rounded a corner, and the trees opened into the town proper. The church stood in the center with the small school just behind it. There should be children inside of that school, their heads bent over books, lips moving soundlessly as they stumbled through the words.

But they weren't in the school. They stood outside in small groups, quiet and pale-faced. Huddled among them, the adults clustered together: mothers with their arms around the younger ones; men with their hands in their pockets looking on silently.

Cora parked the car and got out. Some of the townspeople turned and watched her, but they did not keep their eyes on her for long.

Walking among them, she picked out snatches of conversation. Bits and pieces of the words they passed between them.

"No eyes."

"He didn't find her."

"The girl."

"Snakes got to her."

"Found her in a hole."

At the steps of the church, Cora paused. She wanted to talk with Pastor Wayne, but he may not be inside, and she wondered if the crowd would even let her enter. She was an outsider, a smear of sin and filth, unworthy of entering their sacred place of worship, but as she went up the steps, they made no moves to stop her.

A blast of cool air swept over her face when she entered the sanctuary. And there was something else. A smell that crept into her throat and clung there. Smoke. There had been a fire here. Glancing at the ceiling, she took in the sickly brown marks that resembled two eyes staring down as if something just above her head was casting down its judgment.

"Ms. Mayburn," Pastor Wayne said, emerging from the back of the church.

It was as if a shadow had come out of the gloom. His face was gaunt and pale, and a mottled purple darkened the skin under his eyes.

"You haven't slept," she said.

"Very little. If you've come to ask more questions, now isn't the time for them."

No shit, she thought, but thought better of saying it aloud.

"Why is everyone outside, preacher?"

He closed his eyes and sighed. She knew any other woman would pity him, but her disgust poured from her like water. She couldn't explain it, looking at him—this man who appeared to have aged ten years overnight—Cora thought of her mother. Those first months after the diagnosis when the physical manifestations of the cancer were slight. The changes so small you could think that it was only fatigue or poor diet.

She bared her teeth. He deserved it. All of the pain and anxiety of these moments.

"Ruth McDowell is dead," he said, and Cora took a step backward. He moved away and sank onto the top step leading up to the pulpit, and she followed and stood before him.

She spoke before she could think. "What the fuck do you mean, she's dead?"

"You were there. With us. You saw. How strange everything went. How it died and then came back to life. And then there were the snakes, and then they came in and said they'd found her in the woods. Her eyes…"

She sank into one of the pews, her fingers twitching against the rough wood beneath her. If she pressed hard enough, she imagined it would splinter beneath her touch. Chaos and confusion underneath. It was a fitting metaphor for everything that had happened in the past few days.

Pastor Wayne looked up at the ceiling, those two brown spots still staring down, and his eyes went glassy, vacant.

"Whoso diggeth a pit shall fall therein," he said.

"Preacher, I'm not sure what you mean."

"She dug a hole. Covered herself up with leaves and dirt. And the snakes. They were inside of her. Moving in and out of the holes they had torn."

Ruth had committed suicide. Or someone had killed her. Those were the only explanations. Whatever floated through the air or in the water of the town had twisted Ruth's already disordered mind into something more sinister or had led one of the townspeople to murder.

"She had no eyes," he said, and Cora shivered, the darkness of the sanctuary closing in around them. Just outside of the doors, sunlight washed over everything, but here night held dominion over all. She took a deep breath.

"Preacher, can you think of anything, anything at all, that might be contaminating the town? Anything in the water? In the air? A weed or a plant that people are eating? Anything that could lead to confusion or hallucinations? What we saw yesterday," Cora said, but he turned to her, locked those dead eyes to hers again, and she stopped.

Pastor Wayne looked up at the ceiling again, lifted a finger and traced two imaginary circles in the air, outlining those two brown spots. Cora thought of that old line in *Gatsby*. Something about God's eyes. How they're always watching.

"The whole world was filled with wonder and followed the beast. All that darkness set out to tempt the holy. Did you ever go to church, Cora? When you were a little girl?"

"Yes," she said. Her mouth went dry as he watched her, waited for her to say more. But there was nothing else to say. He nodded.

"If I wanted to leave here, Cora, leave everything behind and never come back, would you help me? Would you help me burn this place to the ground? Set every last thing and person in this forsaken place aflame?"

Cora stared back at him. She hoped he died inside this church. "Where's Leah McDowell, preacher?"

"Would you help me?" he repeated, but she stayed silent and waited for him to answer her question.

"She's gone. No one can find her."

"I don't believe you."

After finding Ruth, the men in the town would have looked for Leah. They would have combed the surrounding forest, the homes of the townspeople. If she was alive, it wouldn't take them long to find her unless she'd hitched a ride on the highway. Or if Pastor Wayne knew where she was hidden.

"I don't know where she is, Cora," he said.

Cora thought back to the townspeople gathered around the church. If there had been a death coupled with a missing girl—a girl that no one could find—police should be swarming the area. Officers would be talking with everyone, asking questions and gathering information. Who had seen her last and where? Had either mother or daughter exhibited any strange behavior? Anything suspicious? Had anyone strange come through the town lately? Someone who expressed odd or excessive interest in either Ruth or Leah McDowell?

But there had been no officer presence. Only the people gathered around the church house.

The air seemed to swell around Cora. "Preacher, where are the police?"

"They brought Ruth here. To me. To prepare for the service and the burial. Left her body in my hands, and I covered her. Covered her shame, and I swear to you, Cora. Three times I've watched that sheet move," he said.

Standing, Cora moved away from him and toward the doors. The gloom was suffocating her, and she had to get away. She needed open air and sunlight, and she burst through the front of the church as her gorge rose to the back of her throat.

Gagging, Cora tumbled down the steps, and the congregation parted for her. *Like the Red Sea,* she thought and pushed herself to her car. She would not be sick in front of these people. She would not.

Throwing open the car door, she vomited into the grass, the door screening the thin stream that dribbled from her mouth. Again and again, her stomach heaved, and she clung to the handle as if it would anchor her to the earth and keep her from tumbling forward into her own sick.

Spitting, Cora reached into the car, her hands searching for a bottle of water, anything to wash away the foul reminder of whiskey, but there was nothing, so she threw herself behind the wheel and leaned her head against the steering wheel.

The preacher had not called the police, but the entire town knew. Whoever found Ruth's body had surely told, and now they waited on their preacher to *do* something.

"Fanatical piece of shit," she said. She dumped her purse upside down on the passenger seat and hunted through wads of tissues, loose gum wrappers and receipts, and tubes of lipsticks she had only used once.

A telephone. She needed to find a telephone and alert the police. She glanced back up at the church. It was likely there would be a phone inside, but she couldn't go back into that place.

The store. Surely the store would have one. She got out of her car, walking quickly and half expecting someone to shout after her, but no one did. The store was empty, and she went behind the counter to look. Tucked under the counter was a faded yellow phone, and she grabbed at it, her heart in her mouth. As she dialed, she watched the townspeople through the large window at the front of the store. Still in their small groupings. Still whispering to one another. Still waiting.

The phone clicked, went quiet, and then clicked again, and Cora worried that the phone wouldn't work at all, but then there was a raspy voice on the other end asking what her emergency was.

"Yes, I'm in the town of Hensley. There's been..." she paused, unsure of what to call what had happened to Ruth McDowell, "a death," she said, and the operator, paused, and Cora feared that the woman would tell her to call the morgue and disconnect the line. "And a girl missing."

The operator asked again for her location and promised to have officers out to her.

"Thank you. Thank you," Cora said and put the phone back in its cradle. She looked back at the church. Nothing had changed, and she presumed Pastor Wayne still sat inside mired in his fear and confusion. She could not go back inside that room. She would suffocate if she did.

Cora scanned the crowd. A large group huddled around two men. They were tall. Bulky. Dressed in dark flannels with hats pulled low over their ears. These would be the ones who had found Ruth then. It would be stupid to approach them now, but Cora locked their faces in her memory. With any luck, she could talk with them later.

The police, of course, would be helpful once they arrived. It had been awhile since she was able to stretch her watchdog journalism muscles. Regardless, someone would talk, and if this was a case of some kind of hallucinogen or toxin, she wanted to get to the bottom of it before there was any more bloodshed.

And Leah. More than anything, she wanted to know that the girl had been found, wanted to know that she would be taken far, far away from this place. Away from Pastor Wayne and the way he watched her as she moved.

Somewhere in the distance, a siren started up. The sound echoed through the empty places between the trees, and the townspeople lifted their heads.

A girl with long, curling blonde hair did not look toward the harsh wailing and instead turned away from the group and locked eyes with Cora.

Cora had seen the girl before. On that first day. This girl was the one Pastor Wayne had sent to find Ruth when Leah had opened herself up, her skin tearing away like tissue paper. Cora could not forget the delicate, wet sound of Leah clawing at herself.

Mary. Pastor Wayne had called her Mary.

The girl and woman looked at each other as if they shared

some secret. Some dirty thing they had to keep quiet. As if to verify this, Mary brought her finger to her lips and winked before turning back to face the church.

And then the sky exploded with the sound of sirens.

Chapter 27

It was dark when Leah woke up. Her clothes were gone, and leaves clung to her bare legs and chest. Her mouth tasted of blood and dirt, and her stomach hurt.

"Momma?" she called and pushed herself onto her elbows. Her legs felt wobbly, and her head felt like there was air inside of it. She didn't think she could stand.

Tucking her legs beneath her, Leah peered into the dark but could see nothing. The sky was a vast ribbon of black that stretched on and on. New moon. No stars. All quiet and sleeping.

Delicately, Leah stretched out her hands and felt the ground. Circled around her were sticks and wet leaves and every few inches a slick, furred lump gone cold in the night air.

Leah drew back and tucked herself in tight. Whatever it was that lay beyond her, she did not want to touch it or it to touch her.

Her lips and chin were wet, and she drew her hand across her face and then rubbed whatever moisture was there onto her stomach. Her stomach. Why did it hurt so badly? It had never pained her like this before. Not even the time she had eaten all of those crabapples that hadn't ripened despite Momma telling her she shouldn't.

Another cramp ripped through Leah, and she doubled over and clutched her fists to her abdomen. How had she gotten here? She remembered walking home, Momma bathing her, tucking her into bed. She remembered dreaming there was something inside of her. And the snakes. Had she been sleep-walking? And if she had, wouldn't Momma have noticed by now and come looking for her? Leah couldn't be that far from the house, and she tried to stand, but her knees buckled, and the pain in her stomach doubled.

Was this what it was like to have a baby? This was Eve's punishment for talking to the serpent in the garden. Women were bound to her suffering. Punishment and payment for the temptation. Momma had told her so. Sister Kirk had talked about it at Sunday School. The day the teachers had separated the girls and the boys.

Somewhere beyond Leah's small circle came the sound of leaves rustling, the sharp crack of a stick breaking, and she sobbed.

"Momma?" she called again and whatever moved came forward. It sounded as if it crawled, slid through the underbrush on its belly, and as the pain shot through her, she screamed.

"Stay away from me!"

Between her thighs, something hot and sticky flowed, and she scrambled backwards. *Run away. Get away.*

Something brought a cool tongue to Leah's calf, and she kicked at it, pushed herself further away, but her back bumped against one of the furred lumps, the wetness clinging to her bare skin, and she shrieked.

All around her, the forest came awake. Birds screeching in the canopy above. A bobcat snarling in the too-near distance. Everything coming to life at once and screaming. Leah's head swelled with the sound, and she thought that it would crack her open. When she opened her mouth, she could not hear her own voice as it joined the cacophony.

There, under the sound of the world coming apart, Leah McDowell fainted, and her first blood poured out of her and into the earth.

Chapter 28

"We found her not twenty yards from where her mother's body was found. Completely unconscious and in the middle of a bunch of dead animals. Squirrels and chipmunks and the like. She was catatonic when she came to. From what we can tell, she has some minor cuts and bruises. Nothing more. She's a lucky girl."

The police officer that stood before Cora spoke a series of clipped commands into the speaker mic on his shoulder before he turned his attention to Pastor Wayne.

"We'll need to contact the next of kin. Once she's been treated, she'll be released into their custody."

"There's no one," Pastor Wayne said, and the officer darted a glance over Cora's shoulder, licked his lips, and smiled.

"Ruth's husband passed before Leah was born, and Ruth's parents have been gone for some time. Thomas' parents, too."

"I see," the officer said, his eyes still trained in the distance. He swiped at his hair—blonde and clipped close—and smiled again, shifted his weight from one foot to the other.

Fidgeting. He's fidgeting, Cora thought and wondered if she could turn and take a quick look at whatever distracted him without his noticing.

"A will," the officer said, but he stopped there, and Cora took advantage and tossed a look behind her.

Mary Pharr leaned against a poplar tree and traced a finger over the bark. A long line of red streaked down her arm, snaked up and over her hand, and she smeared the clotted blood against the tree. As Cora looked on, Mary pressed her fingers to her lips, her pink tongue lapping at the crimson drops, then turned and disappeared into the forest.

She turned back. "Officer," Cora said.

"What's that?" he said and looked back at Cora.

"The will?"

"Yes. Of course," he said and shook his head.

"Would Mrs. McDowell have had a will?"

"Actually, she did." Pastor Wayne spoke in a voice barely above a whisper. When the police had come into the church, he had not moved from his spot on the pulpit, merely pointed when they asked him the location of the body.

He'd answered their questions calmly, as had the men who found Ruth's body, and slowly, the townspeople drifted back to their homes. Death's cold fingers stretched over the town, and Cora imagined them locking their doors against whatever evil had crept among them and mothers allowing their children to sleep curled next to them if only for that night.

A few small groups remained, and they watched with wary eyes as the police brought out the body draped in its white sheet. Mary Pharr had stood among them. Floated from group to group without talking. Whatever had infected Leah and Ruth seemed to have taken root in Mary as well, and Cora wondered how long before another person lost themselves inside the maze of his or her own mind.

"She had it drawn up shortly after Thomas died. It would be in her house," Pastor Wayne said, and the officer nodded, looked past the two of them once more, but the girl he hoped to see had gone, and his face fell.

"You understand that we need to get our hands on a copy of it. For the girl. We'll be in touch," the officer said before walking to his vehicle. The sirens gave two short blasts, and then the car pulled away, dust trailing in its wake, and the town was empty once more.

Pastor Wayne turned and looked up the mountain.

"I've lived here all of my life. Grew up on this mountain. The movement of every tree, the sound of the wind moving through the trees is stamped on my skin. When I was a boy and couldn't sleep, I would sneak out at night and go walking. I never thought to be afraid. But I'm afraid now. It's like something terrible has been sleeping. Sleeping just under our feet. And now it's waking up," he said.

Cora looked up. The sun told her that it was late afternoon, and their shadows streaked away from them as if in flight. Cora thought again of Mary, the bloodstained lips parting to lick at her fingers, and a chill ran over her.

"Something is wrong with Mary Pharr, preacher. Something's wrong with this town."

"Would you go with me? Up the mountain?" Pastor Wayne turned to her then and extended his hand. She recoiled, her lip curled in disgust.

"For what reason?"

"To find the will."

"I don't think so," she said.

"Please, Cora," he said.

"I'm not going there with you. I know what you are, preacher. Wrapped up in your fake holiness. I've seen the way you look at her. She's a little girl," she said.

He stepped forward. "That little girl? She isn't little. Not anymore. I've known her for her entire life, and I've never laid a hand on her. I owe this to her and her mother. Please."

But you've thought about it, haven't you? How long had Mr. Burress thought about his hands around her neck, her waist before he'd actually put them there?

If she went with him, she could maybe uncover more information. The thought of walking with him into the dark made her queasy, but it could be worth it. She sighed. "Fine. But this isn't for you. This is for Leah."

"Okay."

When they reached the house, it had grown dark, and Cora looked up, marveled at the endless black expanse above her.

After her mother died, she'd driven six hours to the coast. It had been night then, too, and she'd stripped off her clothes and walked into the water until it was deep enough to take her under. When she came to the surface, there had been no difference between the sky and the water. There was only the dark, and she floated in it, hoped that the sky and sea would open its maw and swallow her down, but there was the sand under her feet, and no matter how she tried to swim farther and farther out, the ocean spit her out. She walked the beach until the sky went grey. Even though the water had not taken her, there was still some tenuous string that held her in place, and she walked, shivering, toward what she hoped held that string, but morning broke, and she was still alone.

Cora had that same feeling of suspension now. As if something vast held her in its grip and dangled her over a precipice she could not see. That same inky blackness pressed down on her, but Pastor Wayne's hand went up onto the front porch. The stairs were rickety with peeling white paint and she climbed them carefully.

The porch had been recently swept. There were no leaves, no dust or dirt, and a mason jar filled with a handful of straggling black-eyed Susans sat next to the front door. The wind picked up and carried with it what seemed like the faint sound of a radio station turned to static. Cicadas? Cora remembered reading something about them once. How they slept in the ground, quiet in their husks, and every twelve—or was it thirteen?—years they emerged, eyes glowing red to terrorize nice towns filled with nice mothers who raised perfectly nice children. Demons from the dirt set loose among those who would rather not understand what lived beneath them.

Pastor Wayne knelt, popped up a floorboard, and withdrew a key. Standing and brushing his knees, he inserted it into the lock, and the door swung open. He paused at the threshold, but then moved inside. Cora followed and pushed the door closed behind them.

The air had gone musty as if the house had been closed up for years rather than a day, and Cora longed to open some windows, let the night air sweeten that dank odor, but she could still hear that faint static despite being indoors and thought it better to keep them shut.

A single wooden rocking chair faced a large picture window, a faded afghan draped across the arms, and a small table stood beside it. A glass of water sat on the table, the glass chipped along the rim. A coffee table in a different wood—darker and more solid—stood in the center of the room, and a large Bible lay on top. A long hallway opened into a dark, yawning entry to the right of the rocker and another room opened a bit further beyond that. The kitchen, more than likely.

"No lights." Pastor Wayne spoke from across the room, his hand moving the switch up and down without effect. "Stay here," he said and disappeared down the hallway. The darkness seemed to swirl about him, snatching at his clothes, and then Cora could not see him.

Alone, she stood in the center of the living room and watched that darkness move, licking upward like tongues. She opened her mouth to tell him she could do what she wanted, but when she did, the faint static grew louder. As if whatever it was had come into the room with her and grown quietly in the corners.

She could hear Pastor Wayne in the back rooms, a soft rustling followed by a sigh, and then there was music. Violins climbed up and down strange arpeggios, and underneath was the sound of a baby crying. But always there was the static.

"Sisters," Cora heard him say, but he sounded far away, as if he spoke from somewhere deep underground.

"Preacher?" she called and moved toward the hallway, but behind her, a loud thump shook the room, and she turned back. The Bible had fallen open on hardwood. The pages writhed, a living abomination among the holy. Black snakes spilled over the pages and onto the floor, the bodies bloated and teeming with maggots.

"Diseased. Boiling down below. Like blood in the veins. Cut it open and draw it out. Pull them apart. Slit their tongues." Pastor Wayne spoke again; his voice dropped low, the words melting away into something unintelligible. Cora moved toward his voice. Anything to get away from the terrible, coiled mass in the living room, and she walked into the darkness and followed the sound of his murmuring.

Three doors flanked the hallway, and Cora saw them despite the darkness. Reddish light seeped out from beneath the doorways, and the light flickered in time with the static that was now a deafening roar in her ears. Still, she could hear Pastor Wayne beneath the sound, a whisper that was almost a chant, and she stumbled forward.

The doorway at the end of the hallway opened as she approached, and Cora looked into what was surely a young girl's room. The bed had been neatly made, and there were porcelain dolls leaned against the pillows, their lips perfect red bows and eyes wide with expressions of perpetual surprise. A hardcover book lay open and face down on the white coverlet. Fairy tales. Sleeping Beauty in her eternal slumber painted on the cover.

Leah's room, she thought and moved inside, the door clicking softly behind her. She took up the book and ran her fingers over the cover. On it, Beauty reclined on a bed of pink roses, thorns pricking against her pale flesh as the petals absorbed the small pinpricks of blood that fell. She was nude, and her hair fell beside her breasts, the crest of her sex just visible. Why would Leah have such a book? Surely her mother wouldn't have allowed it.

Looking at it made Cora feel uncomfortable, and she set it down again, glanced up at the carved crucifix that hung above the bed.

"The old King opened her up, you know. Her name was Talia before it was Aurora. Took what she would not give. His own daughter." Pastor Wayne's voice came from above and below, and Cora whipped around. A larger armchair stood in the far corner of the room, a corner she had not looked into when she came in, and he sat in it, his back stiff and straight.

"They clawed their way out of her. Out of Ruth. Ripped and tore and bit. Took little pieces of her for themselves. Flesh and bone and blood. The things a mother gives her child. What will you give, I wonder?" Pastor Wayne looked at her. His eyes were hazy, the filmy coating of a cataract come early.

He crawled down out of the chair, moved toward her like an animal, and Cora shrank back. "You get the fuck away from me," she said, but he paid no mind. His tongue traced over her ankles, up her calves, and she shuddered and tasted blood in her throat.

"You taste like honey," he said. Christ's face looked down at Cora from his crucifix, the lips open and parted, and she moaned. Fear and desire mixed hot and feral inside of her. She arched her back, but he withdrew and slunk back into the shadows.

The static grew even louder, and the walls flexed and shifted, the surface covered in the luminescent wings of flies, their dark bodies bulging outward as they crawled over each other.

"Ruth left her to the church. Leah. A ward of God." Pastor Wayne clasped a loose grouping of papers in his hand, and he brought them to his throat, drew the sheaf across the skin there as if it could slash the delicate tissue, and giggled.

"I could take her in. Like a father. Be her guide. Her ruin."

The room shrank and swelled as if they were inside a living, breathing creature. Now, underneath the frantic buzz of the flies, there was the sound of something wet, of a mouth opening and closing as it devoured a meal.

Cora was so tired. Confused. Everything she thought she understood had gone strange. The bed looked so soft. She could lie down. Just for a minute. Let her head stop spinning.

"Lie down. Sleep. Perhaps a prince will awaken you with a kiss. Perhaps not," he said, and a single fly crawled into his nose. Confusion threatened to overtake Cora, but she looked again at the cover of the book. Traced the contours of the sleeping princess's breasts, the subtle rise and fall before the curved bowl of the belly. Gulped air until her stomach hurt.

"Didn't they call Satan the Lord of the Flies?" Cora said.

"Tricky girl. You know more than you let on." He smiled without teeth. "Would it really be so terrible to reign over such a Kingdom? So full of life. The cycle quick. Regenerative. A neverending birth and death, and when that happens, how can death ever truly declare itself the victor? The Conqueror Worm defeated.

"How could Ruth have known? That her lamb was in the jaws of the wolf. Waiting. I've been waiting for so long. Hoping for the smallest taste, and now the meal laid at its doorstep." Panting, Pastor Wayne opened his mouth, and three of the insects crawled out, and Cora shrank away, the full impact of his words settling heavy and sour against her.

"She's just a girl," Cora said, and Pastor Wayne pulled at his hair and screamed, but the sound drowned in the frantic buzzing of the flies.

"How many nights have I fallen asleep begging whatever could hear me to not let me dream of her? How many nights have I heaved and sweated and passed the snakes over my neck and dared God to punish me? And still, my heart keeps beating, and my blood grows darker with every breath."

Cora's head swam, and his form doubled, tripled, winked out before reappearing again, and she leaned against the pillow. When had she sat down?

Close your eyes. Sleep, she thought, but then Pastor Wayne's body loomed over her, and his tongue passed over his lips. She watched as the flies dipped in and out of his mouth, his nose, his eyes.

"How old were you, Cora? Just a little girl, hmm? Just a little girl and Mommy was far away and didn't understand what it meant when Mister Burress—that nice man who taught Sunday School—looked at you for just a fraction of a second too long. Your mother thought it was sweet. The way he doted on his own little girl. On you. Didn't question when he set up the sleepovers instead of his wife. Asked for her to pack you a white nightie. Claimed it was for a themed tea party Becca was desperate to have. And you bled, didn't you? Didn't understand how something could hurt so much. Everything pulling apart, but you were still there. Still underneath him as he moved. And he gutted you. Pulled you inside out and cried when you cried. Licked the salt from your cheeks."

"Stop it," Cora said, but sleep pulled at her, and the flies droned on and on.

"Did you tell her? Before Mommy died, did you tell her what he did to you? How he pulled down your panties? Looked at every part of you, crying the entire time, saying 'I'm sorry. I'm sorry' over and over, but he always did it again. Didn't he? Over and over and over. And you learned to stay quiet. To let him do what he would because if you didn't fight, he wouldn't take as long, and the hurt would end more quickly."

Tears pooled at the edges of Cora's lashes but did not fall. She had learned long ago not to cry. Not for him. Never for *him*.

"No. I didn't," Cora said. Pastor Wayne smiled down at her and reached out his hand, wiped at the wetness trailing down her cheeks, and brought his fingers to his lips.

"Still like honey," he said. "He wanted you. So much more than he even wanted his own little girl. Did she ever tell you that? That before it was you, it was her, and she was so glad that he found you. When they moved, she cried. Not because she would miss you. No. Not that."

The room swam. Colors erupting blue and red and green as the flies lifted their wings. "I should have told Momma. I wanted to. So many times the room would go quiet, and she would look at me, and I swear it was like she already knew, and she was waiting for me to tell her. That she wasn't so broken that I couldn't, but then she would smile and laugh, and I would swallow it all back down. All of that darkness.

"So many times, I felt like there was nothing underneath my skin. Only bone. Muscle. Some automatic force that made them move. Too many times I parted that skin. Opened it up and looked beneath to be sure there was still something down there. Bleeding. Breathing," Cora said, and Pastor Wayne watched her.

"He was a wolf. As am I. We seek. We devour." He brought his mouth to her neck, and she lifted her hands to push him away, but they were too heavy, and she was so tired. Her eyes fluttered. Once. Twice.

Sleep overtook Cora, and she tumbled down, down, down, and something moved above, and she cried out. The flies answered, their droning lifting into ecstasy.

Everything converging all at once.

Chapter 29

Leah woke in a room that smelled like antiseptic and urine. Her wrists hurt, and she went to rub at the burning flesh, but her arms did not respond. Someone had strapped her down, and she flexed against the restraint, but it did not yield. If her throat was not so dry, she could scream until someone came to undo the straps, but when she tried, only a thin wail escaped her lips.

"Leah? Can you hear me?" The voice came from some foggy place just beyond her sight. A place she could not yet see, and she blinked her eyes rapidly, tried to clear her vision, but the room swam in bland color. She could not focus on anything, and the shapes were vague blobs that moved through empty space.

"She's awake." The voice came again, and Leah could not determine if it belonged to a man or a woman. There was movement around her, hands fluttering over her body, and something sharp pressed into her arm.

"Leah, you're in the hospital. We're going to take good care of you, okay? There's nothing to worry about," the voice said, and she felt a hand on her arm squeeze a bit too hard.

Leah opened her mouth to speak, to ask for her mother, but her throat rattled, and she coughed, and the feeling was like a thousand moths fluttering inside of her. As if little pieces of her had broken off and floated into the back of her throat.

Turning her head to the right, Leah tried to focus on the blurred form closest to her, but it made her eyes hurt, and she closed them and tried to ignore the slow throb building in her arm.

"You had quite the accident, but we've examined you. Looked in every nook and cranny." The voice laughed at its own joke.

They had *looked* at her. All of her. The thought made Leah burn with shame, and again, she tried to move her hands to cover herself. Once more, the restraints held her, and she twitched beneath them.

"Those need to stay on for a bit longer, dear. I'm so sorry, but you gave us quite the scare when you came in."

Leah's lips were cracked, and she poked her tongue at the raw spots, swallowed, her throat clicking as she did.

"Hold still now," the voice said, and something poked against Leah's lips. She tried to push herself away, but there was nowhere to go.

"Take a sip, dear. You'll feel much better. I promise," the voice said, and Leah opened her mouth and drank greedily. Her stomach flopped as the water settled. When was the last time she had eaten? She felt as if she could remember eating something before she woke in the woods. Remembered her teeth tearing at meat, and her mouth warm and slick as it worked against her meal.

She remembered the voice. The one that spoke from inside of her.

But all of that had been a dream? Hadn't it?

"That's a good girl," the voice said. Leah pictured a woman with graying hair, a grandmotherly type with kind eyes that crinkled in the corners when she smiled. The kind of woman who baked cookies and knitted sweaters for her grandchildren.

The thought was comforting, and Leah stopped fidgeting and let herself fall back into the flat pillow beneath her.

"Momma. Where is," Leah began, but her voice gurgled and died.

"Hush now. Don't worry about her. She'll be along shortly," the voice said.

All around Leah the colors began to sharpen. Indistinct forms coalesced into the outlines of a television mounted to the wall, the shadowy form of a chair tucked into the left corner, the walls painted a dull, powdery blue.

"She wears the crown of filth. Under the world they have wed her. Their seed shall be fruitful. Her body the first womb. The cocoon," the voice said, and Leah turned to the sound and gasped. The woman before her was young, her skin perfectly smooth, dark hair piled atop her head in intricate braids and twists, the eyes an impossible silvery gray.

"Beautiful," Leah said, and the woman laughed.

"They tell stories about me. They whisper the myths of my existence to children. Set them quivering in the dark, and they lay there under hot blankets waiting for something terrible to emerge or for something to reach out from beneath their beds and gobble them up. Were you ever frightened, Leah, when the children told those scary stories?"

Leah nodded and thought of the book of fairy tales she had left under her pillow.

"In the night, when the little children rolled their tongues over my stories, did they tell you my name? Did they say it aloud, daring each other to say it again and again? Louder and then louder still? Did you ever say it, Leah?"

"I don't know." The woman leaned forward, licked at Leah's lips, drew the small droplets of water that clung there onto her tongue.

"You would know if you spoke my name, little one. Your mother knew. She heard it when she was young, and she trembled as she watched her own foolish mother try to open the door. Did she ever tell you, little Leah? Did she tell you that her mother was a whore? A witch? That again and again she spoke my name into the dark, and when I finally came to her, how she screamed?"

"No. That didn't happen. It didn't," Leah said. Her grandmother had died before she was born. A heart attack. Momma had told her. Before Daddy. Before Momma moved to Hensley to marry him. It had all happened such a long time ago, and there was no use in mourning those who had gone on to a place without any suffering. That's what Momma said.

"Your grandmother knew me. Your mother knew me, too, but for so long she tried to deny it. And now, she is in the realm of dirt with our King."

The woman leaned in close, and her breath smelled of honeysuckle and fresh rain on grass. Lush and verdant. Smells of deep summer when the night drew on slow and late, the shadows leaking across cool earth.

"The forest of every heart is filled with strange devils," the woman said, and her fingers slipped under the straps that held Leah to the bed, and Leah felt her touch against her bare skin, and she remembered.

"It was you," Leah said.

"Yes. And now I'm here. As I should be."

"Please," Leah said. She knew what it was she was asking for.

"Now, now. These nasty things are hurting you. Those men with their white coats and black minds. You should have seen them with their scissors. Snip, snip, snip. So eager to pull that flimsy cloth away. See what secrets you carry underneath that blue dress. Maybe taste them, too. But I didn't see. They drew the curtain then. What a shame."

Turning her face, Leah sobbed. Salt on her lips. Like Lot's wife. A pillar of salt. Too long had Lot's wife lived among sin, and she had turned to look back . So, too, would Leah change. She longed to change. To sprout feathers, scales, claws, teeth. To run. Dig a hole and cover her head with dirt like a bridal veil. Forget all that came before.

"There are so many who listen now. More and more who turn their ears to the earth and listen as it cracks open. Those devils pouring out and filling all of the empty places they only think of in the night. Those dark thoughts that hollow out secret places are brimming over now. Their cups runneth over. Isn't that how it goes?"

Behind the woman, the door opened halfway and paused as if the person had changed her mind, decided to turn back.

Before, Leah would have been afraid. Not anymore.

"Don't you want to see your Momma?" the woman said, and the door swung wide.

"Her eyes," Leah said and opened her arms to the other woman, the woman she had known her entire life, who stood before the door.

Chapter 30

"Michael the archangel. He fought the dragon. Threw him out. Condemned him to burn."

The woman who spoke had dark hair that twisted like snakes. Like worms alive in dirt. The sight of it repulsed Michael, but her face was beautiful. Every feature a delicate tracing. Cheekbones lifting upward. A Cupid's bow mouth that twisted into something that looked like a smile and stained berry-red.

"They named you for him. Your parents. Hoped that his strength would flow through your blood when you took up the snakes. It did at first, didn't it? Didn't it feel good the first time your father asked you to open those boxes? The way the people looked at you? Anointed. Holy."

The walls hummed. Something breathed and lived and *fucked* inside of them. The thought made Michael burn, and he groaned.

The woman smiled. "Have you ever known a woman, Michael?"

There had been a time, when Michael was young, when he had thought of leaving his father and mother behind. All that he believed like so much dust. Something he could wave away and forget. Day after day dreaming of what it would be like to bury himself inside something sweet and hot. Late nights sweating under the quilt his mother had pieced together with the church's quilting group, his erection pressed against it.

Michael had been afraid then. He was afraid now, and of course, the woman knew. He reeked of it. Sweat on his forehead darkened his hair. The woman would smell it on him, that dark stink of fear. Draw it inside of herself and taste it. Perhaps laugh at his weakness.

How easily Michael wanted to give up everything his father had fought for. He waited for the woman to tell him he was weak. That he had been weak since he had been small. Something that should have been crushed before it grew. Like a worm under the heel of a child.

The woman stayed silent and watched him. Eyes the color of the sky before a storm.

"How did you get here?"

She didn't answer, and the woman stretched out on the bed that another woman slept on. Dark curls clouded and obscured her face.

Michael knew her but couldn't remember her name. She was important, but he couldn't place his finger on the spot that told him why. Not his mother. The face was far too young. No wrinkles beside the eyes and mouth. No silvering hair or crepe paper skin. Not a sister. He felt he would recognize his own features reflected in the face below him.

"Ashes to ashes. Isn't that how we all come into this world? Springing up through the dirt?" the woman said.

"No. That's how we die," Michael said, but the Bible verse was muddled in his head.

"All the same. Birth. Death. Shitting and pissing and bleeding into the ground."

"Our home in heaven," he began, but the woman's mouth crinkled at the corners, and she laughed.

"Worms eat at the dead. Pull apart muscle and bone until what's left is so small. Inconsequential. Food," she said.

The woman—Cora, her name was Cora—shifted and moaned in her sleep.

"She doesn't deserve this," Michael said, and the woman stood.

"You all deserve this." Her voice was the hiss of a hundred snakes.

The flies had long fallen silent. Their blackened forms bumped against each other blindly. Michael wished—not for the first time—that they would awaken, lift their wings, and erase the sound of the woman's voice. Beat their wings against the filth on her tongue. Then he could sleep; let himself be pulled under until there was no more death. No more darkness.

"How old was she when you first saw her beneath you? The girl. Leah."

"Stop it."

"Ten? Eleven? When her womanhood first began its blooming. And you passed your snakes among the others, and you burned. Beneath the holy garments you cloak yourself in, you watched her grow. Watched her become a woman, and you wondered how you could lay claim to her."

"No. Not like that." The lie formed without thinking. Ready made to fall from his lips. So easy.

"Of course not. No one would dare dream that their holy man—their *preacher*—would look upon the body of such a young girl and think of himself moving inside of her. Desecrating what her mother, what her God, told her to save for her husband."

"Tell me your name."

"It doesn't work like that, preacher. Not the way you learned in your storybook. There is no divine halo around you that makes me blink in confusion and bend to your will. I am no young girl led into the teeth of the beast."

There was blood on the bed. It dotted the quilt and swirled into strange, serpentine patterns, and Michael thought he could see the outlines of teeth, scales in their undulating, neverending patterns, an eye wide and staring, the iris shining red, but the more he looked, the more the shapes twisted away from themselves until watching their movement made his head hurt.

The woman moved away from him, away from Cora's sleeping form, and went to the window. If she saw anything in the darkness, she did not turn back to tell him or ask him to look upon the horrible things coming up from the earth.

"The hole in the bottom of the world has opened, preacher. The Great Worm moves. I am only what comes before. I only make the path ready."

Michael watched as the woman scrabbled up the wall and onto the ceiling like a spider.

Michael followed the woman's movements to a corner, then another. When she crawled behind him, her breath on his neck, he did not turn his head to see, and soon she was before him again, and the room seemed to expand. Angles and corners where there should be smooth walls. More than four. He could not count them, she moved so quickly now. The ceiling vanished and night sky poured down upon them, and a red moon cast its glow over everything.

"Harvest moon," Michael said, and he heard his father's voice, saw the old man pointing into the sky as the young boy Michael had once been looked to the sky.

"Means the equinox is on us, Michael." Again, his father's voice. Slow and steady.

"Dad," Michael said, and the vision shimmered. The boy and the man who raised him turned to look upon Michael's ruin, their eyes drowning in blood.

Michael ran. He looked for a door, but there was no door. Only walls and sky and the sleeping woman who had come with him. Cora. And above all of it, the woman who had come to usher in something greater.

"Where's the door? Where is the door? Where is the *fucking* door?"

"Oh, preacher. The tongue is a fire of profanity. Opens the mouth of the pit," the woman said from somewhere above him, and he screamed. The sky and the ground screamed back, and Michael fell, curled his body inward and covered the soft flesh of his belly with his arms.

"Keep your eyes closed, preacher. Tight. You don't want to see," the woman said, and he pulled himself in tighter. A grown man returned to the womb.

Michael kept his eyes closed and listened as the world around him came undone.

Chapter 31

Yellow. Everything was yellow. Bright and cheery and singing birds and dust motes floating through sunshine. Like a morning from Cora's childhood. Her mother in the kitchen. The smell of coffee and toast. Her arms and legs heavy with sleep.

Cora brought her arm over her eyes, tried to block out the light prying at her. Her mouth tasted foul. Copperish. Her body ached. Every limb a throbbing extension that felt as if it had been battered and bruised the night before. What the fuck had she done last night? Could she have really drunk so much that she blacked out? She hadn't done that since college. Stupid. *Stupid.* She was supposed to be on assignment, not out partying like some sorority girl.

Blinking against the light, Cora opened her eyes. The ceiling was low, popcorn plaster with a deep brown water stain.

This is not my room. Not my hotel.

Cora sat up, looked at the dresser across from her, at her reflection in the mirror that hung on the wall. Disheveled. Pale. Mascara smeared beneath her eyes.

Leah's room. She'd followed Pastor Wayne here. He'd asked her to help him find Ruth's will. After that, her memory blinked out. Brief flashes of snakes. Pastor Wayne's face. The cover of a book.

The muscles in Cora's legs protested, but she swung them over the edge of the bed and surveyed the room.

The chair. He was in the chair, she thought and turned.

Pastor Wayne was curled in the fetal position on the floor in front of the armchair. His breath rose and fell in the regular rhythms of deep sleep, and his hand covered his eyes.

Somehow, they had both come here and fallen asleep. Had they searched the house? Did he find what he came looking for?

"Preacher," Cora said, but he did not stir.

Twice more, she called him, but he did not move. She crossed to him, bent down, and took his shoulder. He felt spongy beneath her touch as if there were no bones to prop up the skin he wore.

"Michael," she hissed and quelled the urge to kick him awake.

"Cora," he said, and the suddenness of his voice echoing through the small room startled her. She jerked away from him. Still, he did not move.

"How long have you been awake?"

"I don't know. I don't know," Michael said. His voice was a heavy, hollow thing.

He spoke again. "Can I open my eyes, Cora? Has it finished?"

"What happened last night, preacher?" Cora fought to keep her voice steady. She needed him to stand up and tell her what happened the night before. Explain why he was on the floor, his eyes covered. Why she had agreed to come here with him.

"Are your eyes open, Cora?"

"Of course they are," she said and watched as he pulled his hand away from his face, his eyelashes fluttering as if he was working up the courage to open them. A single tear fell from his right eye, and she watched it trace down his cheek before disappearing.

"Open your eyes. There's nothing here."

"Yes. Yes."

Slowly, Michael opened his eyes and squinted into the sunlight.

"Can you sit up?" she asked him, and he brought his arms beneath his chest and pushed himself upward, his eyes sweeping the room as he did.

"What happened," Cora said, and again his eyes flicked across the room. He looked unsteady and confused as if at any second he would bolt from the room screaming, but if he remembered anything that she could not, she needed to know.

"Preacher? Listen to me now. I remember coming up the mountain and coming into the house and to this room, but beyond that, it's all just little flashes of random things," Cora said, and he cowered into himself and shook his head.

Anger burned in Cora's throat, and she bent down, caught his gaze and held it. "Tell me. If you know what happened here, stop acting like a fucking child who's pissed his pants and say it."

"I *knew* things about you," Michael whispered.

Cora rocked back on her heels. Her skin crawled into gooseflesh.

"Something happened to you. When you were a girl. It happened, and you never told," he said, and she felt as if she had slipped underwater. Her fingers went sluggish as she moved them over the splintered wooden floor and picked against the disintegration there.

"And I knew about it. I saw it happening. Like I had been there, and that little girl looked up at me. She saw me, too. You saw me. And your eyes. Your eyes. Asking me why I wasn't doing anything. Why I wouldn't stop it."

Cora remembered now. The flies. The full, terrible knowledge of what happened to her when she was a girl laid bare and bleeding.

"How? How could you have known?"

"You slept. And *she* came. Through the walls. The floor. I don't know."

"Can you stand? Walk?"

"Yes."

"All right," Cora said and stood, brushed herself off. She couldn't stay here. Not in this room full of the smells of wood and dust. Not in this place where she had lost herself only for the darker parts to be found.

"Let's go," Cora said and hooked an arm beneath his shoulder. Touching him made her stomach heave, but she did it anyway.

"On my count," she said. Michael tipped forward, and she almost lost her grip, but then he stood beside her, and the need to escape filled her up, stretched beneath her skin until she thought that it would break through and take the lighter parts that remained of her with it.

Shuffling forward, they found the door, and Cora opened it. She closed it behind them, and the lock clicked from the inside. The sound of fingernails tapping against the wood floated to her, and then whatever lived behind the door fell silent.

"It won't open again," Michael said, and they went down the hallway, through the front room where the Bible still lay open on the floor. Cora's vision from the night before swam before her, the Bible teeming with creatures, and she looked away, focused on the front door. Would it even open? The idea that they were caught in this house like small, quaking animals in the teeth of a trap flashed through her mind, but then they were moving through the door, and into the hard blue sky of an early autumn morning.

The tree line blazed in a riot of yellow, red, and orange, and above them, crows called to one another in mournful voices.

"Everything is dying," Michael said, and they followed the curving path down the mountain. Overly ripe muscadines had fallen from their vines and stained the dirt a deep purple.

Her car was still parked in the dirt lot just outside the church. It looked strange sitting there with nothing around it.

"I can't go back into the church. I feel like a stranger. Like those walls have forgotten me. Pushed me out. Like something lives just behind the wood, and it sees me. All the broken little parts I've tried to hide. I can't go in," Michael said.

Cora's keys were still in her pocket. She could get back to the hotel, use the phone there, call Jimmy, but before that, she wanted Michael to talk if he would. She wanted to drive for a bit, clear her head, and wait for Michael to explain what the fuck had happened last night.

"Get in," Cora said, and Michael obeyed her, waited patiently for her to unlock the doors before folding himself into the passenger seat. He tipped his head back and closed his eyes.

"You can smell it, can't you, Cora? Underneath everything. Rot. Decay. Like when you're walking along and stumble on something that died long ago, and it gets inside of you. You can smell it even when it isn't there anymore," he said, and she fired the engine.

At the main road, Cora turned left, headed away from Hensley, away, even from the little hotel with its shower, its fresh set of clothes. She realized she couldn't go back there now. It was too close to *here*.

It didn't matter where they ended up as long as it wasn't this place with its white church and quiet rooms and its little house on the side of a mountain full of secret abominations. With a girl and her mother tied to something sordid and dirty, and yet there was also this man so interwoven in the fabric of everything that was happening in the town who rode beside her. Cora wasn't leaving it all behind. Not completely.

They drove for hours. Sometimes, she wondered if she had drifted off, had to roll her window down and gulp cold air to remind herself she was awake. They'd passed perhaps a handful of other travellers, and each time the small highway brought other cars toward them, Cora would stare into the driver's window, try to see the faces of the passengers, but each time, the cars were upon them and past before she could make anything out. It made her feel that nothing was real, and the road stretched ever onward. Pastor Wayne did not speak and stared straight ahead. Eventually, Cora grew easy with his silence and watched the yellow lines race away into the distance.

Up ahead, green metal glinted, the reflected letters promising food and coffee and gasoline. The small vestigial reminders that civilization existed outside of the place they had fled.

Turning on her blinker, Cora took the exit, and Michael glanced over at her and offered a weak smile.

"I could murder a cup of coffee right now," he said, and she almost laughed, but the sound died in her throat.

Cora followed the signs to a tiny diner. The lot was empty save for a faded blue Datsun pickup, but the lights were on. What had once been the silver glamour of a bygone era was now a dull exterior with flashing neon lights that advertised pie and coffee. The lights blinked off and on. Blink. A mug and full pot. Blink. The pot tilted and steam rose from the mug. Blink.

Out back, a large dumpster leaked something brown and viscous onto the asphalt, and two fat tomcats lapped at it, their eyes closed in ecstasy. Beside them, a black man in an apron smoked a cigarette, the cherry tip glowing for long seconds before he exhaled smoke.

Cora cut the engine and closed her eyes. "Funny to be so tired when I've slept so much," she said. The sound of Michael opening his door answered her, and she snapped open her eyes and watched him climb out of the car. Sighing, she followed suit. She didn't want to follow him, but there was still the story.

At the sound of their doors closing, the man in the apron dropped his cigarette and crushed it under his heel before disappearing into the darkness behind the diner. Presumably, there was a door there, but Cora couldn't help but feel that they would enter the diner to find it empty. A place where only ghosts walked.

"Did you ever play that game as a kid? The one where you stick your head between your legs, take the deepest breath you can, and then sit up? Wrap your hands around your throat and squeeze. Wait until you get lightheaded, and right before the lights blink out, when dark spots start to crowd out the color, you let go," Michael said. The asphalt felt solid under her feet, not at all like gravel or dirt.

"Yeah. We called it the pass out game. Stupid what kids will do," Cora said.

"I have that same feeling now," he said.

Me, too, Cora thought, but she did not speak aloud.

The door jangled when they opened it, a bell announcing their entrance to whomever cared to know, and right now, there was no one in sight who would possibly give a shit. Ten tables sat on the dining room floor, each one covered in white butcher paper and topped with a salt and pepper shaker, a sugar canister, and a dusty vase filled with a single, even dustier fake daisy. A long bar top with old-fashioned chrome stools and cracked green vinyl seats flanked the back of the diner. Coffee mugs in lurid hues of yellow and orange hung on the wall behind the bar with more flashing neon signs. We Never Close! they promised.

"Hello? Anybody here?" Cora called into the empty room, and a swinging door behind the bar opened just a bit.

"Have a seat anywhere you like, folks. I'll be out directly," a voice called back.

"Well, preacher," Cora said and jerked a thumb at the long line of stools. "Any objection to sitting at the bar?"

"A table, I think, would be more private," he said.

Given everything they had to discuss, he was right, and she moved to the far corner of the room and pulled out a chair. Michael took the chair opposite her, and together they waited, their eyes focused on anything other than the person sitting across the table.

"We don't get many folks through here anymore. Not since they opened up the bypass. I take it y'all will want coffee," the voice spoke again, and Cora turned, watched as the man in the apron came out of the swinging door and moved toward the wall of mugs before selecting two and placing them on the bar top.

"Just passing through. Was glad to see you were open," Cora said, and the man smiled at her. He was tall and lean, with light brown eyes and hair that curled closely against his skull. Pock marks—long-ago scars of chicken pox or acne—dotted his face as well as a smattering of freckles just under his left eye. A tattoo peeked out from under his left sleeve, but from where Cora was sitting, she couldn't make it out.

"Oh, we're always open," the man said, pointing to the sign. "Just that sometimes I like to forget." He laughed and lifted a pot from an invisible burner behind the counter, hooked his fingers around the handles of the two mugs, and made his way towards them.

"Reckon you'll want the whole pot. The two of you look like you've been rode hard and put away wet." He poured them each a mug and set the pot between them.

"Cream?"

Cora shook her head. "Black is fine. This is wonderful. Thank you," she said, and he turned to Michael who also shook his head, took up his cup, and brought it to his lips.

"Mind you, it's hot. Might not be many people coming in anymore, but I always keep a fresh pot on the burner. Must admit I drink most of it myself. Doc says my heart's like to bust out of my chest one day, but I reckon I've made it this far, and if coffee's my worst habit, well then, thank God for small favors. Course, it isn't my *worst* habit, but at my age, it's nice to pretend that everything isn't falling apart.

"Now, you folks looking for grub or just liquid refreshment? I make a mean hamburger. Of course, we got a menu, but I do recommend that burger. If you are so inclined," the man said and produced a note pad and pen from his apron. His fingertips were stained a deeper brown.

"Just the coffee for now. Thank you again," Cora said, and the man nodded, tucked the pad and pen back into his apron.

"Y'all just holler if you're needing anything else. I'll be out back slowly killing myself. Promise you won't tell old Doc now." He reached again into his apron and drew out a pack of Lucky Strikes before shuffling off, his back hunching slightly as he went through the swinging door.

Lifting the mug to her lips, Cora sipped at the coffee, and the burn settled on her tongue, a bright thing that slid through her mouth before it slipped down her throat and warmed her belly. It was too hot, but she took another sip, and exhaled.

How strange to be inside this mundane situation. Drinking coffee as if nothing had happened.

"I asked you a question before, Michael. About toxins, any kind of waste that could have found its way into the water. A plant. An herb. A weed. Something the ladies in your congregation would have cooked or made tea out of? Maybe even decided that it was good for you to take a mouthful and chew? Anything that could lead to hallucinations. There's an explanation for all of this. Something logical. Something *sane.*"

Michael's fingers fidgeted on the table, and he ripped off small bits of the butcher paper, the white strips floating to the floor like snow. It was almost beautiful.

"How could I have known about you, Cora? What happened to you? Even if there was something there. Something in the water. Something we breathed in or ate or drank, it wouldn't let me *know* you. Not like that."

He was right. A toxin would lead the townspeople to see things that weren't there. Hear abominations whispered in their ears by unseen demons, but it wouldn't plant the seeds of terrible truths. The idea of what he was telling her settled hard.

"You said there was a woman," Cora said.

"She knew my name. Knew things about me, too. The way I knew about you. My sins. Everything I've covered up with my faith. Everything I've spent a lifetime hiding."

While Cora slept, Michael had been there. In the room with her. Doing what? Talking to some *thing* that had come there seeking him? Cora's mind refused the idea, circled back to fungus or bacterial spores floating in the air of Hensley. *Impossible. Impossible.*

But Michael had known about Mr. Burress. Of the three people who had known, no one had ever told, and Cora had never spoken of it. Like a good little girl.

Michael drained his mug, poured a second, and held it before him like a totem.

"A hole in the bottom of the world. That's what she told me. That there were things that had long slumbered behind a door. And now the door was open. The book of Revelation laid bare. The whore of Babylon.

"Satan was thought to be beautiful. A lovely prince who wanted what he couldn't have. We are the same, he and I. In my sleep, I can taste her mouth, and I sweat and I want her, and it's all I can think of. Like a fire that gets inside of me and swallows everything, and I try so hard. I try so hard, but she always comes back."

Leah. He's talking about Leah. The memory floated before Cora. His fingers locked around a piece of paper telling her that Leah had been left in the custody of the church. His confession. The coffee went sour in her mouth, and she fought the desire to spit it out.

Michael's face swam in and out of vision, the dark hair giving way to blonde. Mr. Burress' face. The one that had moved above her. The one that had hurt her, had made her bleed and cry and bite back screams, and she clutched at the fork on the table, flexed her fingers around the metal.

"I should take out your eyes. You son of a bitch." Cora spat the words at Michael and he recoiled, but the vision faded as quickly as it had come, and the face across the table was only Michael's.

"I'm sorry." Cora loosened her grip on the fork and let it clatter against the tabletop. She should be angry, should be disgusted now that her suspicions were confirmed, but all she felt was fatigue and a dull ache in her neck.

For minutes, they sat in silence. Stirred their coffee.

"Looks like you folks could use this." The voice startled

Cora, and she turned to see the man in the apron coming toward them, a small brown bottle in hand.

"Yet another vice we won't talk about." With a wink, the man set the bottle on the table and headed back to the kitchen or the little alley out back or wherever the hell he spent his time during the long hours of the day.

"Some tricks up his sleeve." Cora tipped the bottle into her mug and counted to five. It would burn going down.

"Preacher?" Cora said and extended the bottle. He nodded without a word, and when she poured, counted to two, and stopped, he waved her on.

"It's your funeral," she said and counted to five as she had for her own. They clinked their mugs together, their eyes the only things visible as they drank long and deep.

Michael winced as he swallowed, but he kept it down without coughing and went for more.

"Easy there, tiger," Cora said, and then she was laughing. Laughing because she could not cry. Laughing because she was sharing a bottle of whiskey in some podunk, abandoned diner with a fundamentalist, snake-handling preacher who lusted after a teenage girl. Laughing because she knew there was no poisoned water. No hallucinogenic herb or plant. No radioactive waste or any other superhero-making bullshit in Hensley. Laughing because there was nothing else to do.

When Michael joined her, his voice booming out across the empty diner, the man in the apron poked his head out from behind the swinging door and grinned before disappearing once more.

"An angel in disguise," Michael said, and a fresh wave of laughter broke over her. Despite everything, Cora felt clean. Whole. She could almost forget everything that had happened. Almost.

They sat there together until afternoon sunlight came through the windows and shadows bent around them. Every now and then, the man would check on them. Twice, he freshened their coffee even though they had not drained the pot.

"Keeps me young," he said each time they protested that they were fine, that they really didn't need it.

Eventually, the man brought out two burgers, fully loaded, even though they hadn't ordered them.

"Trust me," he said, and they ate quickly and without speaking. Cora had not realized how hungry she was, and when she finished, she asked the man for another. He laughed all the way back to the kitchen, but twenty minutes later, the second plate he'd carried out with a flourish sat clean and empty, and he whistled when he saw it.

"My wife would adore you," the man told her as he took the plate.

She knew that it was only temporary, this feeling of comfort and what could even be called happiness—a moment of stasis before everything came apart—and she found herself not wanting to leave. To stay here in this big, empty place with its warmth and this man who would keep their bellies full and her temporary peace with the preacher. It wouldn't last.

When the swinging door opened again, Cora did not turn, but she smiled, readied herself for a chocolate sundae or a plate of cookies or another brown bottle.

"It's the worms that pull us apart. Ain't it, preacher man? How's that old song go? A kiddie song, wasn't it? 'The worms crawl in, the worms crawl out.'" The man laughed, a high brittle tittering that sounded nothing like the deep timbre that filled the room only moments before.

"Yeah, preacher man. She told me all about you. That little girl that keeps you up at night. Tossing and turning while you picture her stripped down and shivering. How you think about peeling her open from the inside out. She's ripe, too. Ain't she?" The man licked his lips, and Cora thought she saw something move inside his mouth. Long fingers reaching out from within his throat. Worms sliding in and out of the gaps between his teeth.

"No. Please, no," Michael said, and Cora stood, felt the outline of the keys in her pocket and inched her fingers toward them.

"You've been so kind to us, but it's late, and we have a long way to go," Cora said, and the man swiveled his head and stared at her, a wide, shit-eating grin plastered across his face.

"Don't you though?" the man said, and Cora shifted her weight to her right leg, angled her body so that if she needed to run, it would put her in the most direct path to the door. Even though the man towered over her and had at least forty pounds on her, he was old, and Cora figured she could outrun him. Especially if he didn't expect her to run. Twenty paces would get her to the door. Ten more to the car. She would have the key in the engine before he could catch up to her, be out of the lot before he could scramble far enough to even see her taillights.

"Yes. A long way," Cora said again, and she glanced at Michael, hoped he could read her intent there. *When you see me move, run. Run as fast as you fucking can. Knock him down if you have to, but we have to get out of here. Now.*

Cora's fingers closed around the keys. *Stand up. Stand up right fucking now, Michael.*

"Bet she tastes like peaches on the inside. Isn't that what you've thought—no, *dreamed*—about? Yes sir, preacher man. Just makes you want to gobble her right up. And you, Cora. Somebody already got ahold of you," the man said.

Outside, the cats began screaming.

Turning to the sound, the man continued. "Sounds like you two got bigger fish to fry. She's coming." His eyes flooded with red, the pupil blinking out until there was only a sea of crimson, and he bared his teeth like an animal.

Without looking back, Cora ran. If Michael followed, she wasn't sure, but she propelled herself forward, her legs rubbery and loose from whatever had been in the bottle, but she was moving, and her car emerged from the gloom.

Fumbling, Cora pulled the keys from her pocket. *Come on. Come on, you absolute shit. Come ON.*

Behind her, the bell jangled.

"Go on and drive. Drive as far as you can. Walk until your feet bleed, and your skin pulls away from muscle. From bone. Run until your fucking *guts* fall out of you. Ain't no amount of running that will hide you from everything that lives underground." The man stood in the doorway, laughing, and Michael sprinted toward her, his legs pumping up and down.

"Let's go," Michael said, and Cora opened the door, turned the key in the engine. The back end of the car swung outward as she took the turn out of the parking lot too hard, but then the blacktop hummed beneath them, and the diner faded into the distance. The rearview mirror showed the man with his arms folded over his stomach, and he laughed, great belly laughs, as they drove away.

Cora's hands trembled, but she drove into the gathering darkness, and whatever lived beyond the shadows watched and waited.

"Where are we going?"

Cora exhaled, looked up at the stars emerging, at their steady burning. The moon a slip of white light outlined in the black.

"I don't know," she said, but it was a lie. It didn't matter where they went, where they ran.

"You turned north," Michael said. He didn't need to explain.

The road led to Hensley.

"Take me home," he said.

Chapter 32

They'd been on the road for an hour when Cora turned on her blinker and guided the car off of the highway.

"I need to make a phone call, okay?"

"Of course," Michael said, but the idea of stopping set his stomach in knots. Anything that delayed them, that kept them from moving blindly forward, left room for him to think, and if he stopped to consider what it was he was heading back into, his guts would turn to water, whatever courage he'd tried to conjure up dissolved and wisped away like smoke.

Bright fluorescent light broke through the darkness ahead, and Cora turned into the gas station and pulled into a space up front.

"I'll come with you. If you don't mind," Michael said. Cora didn't respond but opened her door, and he scrambled to follow. He couldn't sit out here waiting. It didn't matter that the place was lit up like an airstrip. Beyond the halo of light, there was darkness upon darkness, and he had seen enough of what lived inside of those shadows for a lifetime.

Michael followed behind Cora. *Like a dog* he thought, and shame burned through him. She hated him. It was a palpable thing that hung over her. He deserved her hatred.

"Excuse me? Do you guys have a pay phone here? I didn't see

one out front," she said when they entered. The attendant kept his eyes glued to a small television screen. An antenna jutted out of the top, and a large-breasted woman jumped up and down before hugging an older man who held a microphone and grinned with a mouthful of too-white, too-straight teeth.

"We did, but some asshole took it out with his truck, and we ain't replaced it." The attendant looked up from his program, and when he saw Cora, he raked his eyes over her, pausing when he hit her chest before travelling down the length of her.

"But I reckon if you were a paying customer, I could let you use the one back here." He gestured beneath the counter and smiled with teeth brown and tobacco-stained. A far cry from the man on the television.

"Fine." Cora grabbed a pack of gum and placed it on the counter.

"That'll be a dollar seventy-seven," the man said, and she dug her hand into her purse.

"Y'all one of those couples, huh? All equal and stuff. Let the lady pay for what she wants," the man said, and Cora pushed two dollar bills across the counter which he picked up delicately and considered for a moment before he opened the register and dropped them inside.

"We're not married," Michael said, and the attendant looked at him sharply.

"Romantic getaway, then?" he said.

"No," Cora said, her voice gone icy. The man grinned, and he raked his fingers through his hair.

"Well then."

"Mind if I use that phone now?" Cora said, and the man stepped backward, bent forward at the waist in an exaggerated mock bow.

"My lady," he said, and Cora lifted her lip in a sneer.

"Thank you," she said and moved behind the counter. Michael wanted to call her back, to tell her they could find another place, another phone, but she had the receiver pressed to her ear. The attendant lifted his eyebrows and winked at Michael. If Michael had been another man, he would have told him to mind his own damn business, but instead, he thrust his hands in his pockets and stared back.

"Jimmy?" Cora spoke into the phone, and the attendant leaned back on his stool, folded his hands behind his head. Cora glared at the man, but he gave no indication that he was going to leave his post, and she sighed.

Michael turned and looked out the large glass windows that flanked the entrance. The parking lot was empty save for their car, and the lights bore down, lit up every corner of the lot as if it was day. If anything moved there, Michael would see it before it saw him.

Where the light ended, there was nothing. A defined line that divided the world from the abyss, and Michael imagined this place floating in a great sea of that darkness, buoyed up by what? By *whom*?

He thought he saw something move off to the left. An animal scurrying across the asphalt, or a piece of trash, a long-ago-eaten candy bar wrapper, blowing across the lot. When he looked, he couldn't see anything moving, but something had changed. The lot was slightly darker. Not by much, but it held shadows that had not been there before.

Looking up, Michael stared into the lights, blinked as the harsh glare momentarily blinded him, but he had been right. One of the lights was out.

As Michael watched, Cora's voice rising and falling behind him as she spoke into the phone, two more lights blinked out. He turned quickly, thinking the attendant was doing it. To mess with him. But the man still reclined on his stool, his eyes trained on Cora's backside. There were no switches that Michael could make out anywhere near the attendant.

He stared again into the lot. One by one, five more lights blinked out. Each in succession as if some unseen force had blown them out like a series of candles.

The left corner of the lot was dark now, and Michael thought he saw something move. Cold fear bloomed inside of him, and he backed up until the display case in front of the counter pressed against his calves.

Another group of lights went dark. Half of the lot lay in shadow now, and Michael turned to Cora.

"Cora," he said, and she looked up at him, then beyond him and into the lot.

"We have to go," Michael said, and she nodded, spoke some hurried words into the phone as he turned back and watched the lot be slowly swallowed by night.

"Aww, you don't have to rush off," the attendant said, but Cora ignored him and hurried toward Michael, her keys in hand, and together they moved toward the door.

Behind them, the attendant shouted, "What the fuck happened to the lights?"

Something vast moved all around them. Michael could hear it creeping on little feet, but he and Cora began to run, and then they were in the car, their headlights cutting through the black that roiled around them.

Something with pale legs moved across the swath of light the headlights cut. *Too many legs*, Michael thought before the vast shape disappeared. It had been like an octopus or a spider, but the legs had been decidedly human. He gagged.

"What the *fuck* is happening? What is it? What the *fuck* is it?" Cora struck the steering wheel with her palm over and over, and her voice pitched higher and higher until she was screaming.

"I don't know," Michael said. She slowed the car to a stop, brought her forehead to rest against the wheel, and sobbed.

"We have to move, Cora. We can't stay here," he said when a few minutes had passed. She sat up and wiped her nose with her sleeve.

"Yes," she said and put the car back into drive.

"It's going to follow us, isn't it? Wherever we go," Cora said, but he knew that he didn't need to answer her. "Jimmy said that I called him. Left a message that didn't make any sense."

"Jimmy?"

"My boss back in Atlanta. Said I called him late last night. Said that it was just a bunch of static at first, but then it was me talking over the static, telling him things I couldn't possibly know. His mother's nickname for him when he was little. How he had accidentally killed their dog when he was sixteen. Backed over it with the car, which he had taken out without permission. Where in the backyard he had buried it. That he hadn't told anyone."

Cora took a jagged breath and let it out. "I knew about his high school biology teacher. How that was the first man he ever slept with. How much he had loved Mr. Nickleson. How Mr. Nickleson beat the shit out of him the night Jimmy came to his house to tell him that he did. Told him if he came near his family again he would pull his tiny faggot nuts out through his mouth and make sure he didn't have a tongue to tell about it. How Jimmy still thinks about Mr. Nickleson when he's lonely. I don't think that I can do this. How do I do this?" Cora whispered.

"Once upon a time, I would have told you about faith. Told you to put your trust in something greater than the sum of our selves. Told you to be quiet and listen. I would have said it, but I wouldn't have believed it myself. When I was a kid, I was so sure of myself. So certain that when the time came, when my faith would be tested, I would be the one who did not crumble. That I would be the steadfast one who stood in the face of the darkness. That the evil that moved in the world was a tangible thing, and that I could fight against it. Demons and devils exposed and trembling beneath my holy hands. When my father took me to see the snakes, to teach me how to keep them quiet, I understood then that faith is like a ghost. Something that haunts you. But it isn't real."

Cora was quiet for a moment before she spoke again. "No. It isn't."

"When did you know?" Michael asked, and she swiped at her eyes before tightening her grip on the wheel.

"I haven't believed in anything since I was thirteen, preacher. My mother went to church. She begged me to come with her, but I couldn't. I just couldn't. The thought of even walking in made me sick."

"Because *he* was there," he said, and she looked at him sharply.

"Is this what they wanted for you? Your parents?"

"This?" He gestured toward the darkness. "My father knew evil in the most concrete ways. He saw it in the ways that people numb themselves against pain. Against the sad realities of their pitiful lives. He said that evil wasn't pure; that it was mixed up in everything and easy to fall into. But he didn't know its face. Not really. No, this isn't what they wanted. They wanted me to take up the snakes. Feel powerful and chosen by God. Even though it was an act, I think they still believed. They wanted me to live and die a quiet life. There was no room for anything else in the vision of their son's years on this earth."

Cora went quiet at that. Strange shapes—proboscis-like

extensions—flicked in and out of the dark as they drove, and Michael thought he saw a wolf—its eyes yellow-bright—but then it was gone.

"My mother wanted me to be a doctor. Said there was no nobler profession than healing the sick. Christ-like."

"She sounds like a good woman."

Cora smiled. "She was. Of course, I did everything she didn't want me to do instead. Because what else should a good daughter do except break her mother's heart?"

"I think that's the rule. Children are meant to hurt their parents."

"Probably why my father left before I was two." Cora looked up into the rearview and flipped the mirror upward.

A mountain lion screamed in the night. It was close, and Michael pressed his face to the window and watched as the trees whipped by.

"He told me to come home. Jimmy did. Get in the car and don't stop. He said there was something wrong. That's what he kept saying. Something's wrong. Something's wrong," Cora said.

"Go home, Cora."

She tightened her fingers against the wheel and accelerated. "There's nothing I'd love to do more. Go home and write up my story. 'Pedophile in the Pulpit.' Has a nice ring to it, don't you think?"

He winced, and she continued. "But there's more story to tell, and I'll be damned if I came all this way and don't figure out what the hell is going on in Hensley, North Carolina. And when it's all over, all of those lies you've spun? The church you've built on deceit? I'll burn it to the goddamned ground."

He went silent at that and watched the darkness flex and shift around them as she drove on into the night.

Michael must have slept because the miles slipped away, and Cora was shaking his shoulder, the car pitching forward onto the dirt road.

"We're here," she said, and Michael peered into the dark road opening before them.

Rolling down the window, he listened. All was quiet. Cora cut the headlights. The car bumped along in the dark and rounded the final curve into the town.

"Preacher," Cora whispered, and the entire expanse opened before him. Small forms stood still in a large ring with linked hands and bowed heads.

"The children," he said, and Cora brought the car to a stop. All of the children stood in the town center. A few of the older boys and girls clutched infants in their arms, and Henry Butler, who couldn't have been more than two, stood next to his sister, his head also bowed. None of them moved. It was as if they had been carved from marble and set down among the town. Something hard and beautiful.

"What are they doing out here?"

"They're praying," Michael said, and the obscene truth of what they had stumbled upon hit him hard. How many times had he stood at the forefront of one of those circles? Clasped hands and sweating brows as he spoke in low, fervent whispers about punishment and reward. Asking for forgiveness or for aid in times of crisis. Asking God to heal the sick or lead the blind back into the fold. And now, as they watched, these prayers morphed into abomination. This was not a prayer circle. This was something else.

All at once, the children raised their heads and turned toward the car.

"I can't see their eyes," Cora said, and her voice was strained.

"Preacher. Come and lead the circle," a lone voice called out from the children, but Michael did not know who had spoken.

He reached for the door handle, but Cora pulled him back.

"Are you crazy?" she said, and tears shimmered at the corners of her eyes. Softly, Michael put her hand away and opened the door.

"I'm going to get out of the car now. You can stay. You can go. I'd like it if you stayed. I know that you have no real reason to, but it's been some comfort having you with me. But I have to do this now. They're only children. Probably confused and scared." He'd hoped by saying it aloud, he would believe he was right.

"We can figure out some other way, Michael. Michael!" she called after him, but he walked now toward the children, and they opened their arms to welcome him home.

"Come and see her. The great Mother." Tiny hands pulled at Michael's clothes and urged him forward. The doors of the church were blown wide, and the children guided him toward them. *The prodigal son returned.*

Michael stepped over the threshold and into the church. Inside, the darkness was cool against his tongue.

Wrong, wrong, wrong. All of this is wrong.

"Welcome, Michael." The voice was sweet, girlish. A voice Michael had heard in a thousand dreams. A row of candles set beneath the pulpit cast shadowed devils against the ceiling and illuminated the two figures crouched there.

"We've been waiting," another voice said, and the shock of recognition ran through him.

"Ruth."

The two women were visible now, their faces glowing in the candlelight. Ruth. Leah. Mother and daughter embracing before the face of God.

"Come and see," Leah said. She cradled a squirming bundle,

and it mewled softly.

"Shhh." Leah began to rock back and forth, her hand slipping upward to catch at the neckline of her dress before pulling it down to expose her breast, the nipple large and swollen. She pressed the bundle to it, and the child rooted noisily, its loud suckling filling the space.

The Virgin and the Christ Child, Michael thought. He wanted to laugh, to howl like a man broken, but he did not.

Ruth smoothed her daughter's hair, and beckoned Michael forward, her fingers twitching against the thin blanket wrapped around the tiny, grunting thing.

Its flesh was raw and bleeding. There was none of the smooth, pale skin of infancy, and its eyes were a never ending sea of red. The arms tapered off into bulbous swellings of flesh. No hands. No fingers. The torso streaming away from the head and neck down into yet another protuberance of loose, flapping skin. More worm than child.

Michael's knees buckled, and he stumbled before steadying himself. *Burn it*, he thought, and as if they had heard him, both Leah and Ruth tucked the blanket tight around the creature, covering it once more from sight.

"What have you done?" Michael said, and Leah regarded him carefully.

"The sins of the father. Look how we try and escape them. We spend our entire lives outrunning something that's in our very blood, and blood will always out.

"*Your* sins, preacher, were always written on your face. In the way you hunched your shoulders. The way you cast your eyes upward to heaven as if that simple act would redeem you. You don't have to pretend anymore. How easy, how wonderful to drop the mantle of pretense."

Behind Michael, the church doors open and closed, and

autumn air cut through the sanctuary, the initial sweetness that had greeted him had become cloying, and he breathed in, thankful for the coolness.

Michael pictured the children streaming in behind him, their small heads still bowed, their faces pales as they found their family pews as they did on Sundays. A terrifying congregation of small creatures waiting for his sermon.

"Hello, Cora," Ruth said, and Michael spun on his heels. Seeing Cora there was enough to make him cry aloud.

"Ah, yes. Little Cora who kept quiet. You've spent your days, every one since that night, running. Same as Michael. Same as all of us. But aren't you tired now? Aren't you so, so tired?"

The bundle squirmed, shifted so it faced Michael for the first time, its mouth a perfectly round O filled with rows and rows of tiny barbed teeth. Outside, the sound of many voices, the high, clear voices of children, lifted in song. A hymn, but not one he had ever heard before, and the words tumbled one over the other until it no longer sounded like singing at all but rather the desperate shrieks and cries of animals led to slaughter.

"Go fuck yourself," Cora spat, and the women grinned, mouths opening wide to expose dark gums.

"Your father would be so disappointed, Michael," Ruth said.

He stepped forward. "My father would have burned that thing. That *abomination*."

"And you are nothing but your father's son. Come and try it, preacher," Ruth said, and the women ran, their arms stretched before them, fingers scrabbling against the walls and then the ceiling as they crawled, their heads and necks bent to stare down as they moved above Cora and Michael and out the door.

"No!" Cora ran after them, and Michael followed.

The churchyard was empty. No groups of children offered up strange, garbled prayers. No mother and daughter sheltered a creature that cried and suckled. Every light in every house was turned off. No candles burned in the windows.

"They can't have just disappeared. Goddammit. *Goddammit,*" Cora said.

Completely quiet. No lights. Where are the adults? Michael went cold.

"Come on," he said. The Warner place was the closest homestead. It had been built with the intent of housing the preacher and his family, but Michael's father thought the house too extravagant with its front porch and large kitchen.

His father's place—and consequently, his *family's* place—was in the church, and that's where they had stayed. Michael grew up in the shadow of the church, in the shadow of his father and the snakes he passed each week. He had learned to play quietly and to hold his breath in the face of God, and then eventually to ignore it.

Cora followed him, and soon enough, the simple structure emerged in the moonlight. A wooden cabin that faced north. A large front porch that wrapped around the right side of the cabin, with two windows that flanked the front door. A single rocking chair sat on the porch, the initials E.B.W. carved into the back.

"I don't think now is the time to come calling, preacher," Cora said.

"All of the children were in town. All of them. Even the babies. Something's wrong," Michael said. He lifted his fist, pounded against the door, and waited. Nothing moved within. "Edward," he called, but there was no muffled talking, no voice calling back asking for just a moment.

Cora went to the windows and cupped her hands around her eyes as she pressed her face to the glass.

"Oh, fuck. Oh, fuck. Oh, no." Cora shrank away from the

window, her hands shaking.

Michael leaned his forehead against the door. Behind him, Cora wept softly. Whatever was inside, he didn't want to see. From house to house, the angel of death had come, and he did not want to see what had been left behind. His heart hammered in his throat.

Breathe in. Breathe out. Better to not think. Better to let the air stream in and out of his lungs. Focus on filling himself up like a balloon. Better to not think as he covered his hand with his shirt; to not think as he put his fist through the window before clearing away the jagged remnants of glass; to not think about climbing through and looking down at the two bodies twisted around each other. A man and a woman. Edward and Bethany. Both of them nude. Torn open. Edward's chest a gaping hole. The heart and lungs missing. Bethany's pelvis split open, butterflied. The legs splayed open like an insect's.

House to house Michael and Cora moved. Where families had eaten their dinners only hours before, where they prayed for health and peace, mothers and fathers lay in various stages of mutilation.

Inside the Pharr house, Vera lay on the floor, her spine snapped in multiple places, her jaw broken and the mouth stretched impossibly wide. Someone had inserted two fingers neatly inside.

As Michael stood there, he became aware of Cora moving away from him, back out the front door until he heard her vomiting into the dirt.

Through each house, they moved quietly, found sheets or blankets or tablecloths and covered the dead, and he did the same here, in the last house, before moving back into the night air.

Cora knelt on the ground, her hands splayed against the earth.

If anything watched them from the shadows, it had not come forward. No children emerged from the dark to observe them. No Leah. No Ruth.

Twice, Cora's body convulsed, but only a thin line of saliva dripped into the dirt, and she rocked back onto her heels, swiped her hand across her lips.

"There's only one house we haven't gone to," she said.

Michael looked up the mountain. "Full circle. Back to where we started."

"Ouroboros," she said and glanced up at the sky. "The snake eating itself."

He had a vague memory of seeing a drawing once. A serpent curving back onto itself, its teeth sinking into its own tail. Remembered reading about it on one of the few excursions to the nearest library. His father engrossed, not paying attention as his boy wandered the stacks, his fingers pulling at the spines of books the older man would have surely forbidden.

"Rebirth," he said, and Cora nodded and followed his eyes up the mountain.

Chapter 33

The ground shifted with every step they took. For what seemed like hours, Cora and Michael picked their way up the mountain, dark rifts opening before them as they stepped, sand and silt scattering wherever they placed their feet; the ground suddenly gone soft as quicksand, and it lapped at their ankles and calves. Twice they stopped and pulled themselves from the muck on hands and knees, a soft sucking sound filling the space as the earth reluctantly released them.

Above Cora and Michael, the moon burned, too large and too close. A huge blazing star that had come unmoored. It would blot them out. Smeared bits of blood and bone and skin were all that would remain to show what they had once been.

Loose dirt covered the steps to the porch as if someone had scattered it there in great handfuls.

Michael moved ahead of her, drifting like a ghost, his movements lethargic. Dreamlike.

"I think that I died that first day," Cora said, and he paused on the steps, his back rigid, the shoulders hitched up toward his ears.

"I think he killed me. I was so ashamed. Big hands over that little mouth. Squeezing and squeezing until I was like a doll.

Soft and pliable. I don't think I ever got up from that place. Everything since then has been a dream. And I'm so close to waking up," Cora said.

"It would be easier. To think that," Michael said, and his words struck her like thrown stones. The air had gone thick, and Cora coughed on the hot, little fingers that reached down her throat.

"But he didn't. I wish he had. So much better to wink out. Like a star," she said, and Michael turned to her then, stared at her with eyes large and wet.

Cora walked past him, up the steps. The door was closed and a dim light burned within, its small glow visible through the windows at the front. A candle burning to welcome the long-lost children home. She tried the handle. It was unlocked.

"The sun's coming up," Michael said, and the light inside went out.

"It can't be," Cora said, but there was the faint grey streaking across the dark, the shadows chased away by the coming dawn.

"I'm opening the door," Cora said, and she felt Michael move behind her, the air around them shifting slightly as he prepared himself for whatever lay beyond.

Grasping the handle, Cora pushed the door open.

Nothing moved inside. The room was left exactly as she remembered it from the night before. The Bible cast on the floor and the long hallway stretching on and on.

Together, they went through the rooms. At each doorway Cora held her breath and listened to her blood pound in her ears. Each room was empty and quiet as a tomb.

"There was someone here. I saw a light," Cora said when they had gone through the house a second time. They stood on the porch and watched as the sun rose.

"I know," he said.

Michael turned and faced the road that led back down the mountain. "I need to go back to the church," he said.

"What about all of these people? You can't just leave them there. We need to call the police. Someone. Tell them what's happening here."

"You don't understand."

"No. You're right. I don't understand. Not for one *fucking* second do I understand. Every adult in this town was torn apart. Presumably by that group of Children of the Corn wannabes. A woman back from the dead, and her daughter cradling some fucked up worm baby, and you want to go back to the church to do what exactly, preacher?"

"There's something there that I need to see," Michael said.

"Nope. Not good enough."

He sighed and bowed his head. "There's a book. A book I never thought I would open. My father left it to me when he died. I'm not sure where he found it. He'd gone away. A trip or a travelling revival. I can't remember. I was six. Maybe seven. But he came home after a week, and it was like a dead man had come home instead.

"My mother tried to hide it from me, but I could tell that there was something wrong. He barely ate. Barely spoke. That Sunday was the first time the church doors hadn't opened in decades.

"My mother told everyone he was sick. Picked something up while he was gone, and no one questioned it, but something had gotten inside of him, and I could see it. Something terrible moved behind his eyes."

Cora's head ached, a deep, grinding pain that felt as if someone had inserted a steel rod in the center of her brain and was slowly rotating it.

"Next few days, I'd hear him moving around the church in

the middle of the night. Walking up and down the hallways. I never got up to see what he was doing. Too scared. Eventually, Momma would get up, go to him, and get him to go back to bed.

"That next Friday night, he still wasn't talking, and Momma was afraid she was going to have to call off the service again. Knew that it would really set tongues wagging if the church didn't open two weeks in a row. Already there were people suspicious.

"I didn't sleep that night. Couldn't. I thought my father had a demon inside of him. That like the pigs in the book of Matthew, he'd attempted to cast one out, and it had entered him instead.

"I don't know why I did it, but I followed him one night when he got up. Followed him into the sanctuary, hid under a pew, and watched him. He sat there for what felt like hours. Praying or sleeping, I'm not sure what he was doing, but I was terrified.

"After a while, he got up and went outside. Walked directly into the forest. He didn't take the path, and still I followed him, hid behind a tree and watched. He was carrying a book."

Michael stared out over the mountain, his eyes distant.

"He was using his hands to dig a hole. He dug it pretty deep. The way you do a grave for an animal. Not as deep as a man's but deep enough to keep whatever he put there down. When he was finished, he dropped the book in. He stared at it for a long time. Like he didn't want to bury it, but then he covered it, packed the dirt tight, and I ran back to my bed, pulled the sheets over my head. He looked in at me when he came back in. I heard the door creak when he opened it.

"The next morning, he was in the office, the Bible and his notes laid out, and he preached that Sunday, and every Sunday until he died. Eventually, I thought that everything I'd seen that night had been a bad dream. A kid's overactive imagination kicked into hyperdrive by his father's odd behavior. Behavior a child wouldn't understand, would perhaps inflate into something strange and inexplicable."

"You have the book," Cora said.

"Before my father died, he called me in to him. Told me that once, when he was younger, he had found a book, had seen things inside of it that had marked him. Changed him. He said that there were unspeakable things in the world, and that he had known them. Read about them. That they slumbered beneath the dirt like worms. At first, I dismissed it as the ramblings of a man on his deathbed, his tongue loosened as the end approached, but then he took me back to that night. The night I followed him.

"He told me where to find it. How many steps to take into the forest before putting shovel to dirt. Everything exactly as I remembered it. All of the things I had dismissed as a dream suddenly real and tangible before me. He made me promise him I would never read it. That I would keep it hidden. Keep it buried deep in the ground.

"I knew then what I had seen was no dream. That whatever my father had found inside that book had leaked out of the pages and infected him. After he died, I went back to that spot. Nothing grew there. No trees. No bushes or flowers or vines or grass. Just a round spot that looked as if it had been sown with salt. Whatever's in that book, I think it infected the town. Leaked into our dreams, our blood. Poisoned us."

"Did you ever dig it up?"

"No. There were times when I thought about it. Wondered what could possibly be inside of those pages that would so mark my father, but I never did."

"Why dig it up now? What good could it do?"

"My father said that evil lived in that book. Marked down in ink on paper. Things that no human should ever see. Ever know. There may be something there. Something that could tell us what to do."

"Ever considered calling the military? Having them roll in here with tanks and guns? Blow this place off of the fucking map?" Even as Cora said the words, she knew that it wouldn't work. She'd built her world firmly on the ground of skepticism, but there were too many strange seeds planted here, and in the face of everything that had happened, her logic wanted to curl up and sleep.

"It wouldn't work. They could scorch the earth. Burn every tree, every creature here, but they couldn't stop it," Michael said, and she thought of the cashier at the liquor store, the man in the apron, the gas station parking lot. Whatever was happening was spreading outward like a disease, the burning height of a fever in the trees surrounding them. Every leaf, every branch was poisoned and rotted; the ground an open chasm waiting to swallow them all down.

"Fine. Fuck it. Lead the way," Cora said, and he stumbled off of the porch and onto the path that led to the trees.

Michael walked slightly ahead of her, the forest coming to life around them. Jimmy's words kept coming back to her. *Come home, Cora. Something's not right. Something's wrong. Something's wrong.*

She'd thought about it. She could have hung up the phone, turned, and slipped out the door before Michael could have caught up with her, left him there with that skeeze ball running the register and been back in Atlanta in less than four hours, curled up on her own couch with a glass of wine and a paperback in her hands.

Cora didn't owe Michael anything. This was not her town. Not her people. There was no thread that tied her here, and yet it was her mother's voice in her ear. That thin, paper whisper telling her to do good for people. To always do what was right in the face of wrong. To be a good girl.

Be a good girl.

He had told her that, too. Mr. Burress. Told Cora she didn't want to break her mother's heart. That her mother and Jesus would want her to be good, and she didn't want to hurt them, did she?

But now, Cora could do more than be good. She could do what her mother had asked her to do. While the world unraveled, she could *try*. It didn't matter that she was terrified and didn't understand. She could *try*.

With every step, every twig that snapped or leaf that rustled, Cora braced herself, waited on the children to emerge from the forest on quiet, little feet, but the only living things she saw were birds calling to one another in the trees.

Where had they gone? There had been at least twenty children. She and Michael had searched each house and there had been no signs of them. She imagined them sleeping beneath their feet, the crust of the earth covering their mouths and noses as they breathed in and out.

The church rose before them, and Michael shifted to the left, curved back into the woods but off the path. Following close behind him, Cora picked her way through fallen leaves and underbrush, stepping carefully to avoid poison ivy or oak or sumac or any other leaf that would blister her skin.

"There," Michael said and pointed. As he'd told her, a pale circle of bare earth the circumference of a serving bowl appeared amid the fall color.

"Don't you need a shovel?" Cora said, but Michael had already dropped to his knees and pressed his fingers into the soil. It gave easily beneath him, and he scooped out large handfuls and placed the dirt carefully next to him.

His breath hitched as he worked, his hands dipping in and out of the hole he'd created. Minutes passed.

The sky above them felt too large, too blue, like an enormous eye staring down. Passive. Uncaring. Beyond that, an explosion of color seemed to shimmer, the edges bleeding together into one mass of overexposed tints that left Cora's head feeling like it had been hollowed out.

"Got it," Michael said and pulled the book from the dirt. It was covered in a cloth that had long ago begun to yellow, wrapped and rewrapped tightly, and then knotted at the corners. Michael shook the dirt from the book and tucked it under his arm.

The tree line stretched on and on, and Cora kept her eyes trained on it as they walked back to the church. Up here, there was only the mountain; only the trees to mark where the earth left off and the sky began. The air a thin, piercing thing that burned as it moved through the blood.

Inside the town and the little houses, the adults slept on, their paper-thin skins wrapped in Death, and the quiet settled on Cora and Michael like dust as they stepped out of the forest. Their footsteps died beneath them as they made their way to the church, the white clapboard dull in the bright sun.

They did not go in through the front door but instead through a side door hidden among an overgrown group of wax myrtles.

"My father planted those for my mother. She loved the smell. In the winter, she'd boil the berries and make candles. For months, the entire church smelled of it. I remember thinking that when I got to heaven, it would smell like bayberry."

"Mine would be White Shoulders. It was the only thing my mother would wear. I'd buy her something else, something expensive, and she would tell me that she loved it and then never wear it," Cora said, and Michael unlocked the door and stepped inside.

Pausing in the doorway, she held her breath. Waited for soft laughter or hurried whispers to drift from the sanctuary, but all she could hear was her heart hammering in her chest.

"This way," he said. She followed him down the hallway, which bent to the right, and flanked the sanctuary. The door that led to the pulpit stood ajar, a thin slip of filtered sunlight leaked through, and Cora watched the light as they went past, but the door did not open. There were other doors that led to unseen rooms, but he ducked inside the first one.

His office. Strange to think that she had been here only a few days prior, seated across from Michael and asking him the canned questions she thought she'd so carefully crafted.

Locking the door behind him, Michael crossed the room to the desk, and laid the book against the worn surface.

His hands trembled, and he brought them to the knotted cloth, dropped them, and then brought them back only to drop them once more.

"I'm afraid. God, help me. I'm afraid," he said, but then his fingers worked at the knots, the frayed edges crumbling at his touch, and the cloth unraveled. Layer after layer pulled away until all that remained was a black, leather-bound book about the size of Cora's palm.

Michael turned it over and over in his hands. "Nothing on the cover. No markings. No etchings. Completely smooth." He offered it to Cora, and she hesitated before accepting it.

It was heavier than she had imagined it would be and hot and slick in her palm. The room tilted and swayed, the seasick

song and dance of a heavy night of booze, and she placed the
book on the desk. Instantly, the feeling subsided, and all that
remained was a rancid film that coated the back of her throat.
None of this should be happening. None of it made sense.

"He looked like a dead man after he read it. Like a ghost,"
Michael said. His fingers hovered over the dark cover, and
Cora positioned herself behind him so she looked down over
his shoulder. Breathing hard, he closed his eyes and opened
the book.

A full moon dominated the first page. Beneath it, a nude
woman squatted, her face obscured. From between her legs,
a worm emerged, its mouth full of teeth and reaching toward
her calf. The fingers of her right hand crooked backward and
pointed away from the palm.

"The Great Worm," Michael read aloud, and the room
seemed to buzz, the air itself pulling apart before coming back
together in strange configurations.

Another page was covered with children, their mouths open
and screaming, their eyes great black holes.

The next page was completely covered in black ink except for
the exact center where a tree put out roots that bled outward.
The heart of the tree was shaped like female genitalia with
thick folds of skin curving inward.

"The worms crawl in," Michael said and laughed—high and
hysterical—and it set her teeth on edge. She looked away, but
Michael grasped at her hand.

"Look. It's me. It's me. And you." Cora's own face and body
were set down in ink, a snake stretching toward the dark
curling hair at her pubis. Her head thrown back in ecstasy as
Michael looked on, his chest pried open to expose his heart,
yet another snake coiled in the cavity.

Again, the room shimmered, miniature explosions of color

coalescing before dropping away into nothing.

"Like a holy bag of skin," Michael said, and she wasn't sure if he was reading from the book or if his mind had broken.

"Close the book, Michael."

"I can't. Not now that it's open. We could take it back to that place, bury it again, but it would never be closed." There was another page beneath his fingers, and she would not look, but he bent close, and a thin line of drool leaked from the corner of his mouth to fall onto the paper.

"Someone is knocking. Open the door, Cora."

"There's no one here. Only us."

"We all fall down. We all fall down. We all fall down," he whispered. From beyond the door came a strange clicking: bones clattering together, the mandibles of great insects opening and closing, fingernails scraping against wood.

"Oh, God," Michael moaned, and Cora shut her eyes, watched the dark waves churning behind her lids.

"Someone is knocking," he said again, and she heard it then and opened her eyes. Quiet. Quiet. Under the floor. A blind, quivering thing born in the dark and waiting to be heard. To be let out.

There was blood on Michael's fingers, and he brought them to his mouth. Lips like cherries. Red clay. Something desiccated like the landscape, locked inside of its dying.

Beautiful.

Cora's body had gone warm, her thighs burning and aching, and she brought her hand to her stomach, pressed whatever grew there flat. The flesh on her belly was soft and silken, and she traced that softness down, caught at her belt and zipper before she found the wetness that gathered between her legs.

Michael watched her. Watched her work her hand against herself, and the line of blood that streaked across his lips grew larger, covered his chin until it dripped down his neck and stained the collar of his shirt.

"Can't," Cora said, but her movements quickened, and the world was too full, everything building to the moment she knew would come. A teetering on the edge of pain that threatened to explode before the wash of hot pleasure that came in waves, a slow throbbing that left behind a feeling of distinct emptiness.

Cora left her belt undone and moved toward Michael, brought her tongue to the blood on his chin and traced the sharp angles of his jawline, followed those angles down his neck and up again.

"It's the book doing this, Cora."

"It's not," she said and brought her mouth to his. Lips that tasted of salt and rain, and he sighed into her mouth, moved against her, and she pressed up into him, fit her body against his.

When Michael pushed Cora onto the desk, she arched her back, and he hooked his fingers against the waistband of her slacks and underwear and tugged them down. His hands wrapped around her ribcage, and she knew that he would leave bruises, delicate purple brushstrokes to remind her of where his body had been.

And then Michael was inside of her, and Cora cried out, closed her eyes as the room dropped away until there was only darkness, the taste of seawater on her lips, waves pushing them under and her lungs filled and aching. The taste of blood and death moved through Cora, and his mouth fed her strange words that burned sweetly in her throat as she swallowed them down.

When Michael groaned, his movements becoming slow and jerky, Cora held him to her, buried her face in his neck and traced her name against the soft flesh with her tongue.

Mine, Cora thought, but she knew it was a lie. This strange man with his faith and his snakes and his dark eyes and terrible secrets. This man who had *seen* her as she had seen him. Everything open and exposed. Even now, she hated him.

Michael brought his lips to Cora's forehead, and she choked back a sob.

And still, beneath them, something knocked.

Chapter 34

Beneath the town, the creatures in the dirt slept on. They called to one another in dreams and spoke in tongues long forgotten. Around them, their skins grew soft and pale, and they burrowed further down, safe in the depths of the earth. Together, they waited for the moon to rise. Now that they were different, the sun would hurt them, and they didn't want to hurt.

Once, they had been children; children who feared the dark and called to mothers and fathers who would check their closets and under their beds for monsters. Children with names like Thomas and Catherine, but now they had no names, and they sank into the earth and slept and shed their old skins. Something new and better grew in its place.

It was nice to not have a name, to not have to remember to mind your manners and do stupid things like say 'please' and 'thank you.' It had been so tiresome remembering to wash their hands before dinner, or to not talk with their mouths full, or to sit still and be quiet all of the time. They hadn't wanted to go to sleep—that much had not changed—but it was lovely here in the ground, and it wasn't so bad once they got used to it.

The mother and her daughter slept, too. Their mouths

pressed together, the baby at the girl's breast, and their legs intertwined. They loved Ruth and Leah and had cried when it was time to sleep, but Leah had smiled and promised them it wouldn't be for long.

It felt good to change. To wiggle each tooth as it came loose and then yank it out until there was nothing left but slick gums. It felt good to be strong, to run on all fours like a dog or slither along the ground on their bellies. Why would anyone want to walk? It felt wonderful to be fast.

It had been hard at the start. So many of them were unsure of what was happening, but then there were more and more of them, and they helped the others along, and it wasn't so scary or lonesome.

In the first house they went into, Annabeth Warner had re-membered her father and cried a little, but then they were on him, and it was the most fun game they had ever played. More fun than hide and seek or tag or baseball. Definitely more fun than Sunday School.

The little ones took longer to change, so at first they only watched, but by the time they'd gotten to the third house, they joined in, and everyone said it was more fun than ever.

They tried to trick each other. Hid bits and pieces where no one would think to look, but they all had the same mind now, so that game wasn't as fun.

When it was time for sleep, they cried and protested, but they all came forward and kissed Leah, Ruth, and the baby.

"The baby will be bigger when we wake up, and we can all play with him then," Leah said, and those who still had hands clapped and shouted.

A baby! Some of them remembered taking care of babies. Little brothers and sisters with round faces and great, fat legs. Making faces and watching their little mouths crack open into smiles. A baby would be wonderful fun!

"Will he love us? Even though we don't look like him?" one of them asked, and Leah ran her hand over the baby's head and smiled.

"You will soon enough. Don't worry."

And so they slept on and waited for night to come.

Chapter 35

"It won't stop, will it?" Cora said, and Michael glanced at the floor, listened to the soft knocking that had not ended since they had broken apart, their arms and legs sticky with sweat.

"I don't know."

Michael had closed the book, wrapped it carefully in the dirty cloth. It sat on the desk between them now. Cora's shirt was still unbuttoned and loose, and Michael thought of what it would be like to trace his fingers across the skin there, but it had been a mistake. All of it.

"I'm sorry," he said.

"Leave it alone, preacher."

"It was the book," he said, but Cora waved her hand.

"I said leave it alone."

His father had been right. Evil was bound up inside of the book's pages. Even now, after Michael had seen every page, he wondered if he opened it again, if the illustrations would change, the words carved there rearranging themselves into other strange incantations.

He had spoken the words carved in those pages aloud. As he moved inside of Cora, he had given them life, but he could not remember them, and the thought made him afraid for her.

What have I done?

The air in the room was thick and heady, and not for the first time, Michael longed for a window. He had found the book and brought it here. All of those horrors poured inside of him, and it had told him nothing.

"We can't stop it," Cora said.

"I don't know," he said and hated his own helplessness.

Cora stood, her fingers moving against her buttons and tucking in her blouse. "I'm not going to just sit here."

Whatever was under the floor continued to knock, and Cora lifted her foot and slammed it down. "Shut the fuck up!" she shouted, but the knocking did not stop, and she brought both hands up, directed both middle fingers toward it.

"You still have your keys?" he asked.

Cora patted her pockets. "Yes. Can't believe it, but I do."

"It's still daylight. Other than the knocking, there hasn't been a peep since we got here. I think that whatever it is, it has to sleep during the day."

Cora studied him, her eyes wary. "You may be right."

"Let's go."

"Go where?" Cora said, and Michael realized that he didn't have an answer.

"Does it matter?"

"No. It doesn't," Cora said, and she turned and threw open the door. He followed her, and the knocking faded into a hollow, empty thing.

As they came through the front doors and down the steps, Cora turned back. "See you soon, you motherfuckers," she said, and something sparked inside of him like flint against metal.

Michael followed her to the car. When Cora turned the key in the engine and pulled away from the church, no one rose to stop them, and she peeled out of the lot and onto the road that led out of the town.

"Which way?" Cora said when she came to the turnoff.

Michael pointed. "Left," and she turned, let the wheel slide through her fingers as the road carried them away.

Cora switched on the radio, and immediately, a voice came through the speakers. A calm, even voice. A voice to calm crying children. Cajoling. Soothing. A voice to restore sanity and faith.

"They've gone to ground now. The children let of their blood. Cut open and left to run into the dirt like food. Hearts and eyes and lungs all bleached out. Bags of meat and bone is all we are. Food for worms," the voice said, and Cora hit the power button.

"How far? How far has it gone? Fifty miles? A hundred? Five hundred?" Cora said, her voice pitching up and up, and Michael reached forward, turned the radio back on, and hit the seek button.

"Don't," Cora said, but Michael hit the button again, let the radio settle on whatever frequency it could find.

Channel after channel all filled with that voice; each station, even the ones Michael knew did not exist, broadcasting as far as the signal would carry it.

"The Great Worm," the voice began, but he shut it off. Cora's hands trembled against the wheel, and he remembered the way they felt against his back. Blood rushed to his cheeks, and she glanced over at him as if she knew what he was thinking. He looked away.

Stupid.

"We need to find a phone," Cora said, and he pointed up ahead.

"There's another town about fifteen miles out. There should

be a phone there. Maybe food. Or at least water."

Cora adjusted the rearview, then leaned across Michael and popped open the glove box. Her proximity made him stiffen, and he stared at the back of her neck, a delicate curve that led him to her shoulders.

"Here," Cora said and flipped him a cassette tape. "Put that in."

An aggressive bass blared through the car, and then drums loud and intense, building as the song began.

"Judas Priest. Devil music," Cora said and lifted an eyebrow.

Michael laughed. "Perfect."

As they drove on, the sun a high cold star above them, Cora sang along, and he watched her mouth shape the words.

Three songs later, they approached the turnoff. "Here," he said and she took it.

"There's a little store up ahead. I'd come here sometimes if Sister Maguire ran out of anything. Bread. Milk. Coffee. Generally, if she didn't have it, they would. People recognized me. Knew I was the snake preacher and were a little wary, but generally they were friendly."

The road forked up ahead, a single yellow light blinking, and Michael directed Cora to the left and toward the small main street that ran through the center of the town.

Crumbling brick buildings lined the street. A broken side-walk led to doorways that seemed too close together. Metal lampposts with finely detailed filigree appeared haphazardly, but no lights shone. A large, carved black bear stood outside one of the shop's doors, a sign between his claws that pro-claimed there were unique antiques within.

"Street's completely empty," Cora said and guided the car down the main drag.

With each store they passed, Michael peered into the windows and hoped to catch the silhouette of someone finishing up her shopping, hurrying out in the hopes she could make it home before lunch.

Cora brought the car to a dead stop in the middle of the street and opened her door.

"What are you doing?" Michael asked, but she stepped away from him and toward the bear that stood sentry at the antique shop.

"If anyone can hear me say 'Fuck off!'"

Nothing came forward. No one emerged from the stores, blinking into the sunlight, to look at the foul-mouthed woman standing in the center of their little town.

Cora turned to face Michael. "You see? It's weird here. Eerie," she said, and she came back to the car, leaned against the doorframe and looked in at him.

Michael's throat had gone dry, and the words hitched there, and he swallowed and tried again. "It's already happened. Already here," he said.

Michael knew what he would find if he went to the windows, his hands cupped around his eyes so he could peer into the murky depths behind the brick exterior.

Cora moved away from him, drifted toward the windows, and he wanted to call her back, tell her not to look, but she pressed her face to one of the windows.

Her sob broke through the silence, a heavy thing in the dappled early afternoon sunlight.

Exiting the car, Michael went to her and pulled her away, his fingers feather-light against her shoulders.

Cora jerked away from him. "Don't touch me. Don't you touch me," she said, and the words were like hollow stones in his stomach.

"We have to…they deserve. We have to," she said, and then

she was through the door.

"Help me find something to cover them," she said when Michael came through the door behind her.

The air in the shop was sweet, like pale sugar spun into fluffy clouds, and beneath that lacy scent, a darker fecundity. The smells clung in Michael's throat.

Three small tables stood at the front of the shop. A display case filled with ice cream and dark slices of fudge sat at the back. Next to it, a copper kettle, a paddle, and a long slab of marble. Sweets and a show for the kiddies.

An elderly woman slumped beneath the kettle. The same woman who turned that paddle the day before, her gnarled hands slow and experienced, a marvel for the children who begged their parents to bring them in and buy them the treats she coaxed from sugar and butter.

Blood covered her scalp, bits of bone exposed, her hair sticky and matted. Someone had taken her teeth, lined them up next to her to create two sets of hash marks. Two horizontal lines bisected by two vertical. Inside of the lines, more teeth. A game. They had been playing a game with her teeth.

"Tic-tac-toe," Michael said, but Cora had not heard him.

She moved through the shop, her hands passing over the tables, over the display case, and then she disappeared behind it, ducking down to search beneath, but she came up empty-handed, and she turned to scan the room once. Twice.

"Goddammit, don't just stand there!" Cora said and swiped at her eyes. "Will they all be like this? Everyone? Every single person in this fucking town?"

"Yes," Michael said, and she placed her hands against the top of the display case, leaned forward so that her head hung between her arms.

"Okay. Okay." She looked up at him, and her gaze had gone

hard, her mouth set in a thin line.

"Here," Cora said and moved to the marble slab, closed her fingers over a large knife. There were still bits of hair and congealed blood on the blade, and she traced it against the marble, the gore piling against the edge.

"We'll search the other stores. Take anything we can use."

"Cora. We can't. These people. It belongs to them."

She laughed. Threw her head back and laughed at him. He could see tears trickling from the corners of her eyes.

"Take a look around you, Michael. You said yourself they're all going to be like this. Every single door in this place is going to lead to another horror show. If we can use it, if I even *think* we can use it, I'm taking it."

Michael thought of the book. The strange symbols that had crowded the last page, the intricate tracings traced and retraced, one over the other, until the page crawled with them like a creature come alive. All the while that voice whispering in his mind. A voice like sandpaper on metal.

"You can't kill it," Michael said, and Cora shifted the knife to her right hand, folded it into the waistband of her slacks.

"Maybe not. But I can sure as shit make it bleed," she said and pushed past him and out the door.

Chapter 36

Cora tried not to look at them as she moved around them. The bodies left to rot. Broken bones bent unnaturally; some popped out of socket. A picture of two smiling children and a sun was traced on the floor in blood. Eyes were plucked out and replaced with rocks and pennies and on one man, the head of a G.I. Joe.

"I'm sorry," Cora told them at first, but soon, the phrase grew heavy in her mouth, and she tired of saying it and stayed silent as she looked through their shops.

Michael followed behind her pretending to help, but each time he picked something up, he put it down, and so she was the one who collected. Knives, a baseball bat, a small butane torch. What she really wanted was a gun, but she checked beneath every cash register, behind every counter, and there was no small firearm tucked away.

Back in college, Cora had dated a guy who'd taught her to shoot. Jacob with his dark skin and dark eyes and beautiful smile.

Someone had followed Cora back to her dorm once, a shape lingering in the shadows just beyond her vision, and she had ran inside and called him. The next day, he drove her out of the city, past pine trees and kudzu until he turned off onto a highway that led them to a dirt road. At the end, a large expanse of cracked red clay.

Jacob stuffed her ears with plugs that made her head ache and walked her through how to remove the safety, how to pull back the slide. When he stood behind her, used his body to guide hers into position, she'd pushed her ass against his groin, teasing him, and he laughed. Told her he wanted her to learn this. That it was important.

He'd been here before, he told her. Teddy bears with black, permanent marker targets traced on their chests stood at a distance, and she teased him about his methods, but he'd shrugged and told her that this was the way his father had done it, and he figured it was as good a way as any.

For hours, they stood in that field. When she'd hit each target at least once, Jacob returned to his truck and pulled out a case of cheap beer. She'd wrinkled her nose at it, but he tossed her one. Said that it was a celebration.

They drank the beer, the alcohol pushing her down into the earth, until she felt as if she had become a part of it. Something hard and integral to the land. Something with roots that pushed down into the dark and drank of something ancient.

When Jacob moved on top of her, her back pressing into the grit, small rocks lodging in her skin, he told her that he loved her. Whispered it again and again, and it was not Jacob's voice but Mr. Burress' voice, and Cora let herself go numb. She watched the stars burn and let herself be swallowed.

Jacob had not said it again, and she came up with reasons to avoid him. A test to study for. A paper to write. She hid herself in the library, lost herself in the stacks, absentmindedly picking up books, reading the titles, and then reshelving them.

Jacob left her messages. Asked what he had done wrong. Said if she needed space, he would give it. She started deleting the messages without listening.

If there was a reason for her sudden, desperate need to with-draw, Cora couldn't name it. She stopped going to class, afraid she would see him on campus, afraid there would be nowhere to run. Out there in the open with everyone watching and all of her shame laid bare.

Eventually, Jacob stopped calling, and one day she saw him with another girl. Blonde hair cropped short; tight jeans and tight shirt, her chest exposed and tan and smooth. Laughing, the girl had slipped a hand into his back pocket.

Cora had followed them for a time. Drifting in and out of students hurrying to classes like a ghost, she watched him kiss her—this other girl that should have been Cora—watched the new girl look up at him and smile, and Cora's stomach felt as if it had twisted inside out.

You deserve this, Cora thought and forced herself to look even when tears pooled in her eyes.

All of that was so long ago, and still, every year she would drive herself to a gun range and pay for an hour. Remember the feeling of Jacob's body pushing her down into the earth. Remembered that if she had been a different woman, a differ-ent girl, she could have loved him.

Cora wasn't a great shot, but if there was something in front of her, moving or not, she was pretty sure she could hit it; at least buy herself some time.

She and Michael were in the antique shop now, dust burning in their lungs, and Michael sneezed.

"Sorry," he said, and she shrugged. Stupid to apologize now. Over something as trivial as a sneeze.

Looking at him, broad shoulders bent to examine a table filled with the unwanted leftovers of someone else's life, Cora wanted to hit him, shake him, anything to get him moving, make him understand what it was she needed to do, but she thought back to the feel of his mouth moving down her neck, over her shoulders, and she shuddered.

"Dammit," she said, and he straightened as if she had caught him doing something he shouldn't.

"Sorry," he said again.

"Stop saying that."

His mouth opened again, but he closed it quickly and flushed, bowed his head again to the table, picked up a small lacquer box. Pale pink and smooth. Like the interior of a shell. The color of a little girl's dreams. Something Cora would have begged her mother to buy her before. Before it had all happened. Before she understood that the world was filled with razorblades disguised as long fingers brushing against flesh and looking for an opening.

"Don't open that," she said, but Michael didn't hear her broken whisper. His fingers caught at the latch, and he lifted the lid.

The room seemed to close in around Cora, and she smelled Pine Sol and dust. Was back inside of that closet while Mr. Burress opened up a music box and told her to watch the pretty ballerina dance.

High, tinkling notes drifted toward her. Inside the box, a young woman with hair the color of ravens and clad in long yellow gown clasped a hand to her throat. Clutched in her other hand, a bright red apple. The small indentation left there meant to indicate she had taken a bite.

"Snow White," Michael said.

Cora clenched her teeth. "Close it."

He looked up at her in surprise, the melody playing on and on grinding into her, and she went to him and grabbed the thing out of his hand. The box was surprisingly light, and she crushed her fingers around it, and slammed it against the table. Over and over and over she brought the box down. Blood dripped down her wrist from a cut on her hand, but she did not stop until the music ended, and she stood shaking and panting before him. Her voice fell out of her. She could not stop it.

"That *fucking* music box. Around and around. The pretty ballerina. She never stopped."

Michael reached out and took the music box from her hand. Let it fall to the floor and crushed Leah to him.

"Sorry."

"Say sorry one more fucking time, preacher," she said, and he moved away from her, crossed the small, crowded room and picked up a fire poker that leaned against a wood-burning stove. He hoisted it above him, testing its heft as he shifted it between his hands.

"Figure this will work?"

"Yeah. Yeah, I think it will." Cora breathed, but the tightness in the center of her chest would not release.

Outside, the harsh glare of early afternoon sun had given way to deeper shadows, and Cora glanced out one of the windows. How much time before the creatures woke? Night came earlier and earlier this time of year, and she figured they had three, maybe four hours tops.

She stared out into the street and counted how many shops they still had not entered. Inside one of the shop windows, something moved. A quick flash of red that scurried past one of the windows.

"There's something over there. Across the way," she said and pointed, but whatever she had seen had vanished.

Michael came to stand beside her and squinted. "I don't see anything."

"I'm telling you, there's something over there. You can stay here if you want, but I'm going." If there was anything else out there, she needed to know, to see it with her own eyes. The door slammed behind her as she left, and moments later, she heard Michael come out, too.

As Cora crossed the street, she scanned the windows again. Third window from the right. Someone had painted a dancing hamburger and hotdog on the glass. The hamburger done up like a fifties greaser complete with tight jeans and white t-shirt, a carton of cigarettes rolled in the sleeve. The hotdog wore a poodle skirt, and the face had been painted with cartoonish eyelashes and overdone, simpering lips.

Maybe that was all that Cora had seen. Her eyes had moved across the storefronts and mistaken a hamburger jitterbugging with a hotdog for an actual person in this abandoned shit hole of a town.

Peering past the garish swirls of paint, Cora flicked her gaze over the room. Booths and a long countertop with plastic red and yellow squeeze bottles lined the edges of the restaurant. A large grill stood at the back, and there was a fryer tucked next to it.

The air still smelled like grease when Cora opened the door, and her stomach growled. She thought back to the burger she'd had at the diner yesterday and hoped that the man in the apron wasn't lying on the floor right now, shrouded in the butcher paper that lined his tables.

"Hello?" Cora called into the restaurant.

Idiot. You're a walking horror movie cliché, she thought and went up to the counter and rapped her knuckles against the laminate top.

Three bodies lay behind the counter. Stacked like children's blocks, one on top of the other, their eyes like glass. Unseeing and staring into eternity. She looked away from them.

To the right of the grill top, another opening led to what appeared to be an office and a large set of shelves stacked with buns, condiments, and napkins. Beyond that, at the very back, a massive silver door with a glinting chrome handle. A walk-in freezer.

Cora turned back to the front of the restaurant. Michael stood outside, watching her. She shrugged, shook her head, and he turned away, looked back out at the street.

She thought she imagined the sound at first. A slight scraping as if something heavy dragged itself slowly across the floor. Someone moving carefully, hoping to not be heard.

Moving past the counter, Cora crept toward the back room. She passed an office that housed a small, rickety desk with a ledger open to a series of indecipherable scrawlings, and an overflowing ashtray. A telephone lay on the floor, the receiver out of the cradle but still connected to the wall.

The freezer. It's coming from the freezer.

Cora walked past the shelves with their carefully organized dry goods and held her breath, reached for the knife she'd stowed away in her waistband, and pulled it out.

All right, you fucker, she thought and reached for the freezer door handle, wrapped her fingers around the cold metal and pulled.

The door did not open. Whatever was inside had locked itself in.

She pulled the handle again, but still the door did not budge.

Whatever was inside began to shriek.

Chapter 37

ichael's father would have fought. Would have gone in with everything he could. Spiritual warfare made flesh. His father wouldn't have hesitated. Even if what he did was corrupted, a lie, he still believed in his work.

There had been the time a pickup rolled into the church's lot. Michael was twelve, on the cusp of thirteen. Old enough for puberty to have begun, his voice dropping and hair sprouting under his arms, but still scrawny, still awkward in his own skin.

His mother with a basket of laundry, white sheets snapping on the line as sunlight filtered through them. The kind of day people look back on with the hazy film of nostalgia and wish for again.

Michael had not thought much of the truck pulling in. People did it plenty of times. Parked there and walked to Sister Maguire's if her lot was full. Even those who were just passing through used the church lot, so he had glanced at the truck and had gone back to his stack of dishes.

His father had gone up the mountain to visit with Brother Ives. The old man had spent the winter battling pneumonia, his frail body giving in to death little by little, and now he'd asked for the preacher to come and pray with him before the

Lord took him home.

And so Michael spent the day working through his mother's list of chores and wishing he could have been outside, running through the trees and shouting with the other kids. He knew better than to complain, though. Honor thy father and thy mother.

Michael was inside, his hands plunged up to the wrists in soapy water, when he heard his mother scream. The sound chilled him, and he bolted from the room imagining a wildcat slunk low in the grass, teeth bared as it snarled. His mother tangled in the clothes she hung on the line and unable to run. He took the side exit out of the church, his feet slipping a little on the dirt as he rounded the corner to the back of the building where his mother had stretched the clothesline between two oak trees.

Two men stood in front of his mother, and Michael could smell them from where he stood. The sickly sweet fragrance of whiskey and sweat.

The taller of them stepped forward and caught hold of his mother's dress. His face and hands were dirty. "You're the snake lady, ain't you?"

"Y'all should leave. Right now. There's nothing for you here," his mother said.

"Oh, I don't know about all that," the other said, his hand brushing against his crotch. His hair was dark but buzzed down to the scalp so that the stubble there looked like ash rubbed into the skin.

"We reckon that there's a lot for us here. After all, there's only the two of us, and you got lots of little hidey holes. More than two, for sure."

Michael had frozen, his blood thick in his veins, and his mother watched him over the men's shoulders, mouthed to him to run as they tore her dress from her, but he could not move, and she looked away from him.

It had been his father's voice that startled Michael awake, his father telling him to go inside, to lock the door and not come out until he said to. No matter what he heard. Did he understand?

Michael had nodded and done as he was told, retreated to his bedroom where he stared at the wall until he heard the men begin to scream. Hours passed and then the truck's engine fired up, the tires squealing as he heard it leave the lot out front.

It was dark by the time Michael's father and mother returned. He had not moved.

"Michael." His father called to him in the dark, but Michael did not go to him.

Instead, his father came down the hallway, paused in his doorway, looked in at the boy sitting on the floor, his pants still soured with urine.

"An eye for an eye, and a tooth for a tooth," his father said with his hands cupped around something Michael could not see, and passed on.

After that day, they never spoke of what had happened.

Yes, his father would have fought, but Michael was not his father, and fear and guilt and shame kept him on the periphery.

When the screaming began inside the little restaurant, Michael had that same feeling as he had that day the men came in their truck. As if an unseen force controlled his body while he looked on helplessly.

But then his feet were moving, and Michael pushed open the door.

"Cora?"

"Here," she said and he could hear the panic in her voice and followed the sound behind the counter into the small area just beyond the grill.

She turned to him, her eyes wide.

Before her stood a walk-in freezer. The sound came from inside of it.

Now that Michael was closer, he could make out words, garbled phrases strung together, but he couldn't quite catch on to what the person—for it was most certainly a human voice—was saying.

"There's someone inside. A person," Cora said and pulled at the handle to the freezer. The screaming pitched higher, and now he could hear the word "no" repeated over and over.

"We don't know what's in there," he said, but she rattled the handle again.

"It's a *person*, Michael. We haven't seen anything out here except for bodies. You said yourself that whatever's doing this must be asleep."

Cora turned back to the freezer. "Hey. Hey! Listen, if you can hear me, it's okay. We're not going to hurt you."

The scream subsided into a whimper, and Cora leaned into the door. "It's okay. It's okay. There's two of us out here. One woman and one man. My name is Cora. The man is Michael. We aren't going to hurt you."

"Please." The voice was soft and male, and Cora placed her hand flat against the freezer as if she could push through the metal and touch whoever was on the other side.

"Do you think you could open the door?"

"Are they out there?" the voice said.

Keep your eyes closed, Michael.

Michael had questioned Cora in the same way. After the woman had come to him, he'd ground his fists into his eyes and tried not to hear. The next morning, he hadn't believed Cora when she'd begun to speak to him, and now he heard that same panic in the man's voice.

"There's only the two of us. No one else," Cora said.

There was a shuffling, the sound of a latch being thrown, and then the door inched open. Inside, the freezer was pitch black.

A young Asian man stepped out, blinking in the sudden light. His hair brushed the tops of his shoulders, and he wore a red, long-sleeved shirt over artfully torn blue jeans. The kind of casual that looked expensive.

"It's okay. You're okay," Cora said, and the young man stared at her before collapsing to the floor. He gagged, his shoulders heaving.

"Everyone," the young man said once his breathing had slowed.

Michael thought back to the bodies stacked behind the counter.

"They got everyone. When they came in, Roger rolled his eyes, complained about having to deal with a bunch of brats, but we didn't think anything of it. Figured their parents would be in soon, so we didn't have to worry too much, but then they were on top of him, and there was blood. It's like they found all of the places where they could get their hands inside. And Roger was screaming, and then the lady at table five tried to get away, but they jumped on her, and there were so many of them. Crawling all over, and more and more of them coming in through the door, and I ran."

The young man pointed to the freezer. "I knew I could lock the door from the inside, so I came here. Cut the power before I let myself in.

"I could hear them out there. More and more of them until it sounded like a fucking playground. Laughing and scream-ing. For a long time, they scratched at the door. Tried to get inside. To me. But eventually, I couldn't hear anything any more, and I figured they must have left.

"I saw you. Across the way. I thought they were still here, that you were *them*, and so I came back. Dragged everything I could to block the door."

He ground his fists into his eyes. "I ran away. Like a fucking coward. Left them. All of them. Roger called my name for a while, but then he stopped, and I just sat in here. In the dark. Listening to everything."

Inside of the shame burning across the young man's skin, Michael saw himself reflected. Flight had always been the only option. The only true danger of his life was a habit, a rote pattern he had learned to numb himself toward. The cool, oiled feeling of snakeskin passing over his arms something he could bury deep. Forget.

"What's your name?" Michael said.

"Aran."

"Aran," Cora said, glancing over her shoulder at Michael. "I saw a phone back there in the office. Does it work?"

"Yeah, but the power's still cut. I could turn it back on, and the phone should work."

"If you could turn the power back on, I would really appreciate it," Cora said, and Aran looked down at his hands.

Outside, the shadows lengthened.

Going to die here, Michael thought. Here in the cooling dark.

"Listen, Aran. We don't know how far this thing reaches. We came from Hensley, and it happened there last night, too. If we could use your phone, we could try to figure out if it's happening anywhere else."

"I have a sister at school in Charlotte. My mother," Aran paused, and his face went ashen, his gaze flitting to the bodies left piled in the restaurant, the spray of blood that fanned across the floor.

She would have lived here. In a little house just outside of town. Kept a garden. Made her son come back and kiss her before he left for his shift. All of the little things that made up the quiet parts of a life, and now, the blood in her body would have cooled and thickened. The worn and tired skin sagging into beige or brown or green carpet.

"Do you think we could use your phone, Aran?" Cora's voice was gentle, but her tone implied the need for action. *I'm sorry, but let's get a move on* it seemed to say.

Hunched and shivering, Aran pitched forward, a clumsy attempt to get on his feet, and Michael moved toward him, caught him beneath his arms and pulled.

"Thanks," Aran mumbled, and together they moved back toward the office. Aran leaned over the desk and popped open the fuse box. The lights went on overhead, and music played from some unseen place. Doo-wop. It felt obscene.

He pointed to the phone still lying on the floor. Setting the receiver back in its cradle, Cora waited for a beat and then lifted the phone to her ear.

"There's a dial tone. Aran, did you want to," she began, but he shook his head.

The day that Michael's father had died, he'd gone up the mountain. Walked and walked until he didn't recognize the trees, the leaves mutating, changing colors from green to purple to black. Walked until the hours ran together, and time bled out of him.

He'd stumbled out of the forest the next day, his shirt and pants torn, his face and arms bleeding, and his mother stopped talking.

Michael knew the dark valley the young man walked through now. Knew the deep pits and snares; the ancient wells of shame and regret and sorrow. Often, he had felt he never emerged from that place.

Always, he felt its teeth at his throat.

"Nothing. 911 just clicks. Jimmy's line goes straight to voice-mail, and the office line is nothing but a busy signal. That's it. Those are the only numbers I know," she said.

"Malee. My sister," Aran said, and Cora offered him the phone, but moments later, he shook his head.

"Voicemail," Aran said and handed the phone back to Cora. "Do you hear that?"

Beneath the ground, something came to life. The low, whin-ing sound of an engine revving; the whirring of insects as they ate their way through the ground, teeth opening and closing; bones breaking under heavy weight.

The sound of a legion coming to life.

Chapter 38

Some of the children were already awake, but Leah told them to be still, to be quiet until it was dark. Their skin was delicate, and the sun would hurt. It would burn and shrivel them up into nothing and then wouldn't they be sorry they hadn't listened to her?

In time, their skins would grow hard and tough, and they would no longer have to hide themselves in the ground. Patience, Leah told them, and they listened with their new ears and told her they loved her with their new mouths, and she drew the words into her like honey.

At Leah's breast, the baby dreamed. When it woke, she would sing to it. All of the songs her mother had whispered when Leah was small, a dreaming, quiet girl tucked tightly against her mother.

Leah could feel the woman—the beautiful woman from the hospital—move somewhere just beyond where they slept. Leah brought her hand to her stomach and traced her fingertips across the skin.

The woman had taught her so many things. Opened the world to Leah and shown her all of the beautiful things that lived beneath.

The woman said Leah was special, placed her fingers against

Leah's cheek, and the woman had kissed her. Burning kisses that slid down Leah's throat and down her stomach, and then further, until Leah lost herself.

When the pressure was too much to bear, Leah cried out, spoke Pastor Wayne's name into the darkness, but the woman stopped at the sound, drew away, and left Leah panting, and she had blushed as the woman covered her face and hands in more kisses.

Pastor Wayne would come back. Leah would make him understand. *They* would make him understand. All of them. Together.

Yes. The woman whispered, and Leah felt dampness between her legs and squirmed. Of all the things the woman had shown Leah, this one thing she had been denied. Final release.

Soon.

It would not be soon enough.

Again, the children shifted, cried out in their desperation. They were so bored! They wanted to play again! They were so fast now, and they'd been so good, and they could feel the sun setting. And hungry! They were so hungry! Wasn't it time, Leah? Wasn't it time, Ruth?

Ruth shifted in her sleep, but if she heard them, she ignored their pleas.

"Hush now," Leah said, and they fell quiet as they writhed in the dirt.

At her breast, the baby shifted. When it woke, it would no longer need her milk. Would hunt meat and blood, and Leah clutched it to her, wished she could keep it with her a bit longer. But this was not the way. Children grew and left their mothers. No matter how it hurt. In the end, there was only the promise of gray hair and wrinkled skin and a cold bed.

But Leah was not a normal mother. She would always be

one of their mothers now, and the children whispered to her as the sun set.

She thought of Pastor Wayne, his lips hot against her ear, his fingers pushing at the hard mound between her legs while she moved against him.

"We love you. We love you. We love you," her children whispered, but she heard only the voice of Pastor Wayne.

Chapter 39

"Come with us," Cora said, but Aran started his car, the engine sputtering when it turned over. It was a feeble offer, one that promised no protection, no security, but she couldn't bear the thought of him driving away and into the gaping, hungry maw of whatever was out there.

"I'm going to find them. One way or the other," Aran said.

Cora understood. That same need had gotten her home from college every weekend, forced her to her mother's bedside to watch as the older woman withered under the disease that held her. She spooned soup into her mother's mouth as quickly as it dribbled out and bit her cheeks so her mother wouldn't see her cry. Yes, Cora understood.

She waved as his taillights disappeared from view. It would be foolish to hope he would find his mother and sister and that the three of them would stumble on a place to hide, but Cora hoped it all the same.

Be safe.

The deep rumbling of the earth grew louder. "We should go," she said.

In ten minutes, Cora and Michael made their way back to her car and were back on the interstate travelling north. She pushed the car to eighty, to ninety-five. There were no other cars to watch out for. No blue lights flashing in the rearview. Everywhere she looked laid the dried, dead carcass of something that had once lived.

She figured they had an hour, maybe an hour and some minutes left before night was upon them in earnest. Cora wasn't sure she wanted to be on the road when darkness fell.

Then again, a moving monster of metal and gasoline with locking doors might not be the worst option. The thought of mowing Leah McDowell down and pinning her to a wall—her legs and arms flopping, dislocated extensions of skin and bone—made Cora smile, and she gunned the engine, took the car up to one hundred and rolled her window down.

The wind tore at her hair, whipped it back away from her eyes and mouth, and she breathed deep, the air rushing into her lungs.

"I've always wanted to do this." She had to shout over the roar of the engine and the wind.

Michael did not respond, and she let her hand drift to her lap. Positions ten and two abandoned. Let the car drift in and out of lanes. Crossing and then re-crossing the yellow lines. Flashing her brights and laying on the horn. Why not drive like a complete and utter asshole at what was probably the end of the world?

They were going in blind. It was something that would have grated against her before. The old Cora. The Cora of deadlines and word counts and a schedule that never deviated from its plan.

She understood now that it didn't matter if they planned. That it wouldn't mean fuck-all in the face of whatever it was these things were. There was no playbook for this. No encyclopedia entry or primary resource that would explain what was happening. No one she could call and set up an interview.

It was just the two of them up against whatever the hell was spreading through these little towns like a disease and eating everything up bit by bit. Really though, it was just her. Like it had always been.

Michael and Cora had piled what they found in the backseat. Seven knives, two baseball bats, one machete, and Michael's lone fire poker. She couldn't imagine needing all of it, but knowing that it was there made her feel less vulnerable.

The interstate stretched before them, and she wondered if she kept driving, didn't take the exit and then the turn into Hensley, if they would eventually find the edge of the world. If she could keep her foot against the pedal as they dropped off into nothingness.

Michael spoke from the passenger seat, and she jumped. "It's getting dark."

"I wish this was a stick instead of an automatic. More fun."

"You're avoiding."

"Of course I am," Cora said and swung the car into the shoulder before crossing all four lanes and driving through a plot of wildflowers planted in the median. The D.O.T.'s idea of classing up the joint.

"We're going back there, aren't we? With a small arsenal of really sharp shit that I have no idea what to do with. Frankly, I'm not certain that I'll see the sun rise tomorrow, so pardon me if I do all of the things I wanted to do when I was sixteen before I don't have the chance any more."

"Cora," Michael said.

"Oh, please." She glanced over at him. Eyes so full of concern. "Don't even ask. Don't even think about asking."

"Asking what?"

"What every man asks when a woman starts to do things he doesn't understand. 'Oh, honey. Are you okay?' That simpering, pandering bullshit that you all do when you think we're on the rag, or emotional, or erratic, or whatever the fuck else box you want to put us in, so you can pat yourself on the fucking back and feel like you were the sympathetic one. Like you did everything you could, and she was still crazy."

Anger bloomed through Cora, hard and fast. Like a machine churning to life, and it was hungry, but she could feed it, pour herself into it until it was satisfied.

"I wasn't," he said.

She hated him. It didn't matter that he'd come through this with her. She hated him. This preacher who touted belief in a God that would save him when his veins flooded with serpent venom and didn't even believe it. A preacher whose father had found a book filled with evils that he had touched and then buried, his son quaking in the face of all his father had hidden, and none of it had even mattered.

"What is that?" Michael said and pointed. Ahead of them, a creature sat in the middle of the interstate. Long and pale with a torso that stretched along the ground, it slithered along like a snake. It turned its eyes into the headlights, and the pupils reflected back bright yellow. Delicate curling hair wisped against its head, and it smiled at them, a perfect row of tiny baby teeth.

"The children," Michael said.

"They're awake."

Gunning the engine, Leah pointed the car toward the creature. Fingers tight against the wheel, she hoped for the sharp jolt of impact, the wheels bumping over and then past its body, but it scurried away into the pines that lined the interstate.

"Shit," she said and straightened the car.

Bloodlust grew thick in her throat, and she imagined herself on top of one the slick-bodied creatures, one of her knives against the translucent flesh as she pressed down and down until the blood ran hot and red over her hands gone slick with gore.

"They're too fast," Michael said, but *fuck that.* She would find every last one of them. Every hole they'd hidden themselves in she would find and press metal to bulging flesh until she heard them scream and scream and scream.

Little shits. Little heaving shits with their open mouths and constant begging and crying. Always wanting. Always needing. Mommy this and Mommy that, and Mommy can I have, and Mommy why can't I?

I'm sorry. I'm so sorry. Don't cry. It won't hurt. It won't hurt at all. Just a little pinch, and then it won't hurt. I promise. I promise. Watch the ballerina. So pretty. Just like you. Watch her. Around and around and around. And it never stops. It never fucking stops, and why did it have to be me?

Suffer the little children. Jesus said that. And Cora had suffered, but Jesus had never come. Never come with his shining robes and beautiful eyes to save her when Mr. Burress' fingers had pulled her open, and it hurt and it hurt and it *hurt.* Oh, please make it stop, but it hadn't stopped, and there was his face again smiling back at her.

That face would greet Cora when she died. Those teeth would pierce her skin, and she would try to scream, but she would have no mouth. His lips would cover hers so she couldn't breathe, and everything would slow down. Her heart slipping into a rhythm she didn't recognize before dying away, and her body floating in all of the quiet that remained.

Jesus had not saved Cora before. He would not save her now. There were only her own two hands and the blade tucked into her palm. If there was a savior for her, it was made up of hard, glinting metal.

Slowing the car, she leaned her head out of the window and

listened to the sound of fingers scrabbling through loose soil. "You hear that? A thousand fingers digging. They were in the ground. Buried."

"Hiding," Michael said. If Cora had known, she would have hunted out their dens and burned them all while they slept. Fed their fat bodies to gasoline and fire.

Up ahead was the exit for Hensley, and the sound grew louder as they approached.

Again, Cora guided the car off the ramp and toward the side road. It felt as if she had always done this. As if she had grown up here—a child of the snakes—and finding her way back was an easy thing.

Twilight was creeping up on them. She'd always loved the word. It sounded like an incantation. Some mystical door opening to a place filled with stars. A place between.

Now, it had fallen, and in the great expanse above them, stars emerged, and the moon bled. Red light filled the car, and Cora looked at her hands, steadied them on the wheel as the wheels lurched through a series of potholes.

Under the ground the creatures had buried themselves. Cocooned and safe while they changed into monsters, and hadn't Cora done the same? For seventeen years, she'd buried herself in finishing school and taking care of her mother and going to work, and all the while, she carefully fed the dark thing that slept in her heart.

Cora whispered to the children, to the wakeful things under the ground, "I'm a monster, too."

Sister Maguire's store appeared. She and Michael had found the owner inside spread out along the floor, her right foot twisted inward and her forehead crushed in so that it looked like a bowl. Her body would still be there, draped in the grimy tarp Cora had found.

Nothing moved. None of the worm-like creatures emerged, eyes blinking against the headlights as they crept along the ground.

"Someone's an early riser," Cora said, thinking of the lone creature they had seen on the highway, and Michael reached into the seat behind her and pulled the iron poker over the seat and into his lap.

With the engine off, Cora could hear them better. The earth opening to let them through, their tiny bodies slithering up and up and up. A soft grinding sound that echoed through the trees. She wondered if they had all gone to sleep together or if they had found their hiding places separately, digging beneath the place their feet last touched before the sun came up.

Michael pointed to her left. "There," he said.

Its head emerged first, the hair choked with red clay, the skin smooth and bloated, tiny hands grasping as it wriggled out of its hole.

Reaching into the backseat, Cora grasped at the largest knife she'd found and opened her door. Four more of the creatures crept upward, and she thrust the blade out in front of her. She would slit their throats before they slithered their way out. One by one, she would mark them for death, leave them squirming and bleeding out.

They aren't children any more, Cora repeated over and over as they turned their yellowed eyes to her, their mouths opening and closing around those pointed teeth.

Hungry. She could smell it on them. Desperation and need that smelled like hot metal. They opened their mouths wider and shrieked. Called to their mother who still slumbered in the earth. *Hungry* they said, and their mother did not answer.

Cora was on the first one in seconds, its head whipping back and forth as it gnashed its teeth and screamed, the hands so shrunken that they could not touch her. Reaching beneath its throat, she drew the blade across in a clean line, and blood, thick and black, spurted over her hands.

They are not children. They are not children. Her hands were slick and the knife slipped as she stood over the second one, and it took two tries this time before the blade bit into flesh.

"Cora!" Michael called to her, his voice distended and empty, as if he spoke to her from the bottom of a deep hole, but it didn't matter what the words that floated toward her were. There was only this *doing*, the feeling of blood sticky between her fingers, the sound of air rushing out of their throats as she cut them.

"You fuckers. You little fuckers," she said and turned again, grasped a third creature by the hair and pressed her blade inside of it. Deeper and deeper until she hit something solid, bone or cartilage, and she let the creature drop at her feet.

By now, more and more of the little holes had opened, and the creatures poured out of them. So many of them. A horde of worms made of children. This was how the world would end, under the weight of a legion of worms.

"There's too many," Michael said. Little fingers brushed the backs of her calves, the fingers dug against muscle, and she kicked them away. Three more crawled to her, their necks tilted their heads upwards and teeth bared. *The better to see you, my dear. The better to eat you.*

Michael crossed to the church and brought down the iron poker against the slithering back of one of the creatures as he went. It squealed and scurried away. "Get inside," he shouted to Cora, but she wanted to cut them open one by one and cover herself in their blood. *Baptism* she thought and almost laughed, but there were those little hands on her legs again, and she swung the knife in a broad arc, and whatever touched her slithered away.

The ground writhed, a roping mass of worm-like abominations, and she ran for the church where Michael stood with the door opened.

"Children," a voice behind her spoke, but she did not turn to look and leapt for the stairs where Michael extended his hand, and together they tumbled inside.

Closing the door, Michael threw the lock. "Help me," he said and pressed his shoulder to one of the massive wooden pews, and Cora went to him, grunted against the heavy wood until it blocked the entrance.

"The other door," she said, but already he was rushing through the sanctuary to the back of the church. Something thumped against the door they had just blocked, but it did not budge.

"Michael?" she called through the open sanctuary: her call like a strange prayer. An offering that drifted out of her like smoke. A request to the Divine, begging for everything to be all right. Please, just let it be all right.

Michael appeared in the doorway, the poker still clenched in his right hand. "Here," he said.

"You okay?"

"Yeah. You?"

She looked down at the blood on her hands. It streaked up her arms like lightning flowers traced in crimson. None of it her own. "Yeah."

Another thump sounded at the door, louder this time, and Cora planted her feet, steadied the knife that shook in her hand. If the creatures figured out a way to come through the door, she would be ready.

"There's a window in the first classroom. We should cover it," Michael said.

Cora watched him go but made no move to follow. Unless he had plywood, a hammer, and nails, the best he could do was tack a sheet over the window. They were in a church, not a fucking hardware store. It wouldn't keep those things out. At best, she and Michael had bought some time. Nothing more.

Cora could hear the creatures outside the door, the wet sound of flesh slapping against itself as if they were piling themselves one on top of the other. The door shook as something heavy slammed against it, and the pew shuddered against the impact. The creatures were slow, but there were so many of them.

Fatigue washed through Cora, and she brought her head between her knees, forced air in and out of her lungs. From the hallway, Michael grunted, the sound of something heavy dragging, and she stood up too quickly, her head swimming as the blood rushed out of it.

Moving out of the sanctuary, she followed the long hallway to the last classroom where Michael was bent over a large bookcase, his fingers hooked beneath the wood as he struggled to lift it.

Light filtered through the window, that same ruddy, blood-ied glow, and she went to it and pressed her face against the glass.

"Michael," she said, and he stopped what he was doing.

Together, they looked out and saw.

Chapter 40

They're here! They're here!

The children could hear them. The preacher and the pretty lady. Could hear them coming back, the wheels of the car crunching just above the places they had slept. Could hear his and her muffled voices, and excitement rippled through their skins, and they fidgeted.

Is it time? Is it time? they called to Leah, called to their mother, but she told them to be quiet and still. It wasn't fair. They had been so good, so patient, and they could *feel* it. It was time to wake up. Time to play.

Leah had said the preacher and the pretty lady would come back, had promised they could play, and now the preacher and lady were here, and it wasn't fair that they had to wait. They'd been waiting forever it seemed.

Hungry. We're hungry they called, but Mother did not answer, and they opened and closed their mouths around darkness, but it didn't taste good. Some of them spat it out, and they could feel Mother frown.

One of them had disobeyed. They could feel it moving through the trees, leaves scratching its belly, a rat caught between its teeth. *Couldn't wait. So hungry*, it said, and then Mother punished him.

They all saw, and it was a terrible, awful thing to hear the screaming, to watch as the skin split and everything inside spilled out into a steaming, stinking pile. Mother sighed. She was sorry, but they must obey.

They all went quiet then, tucked themselves in tight and waited for the moon, for Mother to say that it was time to wake up.

They dozed, and they dreamed, and they pictured the pretty woman, tasted salt on their tongues, and then Mother spoke to them in soft tones.

"Wake up, children. It's time."

Chapter 41

The woman had taken the child from Ruth. The seed that was planted inside of her, the seed that she grew as she slept in the earth ripped from her as it squalled and reached out with tiny hands. Placed the baby in the arms of her daughter instead, and Leah immediately brought it to her breast.

Ruth had hated Leah in that moment, her womb empty and throbbing, but the woman had come to Ruth, smoothed her wet hair from her face, and promised that she would always be the True Mother. The original. The Great Worm would grow to know her, would love her, and Ruth let her new eyes close, swam in and out of consciousness as the baby who would become something larger than the world cried.

Her mind drifted to Leah as an infant, her eyes wide and staring up at Ruth, as she nursed. The red fleck seeming to grow larger every day. Leah spinning in circles as a little girl, her blonde hair flying. Leah sleeping, dark lashes brushing her cheeks, her skin damp with sweat, heat rising off of her like mist.

So many times Ruth had stood over the girl's crib, her hands clutched around a pillow, and watched her daughter. It would have been easy. Crib death was a common enough thing. No one would question it, but each time, she put the pillow down, stroked the downy hair covering Leah's head until the girl slept, and spent the night sobbing beside her.

"Momma," Leah said, and Ruth opened her eyes and looked at her daughter. "Can you see me?"

"Beautiful," Ruth said and reached out her arms. This family that she had knit together with blood and bone was a shining thing in the dark, and the woman smiled down at them like a divine Madonna.

"They are waiting. The children," the woman said, and together they rose and went to them, told them what to do, and the children obeyed.

Chapter 42

They gathered in the moonlight, pale bodies glistening as they moved as one entity, wound their way over the feet and legs of the three women who stood in the center.

The women smiled down at the creatures that milled about them, drew their hands over their backs, and whispered words that Cora could not hear. Beside them, a little boy stood. Light hair that had grown long brushed his shoulders, and he looked up at the window, watched Cora and Michael as they pushed the bookshelf toward the glass. The boy waved to her and smiled.

He looked so normal standing there. As if he was waiting patiently for his mother to finish her gossiping. Obedient. Docile. A good boy. A sweet boy. A boy to make his mother proud.

"Do you see him?" Cora said.

"Yes."

"He isn't like the others." The child that stood beside Leah and Ruth looked nothing like those creatures that had once been children who now crawled along on their bellies.

"The baby. The Great Worm," Michael said and sank to the floor. "There's a Bible verse. 'Where their worm dieth not, and the fire is not quenched.' He comes among us like a wolf in sheep's clothing. Of course he would look human. Of course he would be beautiful."

He stopped there, and Cora did not ask him to explain. It wouldn't matter. Outside, the creatures howled into the night. Their mouths would be open and hungry, and from the sanctuary came the dull sound of bodies pitching against the door again and again.

"They'll get in. It will take some time, but they'll find a way in," Michael said. Cora thought of her car, the knives and other weapons they had assembled still in the backseat. All of that time wasted.

They could pull more pews in front of the door. Drag all of the furniture they could in front of the entrances, but there were so many of the worm-like creatures, and they had teeth to bite and chew, and they would find their way through, and then what? How many of them could Cora kill before they converged on her?

Michael rubbed his palms against his thighs and glanced at the window. "I can hear her talking. Leah."

Cora glanced toward the window and watched as Leah approached. The girl had not changed. Her blonde hair still fell heavy down her back, the green eyes still set deep in her pale face. Ethereal. Something not of this world. The girl's fingers twitched as her lips formed words Cora could not hear.

"She wants me to come out. Says that it's time." Tears traced down Michael's cheeks, but he did not wipe them away.

"Our children," he said, and Cora reached back and slapped him. Her palm stung, and she pulled her hand into a fist and ignored the burning.

"Bullshit. Those are not *children*, Michael. Whatever they are, they are not human. You saw them. Children do not look like overgrown worms or snakes or whatever the fuck they've turned into. They don't kill people. They don't finger-paint with blood. Babies don't turn into little boys overnight. You know this."

Blinking at her, Michael brought his hand to his cheek. "You hit me."

"You're goddamn right, and I'd do it again. Listen to me, Michael." Cora leaned forward. "Leah is gone. You understand? Ruth is gone. The world has gone to absolute shit, and she's out there singing her siren's song, and you know better than to listen."

Outside the window, one of the women laughed and there was a light tapping against the glass. "Cora? Won't you let him come out and play? We've been waiting." Leah's voice.

Michael rose and crossed to the window. "Don't," Cora said, but he brought his shoulder to the glass and pushed. "Michael, you don't want to do this."

"You've dreamed of this moment, Michael. Everything open and parted. Waiting for you. The taste of my tongue in your mouth. Your body wed to mine. All of that sweating and desire come to an end. It's time. Come and take what you've always wanted," Leah said.

Michael groaned and heaved his shoulder against the window. For a moment, it shimmered, the moonlight poured into the room, and then it fell away. The glass shattered outward, and Cora covered her eyes, and there was the sound of laughter.

Gripping the knife, Cora slashed outward, but the blade cut through the air only. "Oh, Cora," Leah said. "Open your eyes."

Michael stood with them. With Ruth and Leah and the boy who stared at back at Cora with eyes the color of deep earth. A family. Behind them, another woman with dark braids stood, her hands clasped before her, and beyond that, framed by the broken window, the legion of children.

"Aren't you tired, Cora? Aren't you tired of the pain? All of that hurt that you've pushed down inside of you. Cutting you like little razors. Every step you take outlined in your blood, and no one understands what *he* did to you. Couldn't tell Momma. Couldn't tell anyone. But we know, and we want to wash you. Make you clean," the other woman said.

Cora bared her teeth. "You don't get to talk about that, you bitch," she said.

Ruth gestured to the little boy. "We birthed him. So many of us listened to his slumber, listened as he woke, and we took him into ourselves. Fed him and brought him here. His teeth are opened and waiting," she said.

The little boy looked up at Cora. Eyes careful and searching. Ancient eyes. Eyes that had seen a millennia of blood and pain and swallowed it all down and then slept under the crust of the earth until it was time to wake once more.

"This isn't the first time, is it?" Cora said.

The woman shook her head. "Of course not. We reign below, and we wait, and we bide our time. We listen and watch, and by our grace alone do you go. And you dream up your own Gods, and you fashion yourself as believers, as these people have done even now. Passing snakes among yourselves and never dreaming of what was just beneath you. There are always those who seek us out, who call to us in our slumber, and we listen. We always listen."

"It's time," Leah said and let go of the boy's hand.

Cora ran. She did not look back.

Chapter 43

*T*he body and the blood. *Take of this. Eat of me. Drink of me. Abide in me.*

Leah's voice was all around Michael. It traced over his naked skin, and her fingers pried him open, stretched him wide until he cried out, but she did not stop and pushed past his teeth and deeper into him.

Bear me. The Bride has made herself ready.

Leah's hair smelled of wood smoke. Fire and ash rained down around them, bright sparks of light that danced and died, buried themselves inside her bare back, and she drew the ash into herself and poured it into him.

Michael lay on his back, and Leah rocked against him, her face hidden behind her hair, but she leaned over him and brought her mouth to his.

"Leah."

"No," she said, and pulled back. Ruth stared down at him, her lips pulled back from her teeth.

"Oh, Thomas," Ruth whispered, and Michael bucked against her, but she followed his movements, and he groaned, unable to staunch the growing need for release.

"Let go, Michael," she said, and it was the woman who strad-dled him now, her voice in his ear. Infecting him. A disease of the blood. Clamped around him, the woman pulled him up and into her, and he came, felt himself drawn up and up and up until there was only her body, only the taste of her blood in his mouth. Everything burned away, hot and clean and good.

Bone of my bones. Flesh of my flesh.

"Tell me your name," Michael said, and the woman bent low.

"Hecate. Lilith. Mania. Namaah. You have many names for me, but none of them are mine," she said, and her face was Leah's, Ruth's, Cora's. The face of one of the creatures, a worm that rode upon him.

"You have always known me. Known us. You fall asleep and the ground shifts and suddenly you are floating, suspended as if everything beneath has dropped away. You are feeling us move," the woman said and pulled herself off of him.

Turning away, he curled into himself. Made himself small, but still, the woman's scent lingered on his skin, and he convulsed.

"You belong to us now," Ruth said.

"All of us," Leah said.

"You have so much to learn, preacher," the woman said, and he closed his eyes and descended into the dark.

Chapter 44

The pretty lady wasn't that much fun to play with. She wouldn't scream or run, and the baby wouldn't let them chase her anyway, so it didn't matter. They didn't think the baby was that much fun either, and Mother had *lied* about him.

He looked nothing like they did. Not anymore. He had legs and arms and normal hands like they'd used to have, and he talked with a loud, booming voice that hurt their ears. In fact, he didn't look like a baby at all but like a full-grown *man*. In just a few hours, the little boy that had been a baby only the night before became an adult, and they sulked as he walked among them.

They caught raccoons and possums and snakes, but those little animals didn't satiate their hunger.

"Why can't we eat?" they whined, but he told them to be quiet, and they skulked away, faded into the shadows and watched, envious and angry that he got to be the boss when he was so much younger than they.

"Mother," they called from their places in the trees, but she was silent. Too busy for her children. Too busy playing with the preacher, and the man played with the pretty lady, and it wasn't *fair*.

"We've been so good," they called, animal blood dripping from their chins, and still, she didn't answer, so they hid themselves away. Tucked into their holes, they waited for Mother to return. They did not dare anger him. The Great Worm.

He didn't even play with the pretty woman right. He sucked at her fingers instead of pulling them off one by one. What good did it do to not bite her as he drew her fingers into his mouth?

"All wrong," they all thought, but he suckled at the pretty woman's fingers anyway, and they tried to ignore him, but the little animals moving through the forest had not been enough. Hunger crawled through their bellies with sharp teeth.

Like carrion gathered around the dead, they stood as far back as he made them and watched him taste different parts of her, wishing all the time that it was them instead feeling her move beneath them like a bug on a pin, but they tucked themselves away and had to satisfy themselves with watching.

It was not enough.

Chapter 45

*H*e moved above her. His tongue inside of her. Cora tried to scramble away, but she was so tired, and she could not move, and there was a deeper part of her that burned with want and need.

Cora could feel them watching. The creatures. Those yellow eyes trained on her twisting body. Her tongue was heavy in her mouth and dreamed of everything she wanted to say. Everything she wanted to tell him, but it was sluggish, and she could not focus.

When *he* spoke to Cora, it was in words she did not understand. His lips curved around the syllables, touched them delicately as he gifted them to her, but she did not hear them as he meant them to be heard, and he grew angry, her skin bruising under his touch.

Cora had been here, in this place, for what seemed like lifetimes. Watching the ballerina go around and around. Not moving. Not breathing. Listening to *him* shudder against her. Again and again and again.

This time, he didn't hurt her, and she was thankful for his mouth as it closed around her fingers. Thankful for his teeth grazing against her skin instead of breaking it as he had long ago. So long ago.

But this was not Mr. Burress. This child grown into a man overnight was not the same as the one who had come to her years before. She had been a girl then: a girl who didn't understand what it meant when someone told her she was beautiful. No, this was not the holy man who had hurt her when she was a child.

The man rising before her had hair that was dark instead of light, and his eyes watched with curiosity instead of shame and lust. His face was hard. Angular. Nothing like the soft, rounded jaw of Mr. Burress.

He suckled her fingers as a child would its mother, and she drifted in and out of consciousness, watched those yellow eyes glowing just beyond the ring of light where he had brought her. Hating her and loving her. The children watched as he moved around her, arranged her as he wanted. Sprigs of milkweed placed in her hair like a nervous, unsure bride waiting for her husband.

And he rose before her, the Great Worm, and Cora parted for him, bloomed into something terrible and beautiful, and she gasped when she took him into herself.

Don't move. Don't breathe, Cora thought, left it to him, and he followed all of the patterns he was supposed to as he moved over her body. All of the things her girlish body had memorized and remembered as it fell into rhythm. She would never forget. Not ever.

Skin to skin, he lay with her, but there was not the sharp sting of him entering her, none of the burning that she had come to expect. He had not forced himself inside of her, and she began to cry, his tongue tracing the salt down her cheek and neck.

Around them, the creatures circled and whined, and he drew Cora closer, covered her with his body, and she breathed into him.

Let go. How easy to sleep, to let go and float inside of the place he had created for them, safe and cocooned. Let the world crumble around them, and would it really matter if it all fell apart?

Teeth moved against her throat and down her chest, and he nipped at her, pulled her blood inside of him, their hearts surging forward and falling back, and the moon was a swollen piece of sky that dipped toward the earth to watch their obscene communion.

Dirt in her hair, her nose, and her mouth, and she could not breathe and beat against his back with weak fists, but he only pressed her further down until there was only the weight of him pushing against her. So much pressure that she wanted to scream, but the air died in her belly and grew stagnant and noxious. Something to poison her from the inside out.

Sleep. Sleep. It was what he wanted. For her to close her eyes and sink into him, lost and dreaming under his darkness. Washed clean and made whole.

Curved around each other, they slept, but Cora could not shed the skin of her old dreams. Her mother pulling her hair into a tight bun, or sitting and reading to Cora night after night, no matter how tired she was. Her mother's hands smoothing Cora's dress before coming to rest on her shoulders. Her mother in her hospital bed, paper skin stretched tight over bone, whispering, telling Cora to not let the dark drag her down.

And so Cora slept on and waited for daylight.

Chapter 46

The sun would rise soon. They could feel it coming. Their bodies had gone sluggish, and they hated it. They'd spent the night waiting and waiting and nothing had happened. There were lots more of them now; they could feel the others coming awake all over, could hear the screams as these others hunted, and they gathered some excitement from that, but it wasn't the same. Not at all.

Soon, it would be time to sleep again, and they weren't tired. Mother had promised they could play, that they would have fun, but no one had come to play with them.

One by one, they returned to the dirt, buried themselves in shallow earth. The next night they didn't want to waste a bunch of time getting out, wanted to be ready. Mother would not like it, but she had not answered them all night, and they figured she didn't care what they did, didn't care if they burned up or if the pretty lady stuck them so that all of their blood came running out.

As the sun rose, they closed their eyes. The entire family sleeping and peaceful beneath the earth.

They did not hear when one pair of eyes opened.

Chapter 47

Pulling herself upward, Cora tried not to breathe. The dirt packed around her was loose, and it tumbled against her face as she tunneled toward the light. He had groaned when she pulled her body from his, but he had not woken, and she moved more quickly now as she clawed at the earth and kicked herself to the surface.

When she had first woken, she tucked herself against his warmth and thought about closing her eyes and going back to sleep, but then she saw the blood on his mouth and the blood streaked against her breasts, and she moved away from him, and there had been no pangs of regret as she did so.

Impossible that he had not noticed, but she wondered if he wasn't strong enough yet to stay awake during the day. So newly woken, he would need to rest as the others did, and she was thankful.

All that mattered was moving, the burning in her arms and legs a wonderful pain that kept her heading toward the light. Several times, Cora's hands brushed against the bloated bodies of the children, and she froze, waited for them to come awake and scream, but they only shifted in their sleep, and she kept going.

In minutes, Cora's head burst into the sunlight and she

gulped great mouthfuls of air. For a long time, she lay on top of the earth and let the sun warm her body as she listened to a world fallen silent.

"Michael." She spoke his name aloud, but there was nothing there to recognize it. Even if the women had not killed him, they would have taken him into the earth as well, and Cora wouldn't know where to look. She could dig and dig, expose those mutated children to the sun, kill the ones she could, but she could work all day and still not find Michael or the women.

Rolling over, she examined the freshly churned earth. Hell, she couldn't even tell any more where she had come through. Glancing up, she gauged the sun. Still early morning. Still plenty of time to do what she could. With any luck, she'd be able to find her way back to *him* and burn his body first.

Inside of Sister Maguire's store, she found a shovel and a pistol. "Where have you been all my life," she said as she checked the chamber for ammunition. Empty, but there were bullets under the cash register, and she grabbed those too, and stuffed the pistol, the box of bullets, lighter fluid, and a box of matches into a cloth sack that had once held coffee beans. The smell made her long for a cup, but she hoisted the shovel over her shoulder and stumbled back outside and into the sunshine.

"Ready or not, you assholes."

Cora dug until blisters formed on her hands, the skin exploding and water and blood running down her wrists and between her fingers. She paused for long enough to wrap her hands with strips she tore from her shirt and then kept going.

When she found the first creature—the body a sleek, pale thing—she brought the blade of the shovel down against its belly. It had not screamed—Michael had been right about the sunlight—and she grinned, threw its small body on the fire she had built and watched as black, oily smoke drifted into the sky.

The sun climbed higher, and still she dug. She unearthed four more and offered them up, the flames licking against their pale skins as they curled inward like burning leaves.

She began working outward, expanding in an ever-growing square, as she brought more and more of them up. Some of them squirmed, shirked away when the sun hit them, but they did not scream, and they did not run. The air grew thick with the scent of their burning flesh, and she gagged against the oily stink of it several times, her hand pressed to her mouth as she tried to keep herself from heaving up whatever was left in her stomach.

Everything hurt. Her shoulders were a knotted mass of muscle that would spasm each time she withdrew another shovelful of dirt. Her hands a bloodied mess of raw skin and pus. She knew better than anyone how to put herself somewhere else, how to take all of that pain and tuck it away somewhere secret. She watched the ballerina go around and around. She kept going.

The sun was directly over her when the sound drew her out of the slow, dreamlike digging. Ringing. Something was ringing. The distant sound of a telephone.

Setting down the shovel, she listened. It was not coming from the church. If it had been, the sound would have been clearer. Closer. No, the sound was coming from one of the buildings behind her. Sister Maguire's store, or what Michael had referred to as the Warner place. Turning, she considered both structures. Likely, it was the Maguire store that would have the telephone. For placing orders. Confirming deliveries. If any of the townspeople without their own line needed to place a call, they would have used the phone down at the store.

Cora wandered in the direction of the store's entrance, and the ringing grew louder. Pausing in the front entrance, she took in the neat shelves stacked with dry goods, canned vegetables, and coffee beans in small, burlap bags.

Next to the cash register, an old rotary phone jangled, the receiver dancing inside of its cradle. For ten rings, she stood and watched, tried to convince herself she wasn't hallucinating, that her brain, in desperation, had not conjured up this last connection to a world that most likely no longer existed.

On the twelfth ring, she picked up the receiver and pressed it to her ear.

"Are you alive?" The voice was female. Young. Cora envisioned herself at eighteen. Nineteen. "If you picked up, you must be alive. I think they sleep during the day. I've been all over campus and haven't seen a single one of those fuckers, so you must be. I mean, you have to be." The girl's voice quavered at the end, and Cora sank to the floor and pressed her back against the counter. There was someone else out there. She didn't know where, but she wasn't the only one left. And if there was at least one other person, there may be more.

"Yes. I'm alive," Cora said, and the girl sobbed aloud.

"There were so many of them, and they locked us in. Came in through the windows. They were just little kids, but some of them didn't look like kids. They looked fucked up, you know? All stretched out with these tiny hands. But their teeth..."

Cora didn't speak, waited for the girl's breathing to slow, and she continued. "I crawled into an air vent, and I saw. Everything. Davis is gone. He's gone. Everyone. They killed everyone."

"What's your name?"

"Audrey."

"Where are you, Audrey?"

"Charlottesville, Virginia. UVA."

Virginia. It had stretched up into Virginia, and as far as Cora could tell as far south as Atlanta.

"Listen to me, Audrey. When you were walking around, did you see places where it looked like someone had dug something up? A lot of loose dirt?"

The girl paused, and then spoke. "Yeah. There were a couple of places."

"Okay. Okay. If you can, find a shovel. They'll be underground. Dig them up. Burn them. Cut them up. Shoot them. Whatever you have to do. Kill as many as you can and then hide yourself before it gets dark. Somewhere where they can't get to you. Or if you have a car, get in it and drive until morning. Don't stop for anything. Not even if it looks human. In fact, if you think you can run it over without killing yourself, do it."

Cora glanced behind her at the billowing column of smoke. With any luck, anyone else who watched the sun rise this morning had figured out what Cora had and built their own pyres, their own pile of ash floating into the sky.

"I don't think that I can. They're just kids."

"No. Not anymore," Cora said. Of all of her sins, she imagined God would forgive her this one. "How did you find this number?"

"My boyfriend grew up there. Used to call me from this line when he knew his mother was shopping. Sometimes the line would drop out, and I'd have to call him back. I've been trying 911 all morning but it doesn't ring at all."

"Audrey, do you think you could call this number again? Same time tomorrow? I'll be here waiting. My name is Cora."

"How do you know you'll be there?"

Cora paused, tried not to think about the terrible possibility behind the girl's words. "I'll be here. I promise you."

"Yes. Yes, I'll call. If I can."

"You will," Cora lied. She didn't know what the night held for the girl, but she needed to trust in the chance the girl would be there the next day.

Cora didn't want to let the phone go, let this one remaining thread snap, but there was more work to do before night fell. For her and for Audrey.

"Be safe, Audrey."

"Same to you, Cora," Audrey said, and then the line went dead.

Flies buzzed over the white sheet that Cora had draped over Sister Maguire the night before, and Cora stood and stumbled back outside, leaving the insects to their work.

If the creatures understood what Cora was doing, saw the slow path of destruction that she carved, they gave no indication, and as the afternoon wore on, their silence began to unnerve her.

Any living thing would rail against its own death. The human body, even in the final throes, thrashed and fought against what was happening to it, but the worm-like creatures were immobile under her hands, indifferent as she fed their bodies into the fire.

The ground cracked open its maw, and Cora put herself in its teeth, forced the jaws open farther, and she was the harbinger of death. In her slacks and blouse now coated with dirt and ash, she was the dark angel that brought the end.

You're losing it. Cracking up. Keep your shit together, Cora.

Still, Cora had not found Michael or Leah or Ruth. Had not uncovered the unknown woman or the man who had cradled her through the night and taken her blood into him. Only the army of worms that stood sentry around them.

She would not find them, their bodies dormant deep in the earth's bowels. Tucked into a place she would not discover in the daylight. Not like this. Not as she burned and slashed her way through their devoted children.

She needed water. Food. She was lightheaded, and the world narrowed into an ever-tightening circle. For thirty minutes she would allow herself to pause in her work. Nothing more.

She found bread and apples in the store, a tin cup that she filled with water from a rusted faucet and drank until her stomach heaved up what she had eaten, and she filled the cup and drank more.

Once her stomach calmed, she would eat more. Slowly this time, waiting to be sure her body wouldn't reject it. She took another loaf of bread and two more apples and drifted back out into the afternoon sunlight.

The landscape before her could have been something on a postcard. Mountains draped in fall color that rose toward a granite sky. Something for a visitor to pull over his car, pause for a moment and whisper "beautiful" and maybe snap a picture before driving on to whatever city he called home.

In the center of all of it, the church rose white and severe in the face of all that beauty. Inside of it, Michael had preached of sin and redemption. Passed the snakes and pretended the sharp kiss of their teeth on his skin was probable, his congregation praying the dark venom would not take them under.

And they had all believed. Believed in the power of judgment and punishment. Among these people, there had been little hope. Little belief in forgiveness. They had known something of evil, and she shuddered to think of the ends they had met. Had they seen the children crawling on their bellies as the snakes finally come to take their final payment as their God turned his face away? Unworthy even at the end of His grace and salvation?

Or had they faced the end with clear eyes and glad hearts?

Certain in their faith that God had come to take them home?

Stepping away from the store, Cora walked toward the church. She wanted to feel the dusty air settle heavy in her lungs as the quiet stole inside of her. She wanted to kneel at the altar with something like a prayer thick under her tongue and be still. If even for a moment.

She wanted a homecoming.

She closed the doors behind her when she entered and went down the center aisle, sank to her knees at the altar, and brought her head to rest on one of the steps leading to the pulpit.

Not a prayer. No. It was please. It was not yet. It was not now. And she offered all of it up to whatever would listen. The broken stars and indifferent moon that would surely rise and bring with it the horrors she had come to know. She spoke, and it didn't matter what heard her. It had never mattered.

Cora waited for something, for anything. A sense of holiness or peace. A sign that she had been heard, but there was only quiet, the faint sound of flames crackling as they swallowed what she'd given.

"Okay." She spoke into the stillness and stood. As she did so, her eyes swept over a dark object that lay on the top step of the altar. Black leather binding yellowed paper. The book.

Michael had wrapped it back in the cloth, and they had left it in his office, yet here it was, unbound and waiting for her.

"There's nothing there," Cora called to whatever watched her. She had seen the book, looked at those terrible illustrations, and it had left her reeling, but it had told them nothing.

She pictured Michael's father stopping in one of the small towns that cropped up here and there on the road that led him home, wandering into a bookstore, and losing himself among the shelves, disoriented as he traced his steps over and over without finding his way out of the labyrinth of books. Saw him descending a set of stairs that led to a dirt-packed floor, a room with a single bulb swinging from the ceiling and casting strange shadows along the shelves carved into dirt walls like a catacomb. A place to leave bones. He would have found the book in such a place.

Perhaps the creatures who lay sleeping beneath her had penned it. Perhaps Michael's father was supposed to find it. Perhaps this was how they had planned it.

The book lay open before her. Onionskin-smooth beneath her fingertips, and she did not remember opening it. Of course she wouldn't. This was how it had been. Before. When Michael had been with her, and her hand moved between her legs.

The illustrations morphed and changed under her touch. Nothing was as she remembered. There was no moon. No great tree dripping with blood. There were other things recorded there. Things that slipped inside of her skin. Things that she would not be able to forget.

The book showed her the Great Mothers. The woman who carried the seed, and the woman who nursed it. It showed her the birth and rise of the Great Worm. It showed her the Bride.

Around and around the ballerina spun. It would not stop. She could not stop it.

Chapter 48

They felt her burning them. The pretty lady. Cora. They had learned her name, heard *him* whispering it like a prayer. One by one, Cora found them and pulled them unmoving from their beds, and they couldn't fight. They couldn't even scream.

Surely Mother knew what was happening to her children and would save them, rise from her slumber, terrible and beautiful, and punish Cora. They waited, listened to their brothers' and sisters' skin blister in the fire, and Mother did not help them. They reached for her with their minds, and she called back to them, told them that it was all for the best, that everything would be right in the end. That this was their sacrifice, and that it would make her happy, and that it should make them happy, too.

Yes. Anything, they thought and swallowed down their screams.

Chapter 49

Cora burned more of them, moving without thought, without feeling. She'd left the book on the altar opened to the final page, the little girl depicted there frozen forever in her white dress and bridal veil. Once, Cora had been that little girl, but that was a long time ago. She would not give herself to him. She would not.

Watching the sky, she worked. There was little time left, and still the earth had not offered up Leah, Ruth, or Michael. It did not offer up the other woman and the Great Worm. When they rose, they would look for Cora, and she would be certain they would find her.

Beneath her, the ground shifted, and she stumbled, the shovel handle digging into her chest as she fell. Pressing her lips to the dirt, she breathed into it, whispered to the creatures sleeping below that she was ready for them.

"Wake up," she said, but they did not listen. The sky was still too light, the sun not yet dipped behind the horizon, but they moved, and she smiled at their impatience. The dirt mingled with the blood on her palms, and she spoke again. "I'm a part of you now."

Cora opened her hands, pushed grit and soil and blood past her teeth and down her throat. A communion of the damned.

"We are the same. I am wed to him. Wake up, you little fuckers."

When the last streaks of light fled, Cora climbed the church steps, the revolver tight in her hand. With the doors at her back, she watched the ground come to life.

"Hello," she said, and they called to her with voices filled with sorrow. They had lost so many. Ashes on their tongues. Death filled the air. She smiled down at them and waited. They were not the ones she wanted.

Behind her, the church doors opened, but Cora did not turn to face what stood at the end of the aisle.

"You've taken from us." Ruth spoke, and Cora smiled, watched the creatures cry out for their mothers to punish her, their screeching voices lifted as one.

"Yes," Cora said.

"What will you give us in return?" Leah said, and Cora shifted the gun to her right hand and pressed her finger against the trigger.

"Metal and fire. Blood. You think you will rain fury down upon our heads? That you will end it all?" Another female voice, one that she did not recognize. The unnamed woman.

Lifting the gun, Cora took aim, directed her shot at one of the many creatures, and fired. She watched as its flesh closed over the bullet, and they shrieked, surged toward her, and she fired three more shots.

"Come inside, Cora," Ruth said, and Cora shook her head.

"Go fuck yourself." Cora had seen the book. Had seen her own small body broken beneath the figure of a worm as it pushed itself inside of her. The same body that had been taken so many times as Mr. Burress ran his teeth over her naked belly and claimed it as his own.

"Cora." Michael's voice this time. The voice of a preacher asking his lambs "won't you come?"

"I won't, Michael. There are more of us. Alive."

"It doesn't matter anymore. We feed upon their screams, open our mouths to their despair, and we drink it down. Drop by drop until there is no more," the woman said.

Cora turned and looked at them. Leah with her arm twined through Michael's, Ruth beside them. The woman behind.

"Was it what you always dreamed, Michael? Those smooth legs wrapped around you? Did she cry? Did it hurt her? Did her blood stain your skin?" Cora said.

Leah drew Michael closer to her, and he looked away.

"I know what you are, Michael." He flushed, and Cora pressed him. "Since I was a girl, I've known you. What you are."

Leah lifted the hem of her dress and brought Michael's hand to the hollow there. "Don't," he said, but Leah moved against him, his fingers dipping inside of her as she threw her head back and gasped.

"Isn't she sweet, Michael?" Ruth said, and Michael groaned, his face darkening as Leah pressed his fingers against his lips. Mother and daughter bent over their preacher, their hands travelling over his thighs, until he spasmed and groaned aloud.

Cora did not hear him, the other, the Great Worm, steal into the sanctuary, did not see him crawl along the floor like a serpent coiled and ready to strike until he was on top of Ruth. His teeth sunk deep into her thigh, and blood leaked from around his mouth as he bit down, pulled away muscle and tendon until white bone gleamed beneath the darkness and the blood.

Michael did not move except to shut his eyes. "I told you once before to look away, but open your eyes, Michael. Watch," the woman said.

The Great Worm slipped Ruth's bones from her skin, her

sternum cracking as he worked at her heart, and he lapped up what remained. Outside, the children shouted in ecstasy and hunger, but they coiled against one another, not daring to rush inside.

Leah reached for Michael, but he brushed her hand away.

Cora could not be sure that the Great Worm wouldn't come for her—this ancient god of deep earth—but then she was moving. She heard something shift behind her, and she glanced back. Michael.

"Don't watch," Cora said, but at the doors, she looked back. The Great Worm was watching her go, the blood a dark outline against his mouth, and he spoke to her in a voice she had known all of her life.

"You taste so good," he said, and Cora ran out of the door, and the creatures cried as they parted to let her go.

Chapter 50

Leah could not stop screaming.

"You were the harbinger. The doorway swinging open when you were a squalling infant, shitting and pissing yourself, and you brought us through," the woman said while the Great Worm sucked meat from her mother's bones.

Michael had left her. Her body craved him, her tongue still curved around the salt on his skin, and Leah looked down at the blood, at her empty hands, and she shrieked. The sound filled up the sanctuary, her voice lifted like a hymn toward a faceless god who did not move to help.

The woman stooped low and brushed a hand against Leah's cheek. "You don't matter, little one. We can close the door now."

Outside, the children whined. *Hungry. So hungry. Not enough. We're so hungry,* they called, and the woman turned to their voices.

"I am their Mother. *His* mother," Leah said.

Again, the woman stroked her cheek, but then her fingers tangled in Leah's hair, and she pushed Leah down, and it *hurt.* Her mother's eyes swam before her, wide and unblinking, and still the woman pushed, and it *hurt.*

"She has fed us, Leah. Her blood. Fed *him.* The Great Worm.

And he will feast upon them all, and the ground will grow fat with their bones. Your children, Leah. Care for them. Feed them."

Their voices hurt her ears, and Leah clamped her hands against her face, but the voices grew louder, more insistent.

The woman clapped her hands together like a schoolteacher calling her students to gather. "Come along, children. It's time to eat, and Mother is waiting."

The doors opened, and the children poured through, their fat bodies glistening in the moonlight, and Leah stopped screaming. *He* stood and looped his arm around the woman's shoulders. A playful gesture. Something Leah had seen the older boys do to the older girls, and he and the woman watched as the children crept forward, wriggled on their bellies faster than Leah could have imagined they would. Much faster than when they had first changed, but she had promised them this, and they came now, quick, quick, quick. Follow the leader and quick and quiet, children, and hands in your lap.

She did not speak when they fell upon upon her, did not open her mouth to let out the pain as they bit and tore, but watched the man and the woman standing above her, eyes impassive as the children took all of her.

But isn't this what it meant to be a mother? To give of your body so that the children might thrive even if you weakened? Your blood and your tears one and the same as they eat of your body, and you smile and give them more. Yes, she was their mother, and she opened her arms to them, and they rushed forward. So eager. Her precious ones. They would not forget her.

Leah imagined her own mother cradling her as a baby, wrapping her body inward so that every inch of her skin covered Leah's. Nothing would harm this girl. Nothing would take her baby, but still the red mark had not faded. Had grown deeper as Leah grew older, and her mother still had protected her. Given Leah her body until there was nothing left. It was what a mother did for her children, and she opened herself to them now as the man and woman looked on.

"Eat of me. Drink of me," she said, and the children obeyed. She sang for them. The soft, quiet songs she remembered from her girlhood, and they listened as they drew her into themselves. To love was pain, and she embraced it fully, took the hurt into herself like vapor.

Glancing down at her mother, the last of the light slipping away, Leah pulled her close, embraced her. "I understand," she said, but there was only the sound of her children eating, and she opened herself further.

It was a mother's duty to love her children. Even when they hurt her. Even when they killed her. And she loved them.

Until the very last moments, she loved them.

Chapter 51

"How long before we have to stop driving?" Michael spoke, and Cora ignored him. Kept her eyes trained on the road before her. The creatures had let them leave, but there was no promise in this head start, no guarantee she would watch the sun slip over the horizon the next morning. The road stretched before her, silent and black, and she counted the reflectors as a way to pass the time. She'd already tried all of the radio stations. Dead. All of them.

Michael gestured at the gauges. "Going to run out of gas soon."

Still, Cora did not respond. As if she had no idea the status of her own gas tank. As if she was some hapless victim driving into oblivion with no clear indication of how she would be saved.

"There are gas stations all along the interstate, Michael. American capitalism. Something sacred in it, right? The Almighty Dollar. When the sun rises, I'll stop. Whaddya say? Sound like a good plan? Or did you happen to come up with something better when you had your prick buried inside of that little whore?

"That's right. You should get a little red. Only natural. But I think I'm fine on what it is I need to do to make it through the night, so you can keep the running commentary to yourself. Unless, of course, you get some itch that needs scratching, and in that case, count me out. Honestly, preacher, if you could just shut the fuck up, it would be great."

"You saved my life," Michael said, and she wished he would stop talking. Fatigue settled over her like a great dark wave, and she fought against the weakness that threatened to take her under. Rolling down her window, she let the wind rush over her, but screams choked the night air, and she hit the button, listened to the whirr of the motor as the glass came back up.

"I didn't save shit. They let us go." Her stomach growled, and she needed to take a piss, but there was no way she was pulling over to take a leak in the woods.

"I'm sorry," Michael began, and she snorted.

"Stop being so sorry all of the goddamn time, preacher," she said, and his breath hitched as he held back his sobs. She wanted to hit him. Put her palm against his face with as much force as she had left. Or maybe open the car door and push him onto the blacktop as the odometer hit ninety, ninety-five. The sycophantic little shit.

After that, they rode in silence for a few miles. Every now and then, one of the creatures would dart across the road, eyes reflecting in the headlights, but it made no move toward the vehicle, did not even look up as it passed, and Cora drove on and hoped that one of them would be unlucky enough to collide with her bumper. Or lucky enough. Lucky for her, anyway. And for now, that's all that really mattered. Michael may be in her passenger seat, but now that she had found him, all of the digging, all of the searching, from the day seemed pointless, and she wished that the man had attacked Michael instead. That it was Michael's blood smeared across the man's face instead of Ruth's. Better to be alone, but Michael was here, and she was thankful for his silence.

Looking up into the night sky, Cora felt as if she was following a black map, darkened paths stretching into nothingness. Trapped like a rabbit. Lost and stumbling as she followed the road as it went on and on and on. Circling back on itself again and again. The snake swallowing its tail. Everything devoured itself. Forever and without end. Amen.

Thirty minutes went by, and the silence that Cora had wanted hurt her ears, grew louder and louder. "What about your faith, preacher?" she said, and the sound of her own voice was strange. Disjointed and harsh.

"Faith," Michael said, and his voice was nothing more than a whisper, a slight thing that threatened to fall apart.

Cora pushed him. "Everything that you've built your world on. Your entire life boiled down into something insignificant. You spent so many years, preacher, ignoring and denying, lifting yourself up above the basest human desires. Human *needs*. Holy and untouchable and clean and pure as a little child's fingers only to dissolve at the first sign of trouble."

"Whatever a person believes doesn't matter. Faith. Belief. Two ideas wrapped up into the reality of how far you're willing to take it. Faith doesn't matter. The ability to suspend doubt is so much more. We walk around this earth blind, Cora. And we lead other people into that blindness. Some call it faith, and they fall in love with the blindness. Swear up and down that there is no way out of that pit, and yet others lay claim to it, but they doubt, and so they *pretend*. For too long, I pretended.

"And once you realize that, you start to think of a way out. A way to either convince yourself that what you should believe is real, or a way to end it all."

"Which one were you?"

"For such a long time, I told myself that if I believed more, prayed harder, that it would be easier for me. That maybe one day I would wake up, and I could be like all of those other people. The ones who passed the snakes, smiled into those faces of death, their hearts settled and knowing that the bite would not come that day."

He shifted in his seat. "And then there was no more evidence. No more people to remind me that I stood as some false god. A pillar. An exemplar for all that was good. And it didn't matter anymore. Everything fell apart, and I forgot what it meant to feel guilt. To feel shame. It's easier than you'd imagine."

What an easy thing. To forget. To take everything that created pain or doubt and tuck it away in a place that was hidden. She had done the same for years.

"I fell into it when Leah took me. All of those things that I had wanted for such a long time. It was like stepping into a second skin. Something that I had always known but never put on. And I could *breathe*, and it felt so wonderful that I never wanted it to stop. Even when I saw the foulness settling on my skin like dust. It didn't matter. I had sacrificed and denied for so long, and didn't I deserve this?"

"No," she said. "Peace isn't anything we deserve. Such a bullshit way to justify our behavior. Deserving to be happy. Such crap. We don't deserve anything. The world doesn't owe us anything other than the certainty that we will die. So, no, preacher. I don't think you deserved any measure of happiness after a lifetime of denial. You don't get to store up your good deeds like points you can cash in for a better spot in the afterlife if you fuck it all up."

She expected a response from him. Some canned, rehearsed section of the Bible that would inform her that she had blasphemed, followed by a thirty-minute conversation regarding exactly how much Jesus loved her, and how she could spend the final moments of her life exalting his name. He remained silent, and she again had the urge to commit violence against him.

A moth smacked against her windshield with a meaty thump, brown and white wings fluttering against the glass, and she bit down on her laughter. How inane. How incredibly *normal.* Life and death in the natural world still subject to the violence found against a windshield. If a dog or a cat were to dart under her wheels, would the same thing happen or would the animal rise an hour later and turn its ears to the sound of the Great Worm emerged from the pit?

"Ashes to ashes," she said, and he glanced over at her, but she did not return his stare and kept her eyes ahead, the yellow lines rushing away from her. "Terrible to think that when they take us, rip us open and use our insides for fucking playthings, that our bodies will go back into the dirt. Our bones feeding them for eternity."

Beyond the interstate and hidden among the trees, they watched. Cora was certain of it. Saw the car hurtling through the dark toward the very edge of whatever small thread still held the world together, and they would be there when it broke, their hands outstretched and greedy as she fell into them.

"She didn't ask for this, you know. None of it. She was just a girl," Michael said, and Cora slowed the car, brought it to a dead stop in the middle of the blacktop.

"Didn't she though, preacher?"

"How could she have known? How could any of us have known?"

"No one is completely innocent. You of all people should understand that, Michael. Not for one second do I believe in this bullshit about her being *marked*. She had a birthmark. So what? She wasn't special. She's not the fucking princess of the dark awakened by her one true love's kiss. She was something they could use, and so they did. That's all."

Throwing the car back into gear, she kept going. If she could, she planned to drive until she hit Atlanta. Even if everything was completely fucked, she needed to see it for herself. See the streets she had known her entire life abandoned. The shops and restaurants quiet, and the interstate crowded with empty cars that had nowhere to go.

More than anything, she wanted to be inside of her apartment. Wanted to take the hottest shower—if there was still water to do it—that she could stand and change her clothes. Curl up with her white down comforter and sleep until night fell and then hide herself somewhere until all was safe. From there, she and Michael could part ways, and she could worry about herself and herself alone.

Checking her gauges, she saw that Michael had been right. She had a little under a quarter of a tank left, and there was no way that it was enough to get her to Atlanta. If she wanted to go home, she would have to stop.

Five minutes. Maybe seven. As long as the pumps were on, she could get in and get out quickly. At the next exit, she veered off of the highway and headed for the first station she saw.

"In and out," Cora said and steered into the lot. Whoever had last been here had left all of the lights on, and she lifted her hand in a mock salute to thank the person who had done so.

Pulling up to one of the pumps, she hopped out and looked. It appeared to be functional, but there was no one inside to turn on the pump, and she wasn't sure she could get it to work.

"Dammit," she mumbled, and Michael opened his door and

pointed to the other two cars that remained in the lot.

"We could siphon it off of those."

The lights were still on inside of the store—some employee diligent right until the bitter end—but after further inspection, she still couldn't see anyone.

"Okay. We'll go inside. Four minutes. Nothing more. Enough time for me to see if I can turn on the pumps with all of my infinite gas clerk wisdom, and for you to find a hose that we can use if I can't." He nodded, and she swept the empty lot twice before she began moving.

When they came through the door, it chimed, and she winced at the sound. She didn't want anything announcing their presence. Might as well ring a dinner bell and holler at everyone to belly up to the table because supper was served. Michael moved away from her and down one of the aisles.

There were no bodies anywhere in the store, no grotesque menagerie of arms and legs waving while mouths stiff with rigor mortis grinned out into nothingness. The thought unnerved Cora, but she went behind the counter and found what she was looking for.

The machine that controlled the gas pumps had been ripped from the wall and repeatedly smashed. Bits and pieces lay strewn about. She groaned.

Michael came up the center aisle, a large green hose and small plastic gas tank clutched before him, and he held it aloft. "Here."

"You ever done this before?" she asked him as they left the store, the bell dinging one final time.

He shook his head. "No. But I've seen someone else do it. Brother Meades got his tractor stuck up on the mountain once doing some work for Sister Burnette after her husband passed. I watched him, but it was only the once. I think I can do it."

The parking lot still held only the three cars. No creatures, no screaming, no mutated children crept out of the gloom. Heavy and bleak, the quiet settled around them like a shroud, and she again felt as if some great eye had turned on her and watched with curiosity and mild amusement.

Michael unscrewed the gas cap off of the nearest car—a navy clunker that looked as if it had seen at least two world wars—and inserted the hose and bent toward it.

"Hold on. There's a better way to do this," she told him and went back to the car to retrieve one of the knives left in the backseat.

She hurried back and bent to the hose, worked the knife through the rubber until a small section came free. Working her shirt up and over her head, she pulled it off and handed him the small section of the hose. The air was cold, and she was uncomfortably aware of the thinness of her bra, but he had seen so much more of her than this.

"Put the smaller section in the tank, too, and wrap the shirt around the smaller hose." She pulled the gas tank forward, unscrewed the cap, and dropped the hose end inside. "Then blow on the smaller hose. That way, you won't get a mouthful of gasoline." He looked at her for a moment, but then he was wrapping her shirt around the smaller bit, and within seconds came the sound of gas flowing into the plastic container.

"Trick I picked up from a story I did once. Shitty freelance job when I first got started for a restoration mag. How to get bad gas out of a project car. Guy I interviewed showed me how to do it. One of those things you forget about until it's staring you in the face."

Michael glanced away as he handed her back her shirt, and she did up the buttons, her fingers trembling and missing the holes. She needed to eat. If she was going to get them to Atlanta, she needed water and food. They both did. The gasoline was still trickling into the tank. She had time to run back into the store, grab as much as she could carry, and make it back out before they refueled.

"I'm going back inside," she said, and he nodded and turned his attention back to the tank.

Grabbing a couple of plastic bags from up front, she headed for the coolers, which were thankfully still working, and filled one of the bags with bottled water. She closed the cooler and turned, started to open the other bag, but stopped. To her right, hidden by the shelves stocked with potato chips and candy bars, came a small sound like paper shuffling.

If Michael had come in behind her, she would have heard the bell chime, and surely he would have called out to her, let her know he was in the store. She looked out of the glass windows at the front of the store. Michael was outside, still waiting for the gas to finish draining.

Again came the sound of paper rustling, and Cora looked up into the corners of the building. There may be surveillance cameras, but so many stores still had convex mirrors installed as a deterrent against shoplifting. A way to keep teenagers from pocketing lighters or packs of gum, or for the enterprising, cans of beer shoved into deep coat pockets.

In the front right corner, the mirror glinted a harsh silver, and Cora stared into it and tried to locate her position in the store against where she thought the sound might be coming from.

The first and second aisle reflected nothing back to her other than rows of snacks, but at the end of the third aisle, a tiny form sat on the floor, scuffling its feet back and forth across the linoleum. A child with long red hair that hung limp and oily against her back. Soft noise for a soft thing. Tiny hands fidgeted against the floor as her head bent back and back and back until it touched her spine, the bones cracking as they snapped under the act of changing, the act of *becoming*. Yellow eyes stared up into the mirror at Cora, and the mouth moved. "Momma," the girl called and reached her arms out, and Cora ran. She could hear the girl moving behind her, a soft hissing that grew louder as Cora reached the door and blew through it and into the parking lot.

The door swung shut, and she did not hear it open, did not hear the girl still coming, and Cora slowed and turned to look behind her. The girl stood at the door, her arms bent at the elbows to point behind her, and there was blood at her mouth as if she had bitten through her tongue. She pressed her mouth against the glass, and Cora looked into that vortex of teeth, saw that the girl, in fact, had no tongue, and she opened and opened her jaw, the mouth stretching beyond what should be possible, and screamed.

Outside, the girl's brothers and sisters answered her. "We need to go," she said to Michael, and he pulled the hose from the tank, left it dripping against the concrete, and hauled the tank with him as they headed for her car.

The children crawled from the dark, and they went to their sister, welcomed her, and comforted her as her bones snapped and shifted to make room for something new. Cora watched them surround the girl as she fired the engine, watched them curl their bodies around her and coo. Together, the creatures turned their eyes toward Cora and Michael and watched them drive away.

Again, they had let her go. It would have been easy to over-take her, but they had not.

The car reeked of gasoline, and the edges of the world shim-mered, danced somewhere between reality and a place where she had started to drown. "Put a cap on that thing, would you?" Cora asked, and she hated the weakness in her voice, the tremor at the end of the question.

"Sure."

She wanted to roll down her window, clear the smell from her nostrils, but she would not. Could not bear the chance that the children were out there, singing to each other in the night. A choir of obscenity.

They would have to stop soon, use the gas can to fill up, but she would push it as far as she could, let the car sputter out before she stopped again.

"They were just kids. Little kids," Michael said.

Cora ran her tongue over her lips and traced the cracks that had begun to form. "I had moments when I hated her. My mother. Was so angry that I couldn't see, and I would imagine that she was gone. Not dead, maybe, but just *gone*. Deep inside some hole where I wouldn't have to see her or hear her or listen to the things she told me when she didn't even understand. And I couldn't tell her. Couldn't explain. If there had been something there, whispering in my ear, telling me all of the ways I could make it better, to make her quiet—with my own hands, with my teeth—I would have done it. In that moment, I would have done it." She glanced over at Michael. "Wouldn't you have done the same?"

"Yes," he said and nodded. "Yes, I would have."

Chapter 52

The girl's mother had brought her inside to take her potty. She'd thought she could hold it before they got to her daddy's house, but her tummy started hurting, and Mommy had gotten mad and pulled the car over because she'd told Mommy that she'd had an accident.

There were other kids in the store. Lots of kids. But Mommy hadn't noticed because she was so busy yelling at her. Telling her that she needed to learn how to hold it. That only little babies shit all over themselves, and that Mommy was sick and tired of having to clean up her mess. That Mommy had always been the one to take care of everything, and why couldn't she have waited until she was with her daddy so he would have to deal with her bullshit for once.

Mommy had taken her into the bathroom and turned on the sink, ran the water until it was hot, hot, hot. The girl could see the steam, and she asked Mommy not to, had screamed, but Mommy had pulled down the pink underwear she had picked out that morning, the pair with the tiny little bows that she liked so much, picked her up, and held her under the water, and it burned, and she tried to get away, but Mommy was so strong, and it burned, and she could not get away.

She had cried, and Mommy had swiped at her legs with paper

towels, and they were scratchy and tore at her legs. When a spot on her leg started to bleed, Mommy rolled her eyes, handed her another paper towel, and told her to press down.

The girl could hear the other kids through the door. They told her they were sorry and they would take care of her if she would let them. Hearing them made her want to cry, and Mommy put on a fresh coat of lipstick. Light pink so that her lips almost disappeared.

She didn't like that lipstick. She never had. What she wanted more than anything was to make Mommy eat it. Eat it until she threw up like the time she had not eaten her lunch, and Mommy had packed the same food the next day, the meat all bad smelling and the bread soggy, and she had still not eaten it, and then she had come home, and Mommy had held her hands down and made her eat it. When she threw it up, Mommy made her eat that, too.

The other kids scratched at the door, and Mommy didn't hear them, pressed a piece of toilet paper between her lips to blot them. *Ugly*, she thought, and the kids asked her to open the door and let them in. They would take care of her. Take care of everything. They promised.

Mommy had not heard when she had opened the door, but she saw the children in the mirror. That pale mouth opening to scream, but then they were on top of her, and she never said another word.

They left her in the store. Told her that they would be listening and waiting for her to change, but they would be near and waiting for her to finish. They patted her hair and told her not to be scared. When it was finished, she would feel so wonderful. So strong and fast and *happy*. No one would hurt her again.

She had not been able to speak when the lady and the man had come into the store, and they had not seen the corner where she huddled, sweat dampening her hair and clothes. Like the very worst fever she had ever had. She didn't like it, and it went on and on and on, and it *hurt*, and the other kids had promised. She tried to call out to the woman and the man, but her voice wouldn't work, and they left the store, and she was alone again.

The children spoke to her from the hidden places among the trees, spoke with voices filled with dirt, through teeth like daggers, and the sound slid over her skin like something soft, and she sagged against it, asked them to make it stop. Soon, they told her, but it had not been soon. It had been so much longer. So much longer.

The lady had come back inside, and she had pulled herself out and into the aisle, marveled at the sound of her bones cracking and breaking as she moved and how it hadn't hurt anymore, how it actually felt *nice*. Like in kindergarten when her teacher had hugged her every day and tucked the girl's hair behind her ear and smiled a big smile just for her. Like it was a secret that the girl was her favorite even though she was nice to all of the other kids, too, but the girl had liked to pretend.

And then everything was so clear, and her muscles flexed and changed, and she was so *hungry*, and the lady smelled so *nice,* and the other kids told her to wait, that she wasn't allowed, but she was so *hungry*.

When the lady saw her watching, she ran, and the girl went after her, but the other children stopped her, and she cried and cried because all she wanted was something to eat, and why couldn't she eat?

We will. Don't worry, they told her, and together they watched the man and woman leave, the taillights vanishing in a matter of seconds, and they wrapped themselves around her, cradled her against their bodies, and promised her that everything would be okay.

Chapter 53

Cora woke to the wheel jerking beneath her fingers and the sound of something scraping beneath the car. Asleep. She had fallen fucking *asleep* and the car had drifted off of the highway and into the longer grass that lined the shoulder.

She pulled the wheel back toward the road, and the car lurched to the left, the back end fishtailing. "Shit," she said, and Michael came awake, his eyes going wide as he grasped at the dash.

The car swung back to the right once more before she was able to bring it under control, and she forced her breathing to slow as the road ticked away behind them.

"I can drive. You should sleep," Michael said.

"No. No, I'm fine."

They'd stopped about an hour before to refill the tank, and she'd counted the seconds it had taken Michael to do it, waited shivering beside him, her eyes searching the darkness for anything that moved smoothly along the ground.

If there was anything out there, it did not make itself known, but they had still hurried, and Michael had spilled gas on his hands so that when they re-entered the car she could smell it in the air and thought that it would smother her.

"Cora," he began, but she looked over at him.

"I'm fine," she repeated and punched the power button on the radio. Again, static and the sound of the children weeping and singing, and their voices slid over her skin like oil. She turned it off. They couldn't be far now, and the sky had just begun to lighten. If nothing else, she hoped to have them in Atlanta by daybreak. At minimum she could sleep and find something to eat before night fell again and the ground slid open to release its filth.

Rubbing her eyes, she refocused on the road and ignored Michael's staring. She didn't need his concern. Driving was the only thing she had left, and she needed it to carry her through whatever came next. So far, they had not seen any other cars. Nothing came or went, and she imagined all of the small towns that lined the interstate torn apart and emptied. The children tucked snug in their beds changing, becoming something terrible as their parents slept in the next rooms, their throats naked and ready for milk teeth pressed against thin skin.

Cora didn't remember passing the state line, but they must have because there was a sign in the distance with the Georgia state outline. Dalton. The Carpet Capitol. In the space of two hours, they would be in her apartment, and she could change her clothes on top of sleeping, and with any luck, take a shower, use the phone to see if she could find the girl at UVA. Audrey. She would not be waiting on Audrey's call as she had promised, but maybe she could find the number in the phone book and call her instead. The thought gave her some hope, and she watched the signs as they passed. More quickly now that they were approaching the metro area. If there were people left, they would be here. They would be hiding. They could find them. Gather together. Fight back.

Surely there were television broadcasts. Newscasters reporting a strange virus affecting only children; a virus that would lead them to murder their parents—those adults unlucky enough to be in their path when the fever took hold. Warning signs for worried mothers. Things to watch out for and where those remaining could go for shelter or for food. All of that plus the weather forecast at ten.

"The sun will be up in about two hours," Michael said.

"Yes. We'll be there by then." She did not add the 'if' that she had locked inside of her head. *If* they actually got there. *If* nothing happened in the time it took for the sun to fully rise and all of the creatures to go to ground. *If* they even needed to anymore. It was entirely possible that they had changed, gotten stronger.

Cresting a hill, Cora looked down at the road that lay beyond, empty and glittering before them. Every second she expected to see thousands of the creatures coiled together like snakes in their den. She was still surprised she hadn't.

"Can we stop the car? Just for a moment?" Michael said.

"No. Not this close to sunrise."

"Cora. Please. It won't take more than a minute."

She looked over at him and sighed. "Fine. A minute. Nothing more," she said and guided the car to the shoulder. Nothing moved in between the trees, and he popped open the door and walked toward the tree line. She thought of calling to him and telling him to stay where she could see him, but she didn't, and he wandered toward the forest, let the long grass swallow him up.

She waited for long minutes, but Michael did not return.

When the voice cut through the dark, Cora told herself not to listen, told herself that it wasn't real, but then the voice came again, and she opened the door and drifted toward what called for her.

"Momma?" she shouted, and her mother guided her forward. The voice settled somewhere deep inside of her, and she took a deep breath and curled into the space the voice created. Something easy and good. For the first time in a long while, this was something easy and good.

It was hard to see. Hard to determine where the trees ended and the ground began, but Cora closed her eyes. Better to follow the voice, let herself surrender, and melt inside of the voice guiding her onward. It would not fail. It would tell her where to go. Momma had always told her what to do, and she would tell her now. The monsters that lived in the dark had been chased away by her mother's presence, and Cora took off her shoes and put her toes in the dirt. Momma would tell her where to go and what to do.

"Cora," Momma called again, and Cora crept through the forest, her skin darkening with dirt and mud as she pushed through the trees and underbrush. She would find her mother at the end of the world, and Cora would pull the older woman inside of herself, mother and daughter cut from the same skin, and she would not let her go. Not ever. Not again.

Once, Cora had stood in a room and squeezed the bony hand, clasped the wrist so hard she was afraid she would break it, but it was not her mother's bones that had broken in the end. There was another, more insidious, darkness inside of her, and it had devoured everything.

The trees pushed against Cora, and she swatted at the branches that tore at her arms and legs and forced herself to keep moving. There was no sign of Michael. No indication he had come crashing through these same trees only moments before her, but she didn't care.

"Not yet. Not yet," she mumbled and watched as the night went pale. "Where are you, Momma?"

"Little love. My little girl. Oh, my lost, little girl."

Cora stepped through a series of small, delicately branching trees, and into a clearing. Dead grass sliced the bottoms of her feet as she walked, and she left her blood behind. A gift for the ones in the ground. A gift for worms.

Inside of that dead circle, her mother squatted in the earth, hands and arms dark as ash, her fingers scrabbling in the dirt as she plucked fat, wriggling worms from their hiding places and laid them across her tongue. Gaunt and pale, her mother was nude, her skin stretched tight against bone; her hair was still long, dark curls threaded with silver, but her *eyes*. The iris, the pupil, the sclera. All the color of old blood.

"There's a hole in the bottom of the world. That's where they found me. Down there at the end. In the cold and the dark," her mother said. She looked up and watched Cora as she approached.

Cora offered up her hands, blinked away the tears pooling in the corners of her eyes. This was the body she remembered. Emaciated. Bruised. Broken. The body she had fought so hard to save, but it had not mattered that she had tried. "Come with me, Momma. Come home."

"Silly. Silly girl. We are home." Another worm disappeared inside of her mother's mouth. "I know about you. They told me all about it. Told me all about *him*. How he pulled you inside out."

"Momma. Please. I have a car. We can get away from here."

"Is that what you would do, Cora? Carry death with you like a trinket?"

"No, Momma."

"There were times I would watch you sleep, and I was so afraid. Wished that I had kept you deep down. Quiet. In the dark. Watching you, I could feel that pain shimmering around the edges of every movement you made. Every sound filled with something like sobbing, and I was so *afraid*.

"I imagined what would happen to you. Lie down at night and watch it unfold in my head. A man taking you apart bit by bit and smiling when you cried. Laughing when you asked him to please stop and then all you could say was 'I'm sorry. I'm sorry.' Over and over again. That little girl voice in my head telling him you were sorry, and then you went quiet, and I would stuff my pillow into my mouth and scream until I choked. Every night I said that night would be different. That night I would fall asleep without seeing you before me. Without imagining those terrible things, and the night would end the way it always did."

Dew beaded against Cora's skin, and she wiped at the moisture on her arms, her fingers trembling in the cold. "But you grew up happy. Beautiful. And eventually, I learned to fall asleep without screaming."

Her mother drew herself onto her knees and crept forward on all fours. "But they told me about him. That holy man with his forked tongue. I should have never let you go, Cora. Should have swallowed you up. Kept you inside of me until you drowned. Come with me. This last time. Down into the dark."

"I can't, Momma. We can't. Come with me. Please."

"There's nowhere else to go, Cora," her mother said and reached out. Cora fell against her and pulled her close.

In the final moments before her mother's death, Cora had wanted nothing more than to hold her mother against her, but there had been too many tubes, too many links to machines, but now there was only the sky and the ground, and she pushed her face into her mother's hair and breathed in the smell of clean soil and rain.

Mother and daughter clasped hands, the older leading the younger to safety, down, down, down into the dark where Cora could tuck her body against her mother's and sleep. Shed the skin that had been so used and be born into something clean and new.

Together, they moved out of the trees and toward an outcropping of rock that swelled out of the ground. A place where ancient ice had once flowed and left an indelible mark on the landscape. A scar that could never be erased. Buried underneath the rock, the ground dropped away and the earth tumbled down into a darkness that did not end.

Cora had read about children and teenagers stumbling upon ancient entrances to caves, seen the tragedies written in their parents' eyes as they recounted what good kids they had been. How much those boys and girls had loved to laugh. How they would never forget. Never. But still the ground had swallowed those children up, their bones buried in the silence of the earth, their bodies crumbling into dust.

Now, she followed her mother, their palms still pressed together as they descended, the light fading behind them as they went down into the bowels of the earth. From somewhere up above, water dripped, and a cool breeze moved over Cora's skin. The opening narrowed, and they went down onto their stomachs, pulled themselves along until all of the light faded, and there was only the dark and the sound of her mother breathing, the ground opening to accept their small movements.

Still, they crawled forward, and Cora felt her chest grow tight as she pulled air into her lungs in small sips. There was not room for any more than that, and she clawed at the earth and rock as her mother led her deeper and deeper into the mouth and teeth of the world. She thought that her heart would give out, that she would stop breathing, but it did not.

She thought back to the moment when she had walked into the ocean at night, the dark waves closing over her head as she tried to take the water into herself. Her alien body tucked inside ocean salt, the surf turning her over and over before spitting her out, and this moment was not completely unlike that moment of trying to drown, but there was nothing here to push her away, nothing here forcing her upward until she emerged coughing and choking and spitting as air flowed back into her lungs, the pain splitting her open like a knife.

"You dug me a grave," Cora said, and she heard her mother turn back to her, felt the warm hand against her cheek, remembered what it had been like when she was a girl. This same feeling. Knowing that everything would be all right. That night would end and that joy would come in the morning.

"No," her mother said, and drew her close. "Not a grave."

"What then?"

"Don't you know, love? Don't you know?"

Chapter 54

It was full daylight when Michael woke. His throat ached with thirst, and his skin burned under the full sun despite the slight chill in the air. He sat up, took in the expanse of trees that stretched on and on. Lost. He was lost.

He remembered a car. Cora. Driving with her. She had wanted to get to Atlanta, and they had stopped. Seen something, but he couldn't quite remember what. It had been terrible, he knew that, and they had run from it, but he did not remember getting out of the car. Certainly, he did not remember wandering into the woods and falling asleep curled inside a pile of dead leaves.

Sitting up, he searched the trees for any sign of movement, a slip of color, anything that would tell him Cora was near him, that she had come with him when he left the car, but there were only the bare limbs reaching skyward. White bark reflecting too-bright sun. He squinted his eyes and looked back down at the ground.

Perhaps she had stayed in the car and was waiting for him at this very moment. She would be irritated with him if he found her. He wouldn't be surprised if she had grown tired of waiting and left him behind. He was a grown man. He could fend for himself. She shouldn't have to look out for him. They owed each other nothing.

He heard all of these things in the ghost of her voice, and even still, he hoped that if he found his way out of the woods, that he would see her, her face twisted into a frown but still there, still waiting. His legs shook as he stood, and he took a moment to steady himself and looked around. There was no discernible path leading to this place. No way of knowing how he had gotten here, and no way of knowing how to get out.

He looked at the sun. It was still early morning, and he figured it was as good a shot as any to walk east, and he headed that direction, thorns and brambles snatching at his clothes as he passed through the wood.

The trees here looked familiar. Like the trees he had hid himself among as a boy, trying with everything in him to outrun the wind, to outrun his mother's voice calling him to come back to the church. Come back home. But he was far from home. Wasn't he? They had driven for a long while, that much he knew, but still, the forest called out to him in tones he recognized and something inside that had been long dormant woke.

Yes. He knew this place. With every step, he was more certain. He turned right and faced a tree that forked in the middle, two trunks reaching toward the sky, the branches meeting again high above him to form a canopy that blocked the sunlight. Beyond the tree, there would be a small path; a path that he himself had carved, his shoes scuffling along the dirt.

It took five minutes for him to reach the end of the path, and then he burst through the underbrush, his forehead slick with sweat, and into the back lot of his father's church.

No, *his* church. His father had been dead for a long, long time. He was the one who had taken up that burden; his hands were the ones that passed the snakes as prayers lay thick as sawdust in his mouth.

Looking down, he saw that his clothes were streaked with red clay. Darker soil clung to his hands as if he had been digging.

A small sound came from in front of him, and he looked up to see the side door of the church opening. His mother was a dark shadow framed in the doorway, but he could see her hands, could see her beckoning him to come inside.

"Come and wash yourself, Michael. It's almost time for the service," she said.

Pitching forward, he ran, twice stumbling over stray rocks, but then she was pulling him against her, and he sobbed into her dress which smelled of Borax and cut grass, and she did not tell him to calm himself but let him weep.

"Come, Michael. It's time to deliver the service now," she said and used her sleeve to wipe his face.

She led him down the hallway. Everything was as he remembered, but there was a strangeness to the place: a picture that he did not recall hung at the end of the hallway, the carpet a slightly different shade of blue, a crucifix painted in lurid gold and burgundy over the side entrance to the sanctuary.

Turning, his mother smiled at him and then disappeared into the darkened doorway. This was how she had entered the space when he was a boy, him following close behind his mother, and she would take her seat at the piano to lead the congregation in the hymns while he would take the first pew and wait for his father to appear. No one else had ever sat in the pew. Not even when he grew older and asked his friends if they would sit with him through the service. They would shake their heads solemnly and tell him they couldn't. It was the preacher's pew, and they just couldn't, and that was that.

His mother started the organ. The opening bars of "Blessed Assurance." His father's favorite. She would always play that song if his father was particularly nervous or had been upset the night before. Her way of providing comfort in the smallest of ways.

Michael stumbled through the entrance, head and eyes cast down, and made his way to the front pew as he had thousands of other times, but his mother hissed at him as he passed by her, and he froze, felt his bladder release as urine streamed down his leg.

"Where you going, preacher?"

He looked up then and saw the congregation before him, the fat, bloated bodies of the children squirming beside the bloodless, gaunt faces of their parents. Ruth sat in their pew, her hand twined through Leah's—but they were dead, weren't they?—and both mother and daughter looked up at him, waited as they had always waited for his words to fall upon their heads.

At the back of the room, the woman and the Great Worm stood side by side, looking out over the congregation, and watched him.

"Go on, preacher," the woman said, and the people murmured in agreement.

He had read about a Black Mass once, and as he ascended the steps leading up into the pulpit, he saw himself as the robed man in the picture that had accompanied the entry. He stood before this congregation, and he trembled, the place he had pissed himself gone cold. This would be the last time. He felt it in the air.

"My children," he said and raised his hands to them.

In one voice, they answered.

Chapter 55

They slept. Cora did not know for how long, but she could feel herself tumbling further into the earth, her mother's arms locked around her as they descended.

She thought of Michael, wondered for a moment where he had gone, if he was still somewhere up there, where the light shone too bright. She thought, too, of the creatures who had been children. Of the woman. Of the Great Worm pulling everything down into the deep, but then she forgot them. There was only the sound of her mother's voice guiding her and the feeling of rock and grit in her teeth as she went further into the belly of the cave.

"Only a few have ever found this place," her mother said and turned back to her. Even in the darkness, she could see her mother's eyes. A faint, bloodied glow reflecting back at her.

"People used to believe in the ground. Before it got all mixed up. Before we looked up to the sky, people looked beneath them, and they believed, and they were afraid." A cave yawned open behind her mother. A vast room of smooth rock, and Cora looked beyond. She looked inside.

The floor heaved and shifted. The white, glowing backs of the creatures, and they sang out to her, and she understood. Understood what it was that they wanted. Understood the trick they had pulled.

"You're not my mother. You are not my mother," she mumbled, and the woman who pretended to be her mother pulled Cora close and passed her tongue over Cora's lips.

"But I am. You came from me. From inside. I fed you with my body," her mother said, and Cora tried to pull herself free, but her mother tightened her grip.

When she heard the sick snap of her wrists breaking, Cora screamed, but her mother ate the sound, took it into the darkness of her body.

Around them, the creatures squealed and surged forward, but her mother raised one hand, and they retreated to the far corners of the cave, their bodies slopping against one another as they went.

"Little girl," her mother said and bit through Cora's tongue. Cora did scream then, but the sound was guttural. The sound a beast made as it was dying, and her mother swallowed her down in small bits.

"Hush now," her mother said, waited until Cora quieted, waited for her cries to become small. A thing she could crush between her teeth.

Above them, something large skittered across the ceiling. "The Great Worm," her mother whispered, and her breath smelled of blood, and Cora was so hungry. So hungry, and she opened her mouth. *Please. Please.*

Her mother fed her. Poured herself down Cora's throat, and Cora ate greedily, and whatever great creature moved in the cave came to rest behind them, watched as mother and daughter fed the other.

Cora felt him move then, felt him press against her back, and she leaned into him and moaned. *Yes. Please.*

She thought again of Mr. Burress. Of that very first time he had come to her. How flattered she had been when he told her how pretty she was, told her that her eyes were exactly like stars and that he could look at them forever. Could get lost in them. Remembered her stomach fluttering when he had kissed her and that first rush of hot fluid between her legs. All of the things she had thought she wanted. All of the things that she hadn't understood. She thought of how good it had felt, his lips against her, but then his fingers had pulled her apart, and it had hurt, and she was so confused because it had felt good at first.

Yes, she thought of him now, but the thing moving behind her wasn't him. It was something much greater, and she turned to him. Turned to the Great Worm and opened her arms.

All around them, the children cried out. *Her* children. She understood that now. Moving against him, she opened herself up, and his mouth tasted of deep earth. It tasted of blood and honey and rainwater, and he pushed deep inside of her, and her children lapped at the hot, sticky blood on her thighs.

He whispered to her in a tongue she did not understand, and she wanted to ask him what he was, how he had come to be.

"I have always been," he said, and she could hear her skin tearing, could hear herself opening up. Blooming. "Always."

Down in the dark, Cora looked up, but her eyes did not see beyond the black that stretched on forever.

"At me, Cora. Look at me," he told her, and she did, watched him as he tore her apart and then stitched her back together. Something new. Something better.

Her new tongue flexed in her mouth, and she passed it over her teeth. When she spoke, she knew it would be in a voice meant only for him.

For another small moment, she thought of who she had once been, thought of the girl left trembling in a darkened bedroom, her panties wet with urine and blood and crumpled inside of her left hand.

"Yes," she said, and then everything fell silent.

They would sleep. Down deep in the quiet places, they would sleep, and one day they would wake again, and she would be with them, would protect them as a mother protects her child. She would be strong.

"Yes," she said again and closed her eyes.

Acknowledgments

This book would not be complete without the input, support, and friendship I've received from so many people. Thanks to Melanie Sumner and Anne Richards for their invaluable feedback and support when this novel was in its very beginning stages and had only just begun to stand on the shakiest legs ever. Thanks to Sally Kilpatrick for her unwavering support and frequent advice. A million thanks to Livia Llewellyn for being willing to take a chance by reading my first draft and not immediately telling me I should burn it. An unending sea of gratitude for Damien Angelica Walters for her offering her constant support, being a sisterhood in scary, and never saying no when I came begging for feedback. Without you, this book wouldn't exist. Honestly, without you, most of my work wouldn't exist. Michael Wehunt, my fellow Atlanta resident, I cannot begin to express how much I value having a writer like you in my corner. Thank you for allowing me to commiserate and for pushing me to be a better writer. Thank you to Scott Nicolay who kindly invited me on his podcast, The Outer Dark, and provided me the avenue that led to this book seeing the light of day. Thank you to Anya Martin for being another sister in the weird. Thank you to Aaron Levy and Crystal White for their feedback and encouragement when I hit the mushy middle. My birch crew. I love all of you forever, and thank you for making me laugh when I think it's darkest and for seeing me through all of my writing adventures and being the best cheerleaders a girl can ask for. I owe all of you a coffee and probably something much stronger. Thank you to Ross Lockhart, who took a chance on this weird little book and has made this very intimidating process so wonderful. Thank you to Marcela Bolívar for the cover. There are so many others who have offered advice or cheer throughout this journey, and if I left your name off here, it's entirely the fault of my addled brain. To my wonderful in-laws and family, Jack, Nancy, Matt, Jessi, Camden, Cassie, Patrick, and Sophie, I feel so privileged to have found genuine family in each of you. Finally, for Justin and my little dude. You two have my heart. Forever. Even if sometimes I dream up spooky things. Love. Oh, so much love.

NOMINATED FOR THE BRAM STOKER AWARD FOR SUPERIOR ACHIEVEMENT IN A NOVEL.

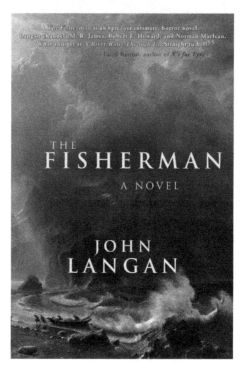

THIS IS HORROR NOVEL OF THE YEAR 2016

In upstate New York, in the woods around Woodstock, Dutchman's Creek flows out of the Ashokan Reservoir. Steep-banked, fast-moving, it offers the promise of fine fishing, and of something more, a possibility too fantastic to be true. When Abe and Dan, two widowers who have found solace in each other's company and a shared passion for fishing, hear rumors of the Creek, and what might be found there, the remedy to both their losses, they dismiss it as just another fish story. Soon, though, the men find themselves drawn into a tale as deep and old as the Reservoir. It's a tale of dark pacts, of long-buried secrets, and of a mysterious figure known as Der Fisher: the Fisherman. It will bring Abe and Dan face to face with all that they have lost, and with the price they must pay to regain it.

Trade Paperback, 282 pp, $16.99

ISBN-13: 978-1-939905-21-5

http://www.wordhorde.com

THIS IS HORROR SHORT STORY COLLECTION OF THE YEAR 2016

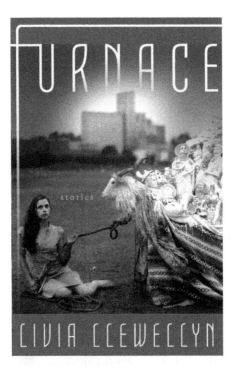

Horror fiction has long celebrated and explored the twin engines driving human existence. Call them what you like: Sex and Death, Love and Destruction, Temptation and Terror. While many may strive to reach the extremes, few authors manage to find the beauty that rests in the liminal space between these polar forces, the shuddering ecstasy encased within the shock. And then there's Livia Llewellyn, an author praised for her dark, stirring, evocative prose and disturbing, personal narratives.

Lush, layered, multifaceted, and elegant, the thirteen tales comprising *Furnace* showcase why Livia Llewellyn has been lauded by scholars and fans of weird fiction alike, and why she has been nominated multiple times for the Shirley Jackson Award and included in year's best anthologies. These are exquisite stories, of beauty and cruelty, of pleasure and pain, of hunger, and of sharp teeth sinking into tender flesh.

Format: Trade Paperback, 210 pp, $14.99

ISBN-13: 978-1-939905-17-8

http://www.wordhorde.com

ABOUT THE AUTHOR

Kristi DeMeester writes pretty, spooky things in Atlanta, Georgia. Her work has appeared in publications such as *Black Static*, *Apex Magazine*, *The Dark*, and several others. Her work has been reprinted in *Year's Best Weird Fiction Volumes 1* and *3*. Her debut short fiction collection, *Everything That's Underneath*, is forthcoming this year from Apex Publications. In her spare time, she alternates between telling people how to pronounce her last name and how to spell her first. This is her first novel. Find her online at www.kristidemeester.com.

CPSIA information can be obtained
at www.ICGtesting.com
Printed in the USA
LVHW040417110122
708076LV00008B/255